DIRECTIVE ONE

ONE

A "Michelle Reagan" Novel
by
SCOTT SHINBERG

SPECIAL NOTICE

DIRECTIVE ONE
Michelle Reagan – Book 2
Copyright © 2019 by Scott Shinberg

FIRST EDITION SOFTCOVER
ISBN: 1622536673
ISBN-13: 978-1-62253-667-2

Editor: Whitney Smyth
Cover Artist: Briana Hertzog
Interior Designer: Lane Diamond

EVOLVED PUBLISHING™

www.EvolvedPub.com
Evolved Publishing LLC
Butler, Wisconsin, USA

Printed in Book Antiqua font.

BOOKS BY SCOTT SHINBERG

MICHELLE REAGAN
Book 1: *Confessions of Eden*
Book 2: *Directive One*
Book 3: *Fly by Night*

DEDICATION

Everything that succeeds is the result of a team committed to making it happen. That's as true in bringing a novel to print as it is in conducting intelligence or military operations. My thanks go out to my publisher, editor, family, and friends for helping me bring Michelle Reagan back to the printed page.

Thanks also to my readers, especially those who keep asking me, "Is that stuff real?" Well, I can neither confirm nor deny it. But in truth, the reality of the Intelligence Community's capabilities is indeed far stranger than the fiction you'll read in Directive One. *If I wrote the truth (and somehow got it past the government censors), you wouldn't believe me anyway.*

And finally, to the real "Evan VanStone" (you know who you are), many thanks for your friendship and wise counsel over the years. You've always said analysts are the engine that keeps the Intelligence Community going strong. This time, you get your just, if virtual, reward.

DIRECTIVE ONE

A Michelle Reagan Novel
Book 2

SCOTT SHINBERG

Chapter 1

Holy shit, that crazy Irish bitch was right! Wendy Green thought gleefully as the young woman in the two-toned blue uniform of a Transportation Security Agency screener waved for her to step forward out of the machine. *This really is easy money!*

Wendy exited the full-body millimeter-wave X-ray scanner in the passenger screening area of Miami International Airport and turned to watch as Rhonda Williams squeezed her large frame into the device. While the post-9/11 security contrivance was tall, its front opening was clearly not built for people anywhere near the four-hundred pounds that Wendy, Rhonda, and their two traveling companions weighed.

Wendy gathered her new Michael Kors purse from the conveyor belt and unconsciously held her breath as she watched the scanner's sensor arm whirl in its orbit around her best friend. Hope turned to joy as the light on the scanner's display glowed green.

The machine didn't find any of it on us. Amazing!

The stoic TSA agent gave the same weary come-on-out wave to Rhonda that she had been giving airline passengers for the previous nine years.

"Watch out, Las Vegas, here we come!" Rhonda said energetically to her traveling companion. Nothing sounded better to her at that moment than an all-expenses paid vacation to Sin City.

"First things first," Wendy quietly said to her friend as they slipped their feet back into their sandals. "Once Monique gets through, let's find that bathroom."

***

Fluorescent lights glared off white painted cinder block walls in Miami International's TSA Screening Operations Center. The musty basement room smelled of stale coffee and the body odors of too many late-night shifts manned by TSA officers who the agency could neither put in front of the traveling public nor fire from their union-protected jobs.

"Oh, shit. Another whale," Tom Gleason groaned to his co-worker with a combination of delight and disgust. He shook his head and pointed to the computer monitor in front of him. "Look at the size of her, will you?"

"What's that, the third?" Ronny Daniels asked with a sneer.

"Fourth in a row. Man, it's not fair. Why do I get the orcas and you got that Barbie Doll earlier? Let me see the picture of her you snapped on your iPhone again. She's smokin' hot!"

"Here you go, you Peeping Tom. Don't get my phone sticky."

Gleason took the cellphone from Daniels and admired the contours of the shapely woman as pictured in the full-body, graphic detail of the high-resolution body imaging scanner. Running his left thumb over the smooth screen, he imagined he could feel her curves through the glass of the cell phone. With his right hand, in a motion he made a thousand times a day, he pressed the green *Clear* button on the screening console, admitting Monique Daniels into the sterile area of Miami International Airport to join her friends.

***

Evelyn O'Doherty stood in front of the ladies' room mirror in MIA's Terminal D, alternating between brushing her ginger hair and pretending to apply makeup to a face that needed no such assistance. While waiting for the four horsemen—horsewomen, in this case—of her planned apocalypse, Evelyn watched with a practiced eye as the rush of self-absorbed early morning passengers came and went, oblivious to the events playing out right in front of them.

Monique Daniels was the first of Evelyn's ensemble to arrive at the choreographed rendezvous. An imposing figure at 410 pounds, Daniels entered the room with the easy ebullience of a naturally outgoing woman not ashamed of her morbidly obese physique. Her sister-travelers followed closely behind and drew their conversations to a close as they entered the restroom. Each was anxious to get on with their business transaction and then into her first-class seat for a five-hour flight to Vegas.

Without a second look at the shapely redhead in the sleeveless white blouse and knee-length blue skirt, Rhonda Williams took the initiative. She entered the large handicapped stall at the end of the row and latched the door behind her.

O'Doherty took her place in the adjacent stall and set her large purse down on the floor. The redhead gently swung the blue door shut, securing it with an audible *click*. She removed the false bottom from her custom-made purse and pulled four small white envelopes from the hidden compartment. She tucked the envelopes into the front of her skirt to await the consummation of the morning's transactions. Finally, she placed an empty Victoria's Secret shopping bag on the stall floor and slid it under the partition to Rhonda Williams.

In the privacy of her large stall, Williams removed her green and white floral-print size 7X dress. She hung it from the hook on the back of the stall door and stood naked in the stall save for the new brown sandals she purchased the previous week with a small part of O'Doherty's five-thousand-dollar good-faith payment. Williams loved the silky feel of her new shoes and would have enjoyed admiring them on her feet but for the bulging abdomen that made seeing them impossible.

Williams carefully lifted her large left breast with her right hand and peeled a magazine filled with 9mm ammunition from the sticky paste that held it concealed underneath. From under her other breast, she removed a small-frame subcompact 9mm pistol and placed both in the shopping bag on the floor, careful to avoid making any incriminating metallic *clink*s.

With her right hand, Williams stretched across her body to lift the roll of belly fat on her left side and hiked the gelatinous mass up the few inches that it would go, resting it on her left forearm. She reached into the cavity created by her overlapping folds of cellulite and skin and carefully extracted several lengths of yellow Primaline detonating cord plastic explosive that O'Doherty had placed there earlier that morning when the five women gathered to put their plan into action. Adding the plastic explosive to the bag on the floor, Williams grinned, glad that this would all be over soon, and thinking about how she was going to rock the casino's world playing Roulette in Vegas with a sky-high stack of green $25 chips. She would finally have money to live like she knew she deserved. From under another fold, Williams removed the metal cylinder it contained. She carefully placed the pistol silencer into the pink-and-white striped Victoria's Secret shopping bag. A wide smile spread across her face as she slipped her dress back over her head.

O'Doherty watched Rhonda Williams's plump hand push the iconic pink-stripped shopping bag under the divider between their stalls. Silently inventorying the contents, the Irishwoman confirmed everything that was supposed to be present was indeed in the bag.

With a hint of a grin forming on the corners of her lips, O'Doherty reflected silently on the success she ascribed to their many practice sessions at Williams's apartment. *Practice makes perfect*, she thought, *or at least it keeps amateurs from screwing it all up.*

O'Doherty kept her end of the bargain by handing one envelope containing a key to Williams under the stall partition and briefly wondered what Williams would do with the twenty-five-thousand dollars waiting for her in a safe deposit box in the MGM Grand casino cashier's cage.

One after another, the three remaining women cycled through the handicapped stall, each in turn sliding her bagful of artfully concealed bounty under the divider. The women exchanged two pistols, another silencer, magazines of ammunition, plastique, detonators, and an explosive initiator for a prized key and the conclusion of a clandestine business arrangement a month in the making.

Chapter 2

Evelyn O'Doherty looked up from her seat in the boarding area to glance at the list of departures on the large electronic display across the aisle. AllSouth Airlines Flight 482 was on time for its regular Sunday morning flight from Miami to Washington's Reagan National Airport— the same route it had been making every day for the past two years.

Around her, the assortment of travelers—families returning from vacation, smiling college graduates sporting University of Miami t-shirts and mortarboard hats, and a medley of business executives— waited to board the 8:32 a.m. flight to Virginia. Some fidgeted in their seats while others meandered around the concourse, stretching their legs for the last time before boarding the plane for its scheduled two-hour flight.

O'Doherty slowly scanned the boarding area. Two uniformed police officers far off to her left seemed more interested in their cups of coffee than watching passengers. Not unexpectedly, she saw no sign of the man who was the reason for her flight this morning.

At the gate agent's instruction, O'Doherty lined up with her fellow first-class passengers to board the AllSouth flight. She followed the passengers in front of her down the jet bridge and into the first-class cabin of the aging McDonnell Douglas MD-90 aircraft. Gently, she placed her all-important carry-on bag in the empty overhead storage compartment and gracefully settled into her well-padded, leather clad, front-row aisle seat next to a gray-haired man who sat down in the window seat to her right.

Passengers filtered in slowly at first. Soon, the line thickened into a steady stream that alternatingly surged and stopped as passengers jostled their bags into overhead bins and slumped roughly into under-padded seats.

As the flow slowed to a trickle, O'Doherty looked down the aisle of the half-full jet. In coach, the bumping and shifting of too-large people into too-narrow seats continued. In first class, the four rows of the small cabin were almost full. Only the seats in the first two rows across the aisle from her remained vacant, although she knew that would not be the case for long.

The clamor of bags being stowed and metallic clicks of seat belts being secured across laps became fewer and quieter. The flight crew in the cockpit, oblivious to the maneuvering of their passengers, continued their pre-flight preparations.

O'Doherty watched with great interest as a gate agent entered through the aircraft's open doorway and handed the manifest and final paperwork to the captain for his review and signature. While the AllSouth agent awaited the captain's permission to close the aircraft's main door, she mouthed to the flight attendant working in the forward galley: "They're coming."

Two twentyish men with hair so short it was practically razor stubble entered the aircraft, flanking an older couple. O'Doherty didn't need to examine the watchful eyes of the pair of handsome young men clad in dark slacks, open-collared dress shirts, sports jackets, and lace-up black dress shoes to divine what their job was. Their radio earpieces made it clear to even casual onlookers what role each served on board—bodyguard.

As the guards settled into their second-row seats, the older couple they escorted took their assigned seats in the aircraft's first row. Across the aisle, a chill ran down O'Doherty's bare arms. She focused her attention on the in-flight magazine, consciously ignoring the newcomers as completely as she seemingly could—with mixed results.

The older woman in the aisle seat across from Evelyn had an attractive face, her wrinkles well-hidden by an artful application of makeup. Her brown hair draped across the shoulder of her white button-down sweater. Her husband, sitting against the window, had not aged nearly as well as his wife. The tufts of graying hair on the sides of his head failed to compensate nearly enough for the horseshoe of bald scalp above. His suit jacket sported a white and blue pin on its left lapel. O'Doherty didn't have to look at the pin's famous blue-and-white logo—she already knew what it represented.

***

The passengers of Flight 482 enjoyed a smooth climb-out, silently praising the gods of air travel for the lack of stomach-turning turbulence. The cries of the smallest children faded as Miami receded in the distance and the cabin air pressure equalized inside their inner ears.

Passengers and crew quickly settled into the universally accepted custom of modern air travel—ignoring the existence of one's fellow fliers to the maximum extent possible.

After the flight attendant cleared the breakfast service, O'Doherty flipped through several channels of the entertainment system. She skipped past the cartoons and satellite news broadcasts in quick succession and stopped on the in-flight map. The white icon superimposed upon the colorful map showed Flight 482 approaching Jacksonville. The flickering of the screen's occasional updates served as the only visible indication of the airliner's five-hundred miles per hour pace.

O'Doherty rose and retrieved her purse from the overhead compartment. She placed her sweater on her empty seat and a stick of chewing gum into her mouth before heading for the lavatory adjacent to the cockpit. Her progress to the restroom was closely monitored by those that could most easily see her, particularly the men seated in first class. Their rapt attention to her form-fitting skirt and pale, taut, athletic legs ensured that no detail of the seven steps she took was overlooked.

When she finished what she needed to do in the restroom, O'Doherty exited the tiny room and stepped out into the aisleway. She gripped her large purse tightly.

O'Doherty glanced at the flight attendant in the forward galley sorting the first-class passengers' used breakfast dishes and trays. Further back, the windbreaker-clad fortyish man in the third-row aisle seat shifted his gaze too slowly. O'Doherty knew he was looking at her with more than a casual interest. His watchful eyes spoke of more than just a man admiring her long auburn hair.

At her seat, she stood with her slim body angled to block the other passengers' views of her purse as she placed it on her seat. She removed the newspaper from her bag and looked closely at her seatmate. His thick gray hair still held hints of its once-dark color running along the sides.

O'Doherty placed the carefully folded newspaper on the armrest between the two seats. She watched the flicker of recognition register in the man's eyes as he saw the barrel of a pistol's suppressor jutting out from the ragged edge.

From her purse, the agile redhead withdrew the other silenced pistol. She spun smoothly on her right heel and fired a single shot from point-blank range into the head of the bodyguard sitting in the aisle seat of the second row. The soft *thwoop* of the shot was quickly followed by a muted *ting-thunk* as the brass casing of the subsonic hollow-point bullet ricocheted off the plastic bulkhead. The 9mm bullet splattered blood across the headrest of the dead man's seat and onto the middle-school-aged girl sitting against the window in the third row.

The bodyguard in the window seat scrambled to draw his weapon from the shoulder holster beneath his jacket. O'Doherty shifted her aim from the dead guard to the one racing to save his life and squeezed her pistol's trigger for the second time that morning. Neither man ever had a chance.

The blood-splashed 'tween girl in the third row howled a high-pitched wail. Her cries were joined by the rising screams of surprise and shock from other passengers in the first-class cabin, all of which combined to muffle the already suppressed *thwoop* of O'Doherty's second shot that ended the second bodyguard's life.

The metallic click of a seat belt buckle unlatching caught O'Doherty's ear through the din of frightened passengers.

O'Doherty spun a quarter turn and looked to her left. She aimed at the third-row passenger in the windbreaker as he grappled feverishly with his seatbelt, plunging his right hand inside his jacket under his left arm. O'Doherty squeezed the trigger of her pistol, sending her third bullet of the morning into the upper abdomen of the plain-clothed TSA air marshal.

Wracked with pain from the rending of muscle and organs the subsonic 9mm hollow-point bullet caused to his left lung, the air marshal let out a slow, deep grunt of torment and slumped back in his seat, holding himself in agony. With another quick shot—this one to his head—O'Doherty put an expedited end to the lawman's short bout of suffering.

O'Doherty quickly stepped aft, past the curtain separating the two cabins of the aircraft. She aimed carefully down the long aisle at the flight attendant running for the rear galley—and more importantly the intercom to the cockpit that it contained. She centered the small rectangle of the pistol's front sight into the notch of the rear sights, steadied her two-handed grip on her weapon, and squeezed the trigger at a deliberate pace. The 9mm slug flew forty-two feet until it penetrated the lower back of the woman dressed in AllSouth Airlines's blue-and-yellow summer uniform. The flight attendant crumpled to the floor, paralyzed by the searing pain.

With no immediate need to kill the now-disabled flight attendant, O'Doherty returned to the fore galley. The flight attendant who had so recently served her a fruit plate and cheese-omelet breakfast with a smile, now stood holding the intercom handset in her left hand. The ashen-faced cabin crewmember's right index finger stabbed the control box wildly, repeatedly missing the button that would call the cockpit.

Adrenaline and the stress of the moment accentuated O'Doherty's Irish brogue more than she would have liked. "If you hadn't gone for the phone, I might have been more lenient with you, dear."

"Please, I...." the flight attendant muttered defensively. Her sallow face shook uncontrollably.

O'Doherty pulled the trigger of her pistol, firing into the chest of the flight attendant. A mixture of the gunshot's *thwoop* and the high-pitched scream of the AllSouth employee's anguished cry reverberated through the small space of the galley. The slow-motion buckling of the fifty-something woman's legs gave her fall to the floor an almost cartoonish quality. Not willing to risk another quick shot at the flight attendant lest it pass through her slim body and puncture the fuselage of the aircraft, O'Doherty pushed the veteran crew member to the floor and ended her life with a bullet straight down into the top of the senior flight attendant's skull.

O'Doherty moved to the cockpit door with a rehearsed tempo and removed the chewing gum from her mouth. She placed half of the colorless wad over the peephole in the center of the door and spread the remainder of the now-flavorless confection onto the lens of the camera overhead. This blinded the pilots' only two views of the passenger cabin from the cockpit.

O'Doherty returned to the passengers. She stopped beside the gray-haired man who had been quietly sitting next to her for the past forty-five minutes. He stood in the aisle aiming his own silenced pistol—the one O'Doherty had concealed in the newspaper and placed on the armrest for him—at the ready. The tall man, several decades Evelyn O'Doherty's senior, kept his firearm leveled at the couple in the first row. The threat of two menacing semi-automatic pistols aimed in their direction and the clear willingness of the people wielding them to use them kept the couple quiet and attentive to their captors. Behind them, a cacophony of screams, shouts, and sobs from other passengers pervaded the passenger cabin.

Evelyn's seatmate pushed his thinning gray hair from his eyes and gestured to the seat she had only recently vacated. On the seat sat the weapons he had collected from the bodies of the air marshal and two bodyguards.

Evelyn nodded her approval. "One more minute."

The man nodded in return.

Evelyn snatched her bag from her seat and walked purposefully to the cockpit door. From the false bottom of her large purse, she carefully withdrew the long, thin yellow tube of "detonation cord" plastic explosive, a detonator, and an explosive initiator. She affixed the det cord in the shape of a large oval to the steel-and-aluminum reinforced cockpit door—a door built to the enhanced security specifications airlines worldwide quickly adopted after the September 11th attacks to prevent future hijackings.

O'Doherty ignored the buzzing of the passengers far behind her. She carefully attached the detonator to the squarely cut end of the straw-thin explosive. She stretched her rig's triggering mechanism along the floor to the galley, gathered her purse, inserted a pair of bright orange earplugs, and yelled a quick "Get ready" towards her seatmate.

Evelyn's partner took his cue and ducked back into his seat for protection behind the bulkhead that separated the first-class cabin from the galley.

"Fire in the hole!" O'Doherty yelled for the fun of it, no longer caring if the cockpit crew was alerted by strange noises from the passenger cabin. Things were about to get considerably louder. Smiling, she was almost giddy with anticipation.

O'Doherty buried her face into the corner of the small galley, opened her mouth to ensure the pressure would equalize in her lungs and not cause a fatal air embolism, and jerked the white plastic ring of the initiator with her index finger. The yellow flash and deafening bang filled the aircraft in an instant, followed immediately by the sharp, choking stench of the residue from the detonation of pentaerythritol tetranitrate—PETN.

In a flash, searing heat—which, for just an instant reached 7,600 degrees Fahrenheit—melted an oval-shaped section from the center of the door. The explosion's shockwave sent a fragment of the door crashing forward into the cockpit. The pilot standing at the door trying to see through the gum-covered spyhole never felt the impact that killed him. The door fragment slammed the body of the forty-two-year-old aviator into the bank of fuses and switches located above the MD-90's flight crew's seats. The door and the pilot came to rest against the edge of the control panel between the pair of cockpit seats.

The deafening roar of the blast and unfurling stench of PETN swept through the aircraft, silencing the panicked passengers. A hundred set of arms and legs shook silently—uncontrollably—now completely unsure whether they would live to see the sunset.

O'Doherty edged her way into the cockpit sideways. She twisted her lithe frame through the oval as she had practiced so many times back home, ever careful to avoid the still-glowing metal along the severed edges where a well-armored door had so recently stood. She grimaced at the sight of the dead captain's bloody, distorted face, the bottom half of which was missing where the door fragment had severed it from his head only seconds earlier.

She maneuvered through the cramped cockpit to reach the co-pilot. O'Doherty watched the uniformed man with three yellow stripes on each black epaulet of his now-stained uniform shirt writhe in pain. Blood seeped from his eyes and ears. At the sight of the middle-aged man's torment, O'Doherty felt a twinge of empathy for the suffering airman, now permanently blinded and deafened. The Irishwoman stood over him, aimed her pistol vertically, and fired a silenced round into the top of the co-pilot's head, mercifully ending his anguish.

She returned to the first-class cabin and looked appreciably at the familiar head of gray hair peeking around the corner of the bulkhead. She looked at him, hooked her thumb back towards the cockpit, and said with pride, "You're up, Declan."

With a nod, the taller man traded places with O'Doherty.

Evelyn looked at the married couple in the first row. The woman's face was frozen in panic, mid-sob, her white sweater now stained varyingly with blacks and grays by the dust and residue of the explosion. Her husband pressed her left hand firmly between both of his. Although appearing to comfort his wife, he sat almost oblivious to her presence. He stared wide-eyed at Evelyn O'Doherty and the pistol in her hand.

The balding man sat as still as a rock. His ears still rang from the explosion and his mind raced in circles as it processed just how quickly his world had changed in so short a time. In less than two minutes, Flight 482 had gone from just another tedious chore for him and his wife to endure on their return home, to an aerial nightmare of blood and explosions.

With time, at last, to pause for a deep breath, Evelyn looked for the first time that day directly at the lapel pin adorning the blue pinstriped suit jacket of her balding prisoner. She smiled in satisfaction, recognizing the bald eagle's head rising above the white shield, both set upon the circular blue background with a narrow gold edge—the official seal of the Central Intelligence Agency.

"So," O'Doherty said with feigned calmness and interest, "how was your daughter's wedding, Meester director?"

Chapter 3

Evelyn O'Doherty stood in the aisle where she could be seen by the passengers of Flight 482 and spoke slowly into the intercom.

"Ladies and Gentlemen, this is your hijacker speaking. You may have noticed that there has been a *teensy* bit of a ruckus up here in the first-class cabin. I can assure you that all the excitement is over for today. If you would so very kindly remain quiet and in your seats, I promise you that we will all land perfectly safely, and this will be over soon. Contrary to what the evening news might have you believe, I have no intent to crash this airplane into a building or anything nearly so foolish as that.

"Quite the contrary, I have plans to meet people at lunchtime, so I want to get this affair concluded quickly and safely, just as much as you do. So please, sit back, keep your seatbelts buckled, and you have my word that we will all land safely just as soon as we can."

O'Doherty returned the intercom handset to its cradle and perched herself on the flight attendant's fold-down jump seat opposite the couple in the first row. She gripped her pistol loosely but kept it at the ready in case a passenger decided to do something stupid.

Director of the Central Intelligence Agency Richard Duncan stroked his wife's arm reassuringly in a loving, if ineffective, attempt to comfort her. Heather Duncan's eyes remained locked on Evelyn's every move, and the older woman's stark-white hands quivered as they clenched the armrests.

"What do you want?" the head of the world's most powerful intelligence agency quietly asked his captor.

"You, Meester director," O'Doherty answered with a grin. "However, I don't need your wife," she said, and pointed the pistol at Heather Duncan's chest.

"Wait, *wait!*" Director Duncan said urgently, raising his hands in surrender. "Don't do that! Just tell me what you want."

"I just want you to do as you're told. If you cooperate, I assure you, you'll both stay alive. If you give me any hint of trouble, just remember... I'm here for *you*. I don't need her. So, until we land, just sit there quietly. If you do that, we'll get along just f*oi*ne, M*ee*ster Director."

"Alright, alright! You'll get no argument from me. You've made your point. You don't have to shoot anyone else."

"It remains to be seen what I may yet have to do today. Now, tell me, Director Duncan," Evelyn said as a sly grin spread across her face, "isn't it the CIA's job to know what's going on around the world? Just out of curiosity, then, how did you not see this coming?"

Chapter 4

Air Traffic Controller Randall Feit cursed under his breath and said into his microphone for the sixth time that afternoon, "I say again, aircraft squawking one-two-zero-zero on short approach to Bermuda International, say your callsign." Since the fourth iteration of his command, he had been leaving off what he desperately wanted to tack on the end: *You asshole*.

His supervisor, Deana Martin, looked over Feit's shoulder at the computer monitor displaying the planes in the airspace around Bermuda. "What's going on with the VFR aircraft at two-thousand feet, Randy?"

"No idea, Dee. It came up on my screen a minute ago and is interfering with scheduled inbound traffic. I'm broadcasting on both approach and emergency frequencies. He's lined up for a straight-in approach, but isn't responding to any of my calls." Feit threw his hands up in frustration. "Maybe it's a private pilot who doesn't know what the hell he's doing?"

"Well, shit," Dee muttered under her breath. "Delay the other two inbounds until we get this resolved. The VFR's clearly going to keep on coming whether we want him to or not. He'll never fly into *my* airport again, that's for damned sure. Vector the other traffic back around, and I'll call the tower. There's nothing else we can do from here, and it becomes the tower's problem once his wheels touch the runway."

***

Declan O'Doherty's fluid piloting demonstrated the expertise he had gained from his decades behind the yokes of larger, transcontinental aircraft—*heavies* in the parlance of the aviation world that he knew so well. He landed the MD-90 on Bermuda International Airport's Runway 12 shortly before noon, local time.

At the end of the runway, a small forward push of the left throttle was all it took for him to spin the airliner clockwise with the thrust of engine number one, beneath the jet's left wing. With a glance out the windscreen to satisfy himself with the aircraft's position, he throttled the engines back to idle and smoothly applied the foot-pedal brakes. The jet settled to a stop at the end of the runway, pointed back in the direction from which it had only just arrived. Declan nodded to himself, pleased, noting that the plane's stubby white nose aligned quite well with the runway's white dashed centerline.

Evelyn O'Doherty rotated the handle of the main cabin door and shoved it outwards, activating the emergency slide. With a high-pitched whine and whoosh of compressed air from its storage tank, the slide inflated and extended away from the aircraft's door.

Declan approached from behind Evelyn. "The helicopter's right on time, Evie. I saw it flying in from the east. It'll be here in fifteen seconds or so."

"Good. We don't have much more than a minute until the Garda arrive."

Declan's face contorted as a wave of pain rippled across his midsection. He grabbed at his abdomen and struggled to breathe through the discomfort.

"You're in pain," Evelyn said softly, and stroked his arm.

"The Percocet I took this morning wore off a while ago. I didn't want to take another and try to land while the aircraft is flying one way and my head is going another. As the old saying goes, 'What butter and whiskey will not cure, there's no cure for.' That may be true, but Percocet ain't a bad substitute. I have a few more in my pocket for after I take off. Pancreatic cancer is a painful way to go, I'm afraid, my dear."

"There," Declan said, and pointed through the open door towards the Eurocopter EC135 helicopter settling down thirty yards from the jet. "Kevin landed."

"Okay, I have to go now." Evelyn looked the taller man in the eyes and said with honest gratitude, "Thank you, Declan."

"Evie, please. Just this one time. This is the last time. Won't you let a dying man hear you say it again?"

Evelyn O'Doherty looked up at the wrinkles crisscrossing the face she had known so much better when it was smooth — all those years ago when his gray hair was as black as the night's sky over their native Donegal. The now-pained smile of the man who used to worship the ground she walked on — and maybe still did — looked upon her angelic face with the love of longing and loss. Evelyn looked up at the man who had agreed to make his last flight one that served her purpose, and the fulfillment of a lifetime's preparation. Her thoughts and fond memories brought forward a heartfelt smile and a distant memory of a warmth in her bosom that she had not felt since she was a twelve-year-old girl. Maybe they were memories of fondness, or perhaps she only had a fondness for those memories — she couldn't quite tell the difference.

"Yes, daddy," Evelyn said as she looked into her father's eyes. "Yes, I'll say it for you. Or Poppy. You always liked that one."

"I think, maybe, that's the one *you* liked the most, Evie. I missed you the whole time, you know that, right?" Declan said, his eyes tearing. "You have to know that. When your mother took you to her people, I... I... I never stopped loving you. Both of you. You have to know that, dear girl."

"Yes, Poppy. I know. I do know it, truly. I love you, too," she said, saying what her father wanted to hear. She kissed the ailing aviator on his cheek to make her parting words ever the more convincing.

A gravelly voice shouted from the bottom of the yellow emergency slide. "Come on, up there. Let's get a move on!"

Declan O'Doherty chuckled, and said to his daughter, "That's Kevin, all right. With that attitude, he's Seamus's son for sure."

Evelyn looked at her prisoner, and said, "Now, M*ee*ster Director, it's time to go." She spat out the rest rapidly, not giving Richard Duncan time to respond. "You first. Down the slide with you, and if you give Kevin at the bottom there any hassle while he's cuffing your hands, I'll shoot your wife. Maybe in the leg or maybe in the head. I don't know. Any questions? No? Good. Out you go, then."

Duncan did not even try to answer her clearly rhetorical questions.

With a look at his wife who sat shivering in fear, Duncan went down the slide as ordered without a word of protest. Evelyn watched as Kevin bound Richard Duncan's wrists behind his back without incident.

O'Doherty turned next to Mrs. Duncan. "All right, now, Heather. Let's join your husband, shall we?"

With a good sight more prompting and fuss than her husband required, the pair of O'Dohertys pushed Heather Duncan down the slide unceremoniously. She sprawled off the bottom of the slide and landed with a grunt on the runway next to her husband. Kevin handcuffed the still-dazed woman and lifted her to her feet.

Evelyn gave her father a final kiss on the cheek as her unspoken farewell and slid down the aircraft's emergency exit. On the ground, she and her hired pilot pushed the handcuffed Duncans forward and dashed to the six-seat helicopter.

Evelyn's eye caught sight of the bright red-and-green logo on the side of a white Digicel van parked next to a cell phone tower a few hundred yards away. Three maintenance workers stood staring at the unusual accumulation of aircraft at the end of the runway. O'Doherty ignored the three jumpsuit-clad workers and prodded her charges forward as the sirens of two approaching police cars grew louder.

Evelyn watched her father pull the emergency slide's quick-release latch and close the airplane's door. The yellow slide detached cleanly and dropped onto the runway.

With the Duncans safely seat-belted into the chopper's rear row, Evelyn climbed in beside the pilot. Kevin lifted the whirlybird off the runway with less than ten seconds to spare before the red-and-blue flashing lights of two airport police cars pulled up on the taxiway behind the wayward AllSouth Airways airliner.

In the airliner's captain's seat, Declan O'Doherty ignored the police and accelerated the MD-90 forward along Runway 30, launching it aloft to the west.

In the helo heading south, Kevin piloted the rotorcraft on an expedited path of its own, offshore over Clearwater Beach and away from the large fixed-wing aircraft and the turbulent jet wash spewing from behind its twin turbofan engines.

Evelyn took a deep breath, held it for a moment, and exhaled slowly. She watched the blue-and-yellow AllSouth Airlines jet recede effortlessly into the distance and wondered if her own plans for an uneventful getaway would go as smoothly.

Chapter 5

The National Reconnaissance Office's RATCHET 15 satellite crested the North Pole and headed south over the Atlantic Ocean, spiraling like a football forever falling across the sky. The small satellite sped along its preprogrammed orbit at over 17,300 miles an hour. Its broad-spectrum electromagnetic survey antennas vacuumed up the myriad signals from military and civilian radars broadcast by hundreds of terrestrial emitters within its line-of-sight.

As the spy satellite came within sight of the North American coast, it found no shortage of complex signals from military aircraft search radars, powerful over-the-horizon ballistic missile warning systems, and lower-power civilian air traffic control radars. The omnidirectional antennas mounted on the front of the spinning spacecraft scooped up each signal with ease.

Each received signal was fed through a series of application-specific integrated-circuit processors and compared to the characteristics of all known signals. Most of the intercepted signals were discarded as being of little interest. Unknown signals were compared in real-time against the Mission Priorities Tasking List, the MPTL, stored in RATCHET 15's memory.

Off the east coast of North America, the satellite's workload was light. Most signals from Canadian and US emitters were all well known. Some days, the occasional new pulse repetition frequency of a Russian naval radar signal would rate a high-enough priority on the MPTL to be reported in real time, but not today.

RATCHET 15 traced a ground track 300 nautical miles east of Charleston, South Carolina. As the SIGINT satellite sped towards the Caribbean Sea, it received a signal classified by the MPTL as TW-PRI-LOW. The low-priority known signal, while nonetheless on the tasking list as one to be reported upon every contact, would have to wait. Its low priority left the report in the satellite's communications transmit buffer for another hour. It sat unheeded until enough additional and higher-priority reports were queued up to justify the use of the satellite's precious battery power to downlink seemingly unimportant information.

Chapter 6

Kevin Riordan landed the EC135 on the gently rocking deck of the *Blue Ayes* and got out to refuel the helicopter.

Evelyn O'Doherty stepped down onto the flight deck atop the hundred-eighty-foot-long superyacht she chartered for the week. She shielded her eyes from the bright mid-day sun, looked appreciatively around the large vessel, and stared briefly out past the stern at the calm sea. The blue water stretched as far as her eye could see, with no land in sight.

She glanced at her watch and did some quick math. She estimated the fifty-mile helicopter flight took just over a half hour. The uneventful trip put them a few minutes ahead of schedule, she noted, pleased with her meticulous execution of a complex plan a year in the making.

Evelyn greeted a blond Nord wearing a crisp white uniform as he appeared from the lower deck to greet his guests. "Captain Nils, we're going to have some company."

"Certainly, ma'am," he said with a smile.

The captain craned his neck to get a good look at the silent pair seated in the rear of the helicopter. He noticed their exhausted eyes that barely blinked as they scanned their surroundings, darting from horizon to yacht to captain and back again. The career seaman looked closely at his new passengers and recognized the look on their faces— confusion. He cast an uncertain glance at his client as O'Doherty walked to the railing and looked out to sea. With the false smile of a professional servant addressing the mistress of the household, the captain assured her that several suitable cabins were available for her guests. Inwardly, Nils Bergan wondered what trouble this week's client might be getting him into.

The sound of rushing water from an otherwise calm sea drew shouts from the lower decks. Crew members of the *Blue Ayes* pointed off the yacht's port bow where white froth bubbled up from the sea fifty yards away. The unfolding scene immediately commanded the attention of all on board.

"Submarine, ho!" came a shout from a lower deck.

"What in the world?" Nils muttered. He rushed to the railing to see for himself what was emerging from Neptune's Deep. A lifelong sailor, he had seen more than one ship succumb to the ocean's depths, but to his mind, no ship should ever come up from the blue—it was a one-way trip.

The glistening obsidian hull of a submarine violently shed water as it emerged into the light of day. It breached the surface of the otherwise calm Atlantic with the rush of an impromptu waterfall. The rectangular, black-matte sail of the Soviet-built Kilo-class attack submarine sat like an afterthought atop the rounded black body of the warship.

O'Doherty stood silently beside Captain Nils as the two watched the iron whale emerge, sailing in formation abeam the *Blue Ayes*.

All hands aboard the *Blue* stood motionless, transfixed by the scene playing out in front of them. Crew and passengers alike watched with rapt attention as the sub's crew appeared on deck and inflated a large, reinforced-rubber raft.

As it headed for the *Blue Ayes* with its crew of four, the new arrival met with a mix of interest and concern from the yacht's crew. Aliens descending from the sky would not have gotten more amazed looks than did the submarine's crew.

"Captain," O'Doherty said, interrupting his wide-eyed gaping, "I did say we were going to have company, didn't I? They're expected. Please have my guests escorted up here when they arrive."

"*Uhhh*... Yes, ma'am," the captain responded, too shocked to argue otherwise. A professional merchant mariner before taking on the far more comfortable duties of a charter yacht skipper, Nils had only ever seen a submarine breach the surface in movies. To be boarded by the warship's crew was a shock to a man who had gotten used to little more excitement than avoiding bad weather while sailing rich guests between beautiful islands.

A crewman on the raft threw a line to an awaiting hand of Captain Nils's crew who tied it off securely. The *Blue*'s first officer, Johannes, a squat, powerfully built weightlifter who occasionally had to duck into one of the *Blue Ayes's* six staterooms to allow another crew member to pass in the narrow passageways, met the raft's passengers as they boarded. He escorted the four newest guests and the cargo they carried up three decks from the waterline to the flight deck, where they met their awaiting hostess.

Almost in unison, the submarine's crew members dropped the duffel bags on the flight deck.

Relieved of his load, the senior member of the contingent, who sported the traditional "scrambled eggs" of a commanding officer on his black uniform hat, smiled at Evelyn. "Hello, Miss Dor'ty," the bearded naval officer said warmly. His heavy accent blurred her name in almost unrecognizably guttural tones.

The officer looked appreciatively at the Duncans in the rear seat of the helicopter. He nodded to Evelyn and smiled so broadly that his white teeth contrasted starkly against his dark complexion and jet-black beard. "Well done, Miss Dor'ty. To tell truth, I had doubt. But now, I see to believe."

O'Doherty got the gist of the submariner's limited command of English. Certainly, he spoke English better than she spoke his native tongue. Evelyn smiled at the career naval officer and nodded, accepting the compliment silently.

The submarine's captain spoke to his three crew members in a language unrecognizable to Captain Nils, and the military men turned to leave. The three junior crewmembers made several trips between their raft and the flight deck while their captain paced about.

While the crew of the *Blue Ayes* watched with rapt attention, the submarine's crew piled twenty medium-sized duffel bags on the flight deck. O'Doherty inspected each thoroughly, careful to not let Captain Nils or First Mate Johannes see the contents.

Satisfied that the bags contained the $40 million in US currency she was due—and not an explosive double-cross—Evelyn nodded to the visiting captain.

The bearded sailor suppressed his displeasure at having to wait for the permission of a woman to conclude the transaction. He bristled at that thought and yelled at his crew to move faster. He stole a glance at Evelyn and smirked. Inwardly, he rejoiced at the foreknowledge that he would be the man in charge at the end of the day. Once back home, the admiral would, no doubt, be thrilled at the success of his mission. The captain's attitude brightened at the thought that a promotion would be his reward upon his triumphant homecoming.

Once Evelyn completed her inspection of the bags, the sub's captain ordered his crew to take the pair of shackled prisoners down to their transport. The submariner forced a smiled as he accepted the handcuff key from O'Doherty.

The crew of the *Blue Ayes* watched in disbelief as the newcomers departed, mouths agape at the afternoon's events. The small raft sailed the short distance to the sub with its pair of prizes—husband and wife—aboard. As the submarine's crew received their new passengers and recovered their raft, O'Doherty gave orders of her own.

"Captain Nils. I'm going below to change my blouse. This one's ready for the wash." She pointed to the dried blood and gray streaks of explosives residue which stained her white silk sleeveless top. "After that, I'm going to return to Bermuda for lunch and business. When I return to the *Blue* late this afternoon, I'd like to have that Atlantic salmon dinner Chef Julienne talked about the other night."

"Certainly, ma'am," Nils responded, slowly recovering from his bewilderment, and at a loss for anything more to say. His eyes remained glued to the sub abeam his own vessel as he watched the deflated raft being hauled aboard and stowed below deck.

In her cabin, O'Doherty tossed her soiled blouse on the bed and took the time to run a wet washcloth over her arms. There was no time to waste, but she needed to get the smell of the explosives off her. She dabbed perfume on her neck and grinned at the thought that she would enjoy showering that night more than she'd enjoyed a shower in a long time. The prospect of finally being able to relax after so many months of painstaking preparation excited her. From the dresser, Evelyn chose a maroon, short-sleeved blouse and pulled it over her head.

She grabbed the soiled white blouse from the corner of the bed, and said, "Pretty little thing, you have one more important job to do for me today." With a grunt, she pulled open the sliding glass door of her stateroom, dropped the stained garment on the floor of the balcony, and headed back upstairs.

Evelyn arrived on the flight deck as the top of the submersible warship's sail disappeared below the waves, hiding its bulbous hideousness below the beauty of the deep blue sea. A rooster tail of water fanned out behind the sub's periscope—the only remaining indication of anything hiding beneath the surface of the otherwise tranquil sea.

As the periscope's spray disappeared and the last remaining evidence of the submarine's existence evaporated in the noonday sun, Evelyn gave Kevin the signal for which he had been waiting.

"Now," she whispered. With the knuckle of her right index finger, she squeezed the crown of her Breitling wristwatch to activate the stopwatch.

The two moved into action simultaneously, as if sharing a single heartbeat. With a deliberate pace, but not so hurried so as to alarm the crew of the *Blue Ayes*, they loaded the heavy, cash-filled duffel bags onto the rear seats of the helicopter.

"How long do we have?" Kevin asked quietly.

"Five minutes. Maybe ten, but let's not be here to find out."

"Roight," he said, his Irish accent matching the strength of Evelyn's as the stresses of the day gripped him tightly across the back of his neck.

After they finished loading the last of the duffel bags, they climbed aboard the helo and he made quick work getting the aircraft into the air. He piloted the EC135 on a southerly heading, caring more about climbing for altitude than putting horizontal distance between themselves and the *Blue Ayes*.

Riordan eased the throttle back and guided the helicopter into a smooth orbit four-thousand feet above and one mile south of the yacht. He didn't have to hover long before he saw the white line form across the top of the dark blue sea below. The streak he had hoped would never form grew longer across the surface aimed directly at the yacht.

"Damn," he said, and sighed, "there it is, heading right for the *Blue Ayes*."

In an instant, the sea lit up below them. Flashes of yellows and oranges turned to blacks and grays as the diesel and aviation fuel tanks aboard the *Blue Ayes* erupted in sequence. A fireball climbed steadily into the air, spreading its ugly stain against the beauty of the pale blue sky. The colorful inferno raged silently on the surface while carbon-black smoke billowed skyward in two expanding, dark columns. The sleek lines of the luxury motor vessel's hull shattered and were thrust up from the sea at sharp, unnatural angles, mangled by the force and heat of the explosion.

The rear of the yacht, heavy with engines and generators, sank quickly while the front took on water more slowly and bobbed on its side as it burned. A few yards to the side of the mangled yacht, two lifeless bodies of the *Blue Ayes*' crew bobbed in the ocean.

Kevin spoke softly. "Oh, man, that was horrible. How long did it take them?"

"Six and a half minutes," O'Doherty replied. She pressed the button on the crown of her wristwatch, stopping the digital counter at 6:32.

"*Hooo*, it all happened so fast. You were right, Evelyn. They blew up the yacht. I can't believe they actually blew up the damned yacht. I mean... the crew!" Riordan paused and glanced over at O'Doherty. "They were really nice people. I feel bad about them."

"*We* didn't hurt them, Kevin. Just remember, that. The submarine torpedoed them. Not us. I had a hunch that the sub's captain wouldn't want to leave any witnesses alive. Including us."

"Sure look it," Riordan said, his brogue in full effect. "But *you* knew it was coming. Well... pretty sure it was coming, wasn't ya?"

"It was just a hunch, but a pretty good one. The smart survive. That's us—the smart ones. And rich, now, too."

"Yeah, I know, but still... I feel bad."

Kevin reached into the leather pocket on the door next to his seat and withdrew a yellow Garmin GPS navigation unit not much larger than a cell phone. He handed the pre-programmed device to Evelyn, and said, "Here, hold this, won't you? Read me the directions and distances every few minutes. We've got a two-hour flight to make and just enough fuel to get where we're going with the weight of the bags, so there's not much room for error."

O'Doherty settled into her seat for the afternoon's flight and focused on reading the small screen of the battery-operated GPS unit. She tried to ignore the growing queasiness in her stomach and hoped to avoid getting airsick in the small cabin. That would most certainly ruin an otherwise perfect day.

Chapter 7

CIA officer Michelle Reagan rolled over in bed and looked at her boyfriend. With an exaggerated motion, she gently drew her fingertips across the hair in the center of his chest.

"Good morning," Dr. Steven Krauss said. "What time did you get in last night?"

"About two-thirty. It was a long flight, and we landed at Dulles about an hour late. How was your business trip to London?" Her voice rose with excitement as she remembered its significance. "It was your first overseas trip as CIA's European Issues Coordinator after your promotion! Tell me *all* about it."

"It went well. MI-6 put on a good conference. Besides a few others from my group, we had some DIA analysts and German BND folks attend, as well. We spent the first few days in London and then went up to the Joint Intelligence Operations Center for a day. Just between us, I'm surprised at what the US military calls an *analyst*. Most of those kids are so young they can barely find Europe on a map. Most of them were born after the Berlin Wall came down. How can they *possibly* know anything about the context of what's going on over there?"

"Well, not everyone has a Ph.D. in history like you, so be kind. Besides, you're just getting cynical in your old age. How was the food?"

"Hit or miss. The Brits fry or boil everything. We did go to this one great restaurant downtown near the Thames, though. There's a carved wooden sign just inside, right near the bar, which says the place is owned by the Seventh Earl of something or other. I thought that was cool. I had the Shepherd's Pie. I enjoyed that."

"Beef and potatoes sound really good right now. I've been living on noodles and mystery meat for the past week, but I did enjoy the Chicken Madeira on the flight home. The red wine was way too sweet for my tastes, though."

"Noodles, eh? Off to Italy this time, were you?"

"Nice try, Steven." Even with his security clearance and super-grade status as a Senior Intelligence Service executive, he was still not cleared to know what his girlfriend of the last decade did for CIA's Special Activities Center—the covert action arm of the CIA. He knew the nature of her work and her operational cover name, Eden, but Michelle most definitely did not want him knowing about the details of her fieldwork nor worrying about her every time she traveled operationally. He'd picked her up from Navy hospitals twice over the years after she had been wounded in action. She didn't want to worry him unnecessarily.

"Okay, then, how's your new partner working out?"

"Alex is doing well," Michelle said. She pulled the covers up under her chin as she warded off a chill. "He has the tactical skills down cold, as you'd expect from a former SEAL. I'm a bit worried about his attitude when it comes to tradecraft practices like wearing disguises, though. He still seems to think that once we find, fix, and finish the problem, it's over and he can just waltz out of there—wherever *there* happens to be. In reality, there's still an entire national police force to evade on our way out. He's so used to only having to deal with military forces that he doesn't think much about the police. So, I'm working with him on that. One photo of him on the TV news and his career's over. Or worse."

Steven let Michelle's euphemism of "find and fix the problem" go without comment. He knew exactly what it meant, having personally seen her kill three people that were holding him at gunpoint on an ill-fated vacation several years earlier. Once she and Alex *found* their target, *finishing* him meant that someone's next of kin would be planning a funeral. Krauss had used the word *assassin* to her face only once. Michelle made it clear that she preferred the military's term, *operator*.

"I'm going to take an exceptionally long and hot shower. After that, how about we go to Bob and Edith's Diner for breakfast?"

"It's almost noon, sleepyhead."

"Yeah, but they serve omelets all day, and I could really go for one with mushrooms and tomatoes right now. You can get whatever you want. My treat!" Michelle threw her legs over the side of the bed, stood up, and stretched.

"Go take your shower," Steven said. He reached over and playfully slapped her bare behind. "I could go for the B and E burger again."

Michelle showered away the vestiges of her mission to Thailand using what she merrily thought to be all the hot water she hadn't consumed in the ten days she'd been out of the country. It took three shampooings until she was satisfied that she'd banished the remnants of too much back-alley café cigarette smoke out of her shoulder-length brunette locks.

She stepped out of the bathroom in her well-worn Terry cloth bath robe, hair wrapped up in her favorite blue towel. Steven stood in their bedroom, buttoning up a dress shirt.

"Did they change the dress code at the diner since I've been away?" Michelle asked jokingly. "Jeans and a polo shirt should work just fine."

"No, it's not that. I got a text message from the office while you were in the shower, and I have to go in for a while. There's a senior-executive recall. Probably just a test of the phone tree, or something."

"*Aww*, that's a shame...."

"Yeah, so I'll have to take a rain check on lunch. Why don't you choose where we'll go for dinner? My treat."

"Sure thing," Michelle said, and gave her boyfriend an extended kiss goodbye. "I'll make a reservation somewhere they don't serve noodles."

***

That evening, Krauss walked through the condo door and dropped his leather briefcase outside the hall closet. The thud of his tan leather attaché on the hallway carpeting was met with a familiar voice calling from the kitchen.

"I'm in here, Steven. It's after eight o'clock. Are you all right?"

"Sorry I didn't make it home for dinner," Krauss said, and grimaced. "I hope you ate without me."

"Mm hmm. I waited a while, but eventually got hungry," Michelle said as she chopped the ends off a half-dozen peeled carrots for her next-day's snack. "Hey, did you hear about that flight from Miami that went missing? It's all they're talking about on CNN." She gestured with her Henckels chef's knife to the television in the living room.

"Yeah, it's all over the news," he confirmed. "I'm sure it'll be the story of the week on every channel."

"Is that why you were called in? After that Malaysian Airlines flight went missing a few years ago, everyone went absolutely nuts for months. What do you think happened to this one?"

"No one knows. And I'd rather not talk about it. You understand."

Michelle froze, knife suspended in mid-air. "Oh, so that *is* why you were called in? Wow, okay, I won't ask. Fair enough."

"I stayed a while longer clearing out my inbox. It's going to be a long week, and I may not get to buy you that dinner for a while. It sucks that this came up just when you have a week off after your mission. It would have been great to get away for a couple of days or a long weekend—just the two of us."

"I'll take a rain check on the weekend get-away, as well, but I'm going to hold you to it this time. I haven't seen you in two weeks. But at least I got to spend this morning with you in bed," she said, as her face expanded into a devilish grin. "I'm planning to work out tomorrow. So why don't I use the headquarters gym in the morning, and then we can meet up for lunch? Even if we just eat in the cafeteria or at your desk, at least we can be together for a few minutes."

"That'd be great. I'm looking forward to it," Steven said, and nodded. Risking life and limb—or at least one of his ten favorite digits—he snatched a freshly peeled carrot from the butcher's block under Michelle's knife and plopped it into his mouth.

Chapter 8

In the basement gym of CIA Headquarters in McLean, Virginia, Michelle grunted out the last five reps of medicine-ball squats as Steven crossed the gym floor towards her. He glanced around the unfamiliar room at the half-dozen employees exercising and fidgeted with the knot of his tie.

"Hey," she said, and dropped the heavy ball onto the padded mat. She removed her iPod earbuds, and asked, "It's too early for lunch, isn't it?" She raised herself up onto her tiptoes, met the gaze of his hazel eyes for a moment, and leaned forward until their lips met.

"Hey, yourself," Krauss said. "Look, I'm not going to be able to take a break for lunch today. We're having a working lunch with a new task force we stood up this morning. There's a big briefing at 2 p.m. that I'd like you to sit in on. I'll have to sponsor you in, so just show up at Emergency Operations Center Two. Ask anyone that's going in to tell me you're outside, and I'll come get you. It's supposed to be senior executives only, but on this... I want your expert opinion on how something like this could have happened and what it might mean."

"You mean the air—"

Steve held up his hand to cut her off and looked around the gym to see if anyone was within earshot. Three employees on the far side of the room continued their runs on squeaky treadmills while a muscle-bound man in the far corner bench pressed what looked like a dangerous amount of weight.

Michelle looked at her boyfriend's raised hand. To her, Steve could not have looked any more like a man about to tell someone a secret if he tried. On more than one occasion during the years they'd been dating, Michelle had remarked that it's a good thing he's such a brilliant analyst because there's no way he'd survive a day in the field with tradecraft skills as bad as his.

Steve cupped his hands over the side of Michelle's sweaty face. Into her left ear, he whispered, "The director was on board. He's missing."

"The director of what?" Michelle whispered back.

Steve tilted his head slightly and stared silently into his girlfriend's brown eyes to let her question answer itself.

Her eyes went wide in surprise, and her face lit up in utter disbelief. "*No!*" she hissed.

"Two o'clock in EOC Two on the second floor." Steve held his index finger to his lips and turned to walk away.

Michelle shook her head and giggled.

***

Just before 2 p.m., Michelle Reagan settled into a seat near the back of the large briefing room, a few steps down from the audio-visual control booth. She watched as her boss, Michael, entered the room through the entrance to her right, near the breakout conference rooms.

He walked to a seat in the second row reserved for Senior Intelligence Service executives and scanned the auditorium-style seats of the EOC. The tall man, white hair slicked-back over the top of his head, did a double-take when he saw Michelle, a GS-13 grade employee, sitting near the back of a room full of executives. She smiled and nodded a silent greeting. Michael inclined his head towards the figure of Steven Krauss who stood on the dais, next to the podium. Michelle nodded at Michael's silent question — yes, she was there at her boyfriend's invitation.

The EOC filled rapidly with CIA executives and senior managers. As the number of empty seats dwindled and the air conditioner struggled to keep pace with the increased demand suddenly placed upon it, Michelle felt mixed emotions about her choice of attire for the day. Having only planned to have lunch with her boyfriend, she wore a skirt shorter than she would have chosen had she expected to sit in a room full of conservatively dressed senior managers. While she didn't really care what they might think of her personally, Michelle would never do anything to embarrass her boss in front of his peers. She tugged at the hem of her skirt, pulling it the little extra she could wiggle it along her thigh.

The facilities manager stepped to the podium and addressed the gathered crowd over the microphone. "Ladies and gentlemen, the deputy director."

The assembly rose to their feet as US Air Force General Barbara Folson entered. The career Air Force Intelligence Operations officer had made it perfectly clear early in her tenure on the seventh floor that she preferred to be addressed as "the General." Folson walked briskly past Krauss and stopped in the center of the dais. Four stars sparkled brightly from each epaulet on her dark blue Class A uniform, and five rows of impeccably arranged "fruit salad" ribbons adorned the jacket below her silver jump wings.

Two CIA Security Protective Officers—SPOs—in dark suits with earpieces conspicuously protruding from their left ears, followed her into the room and took up positions in the front corners.

Above the reinforced exit, a bright red sign illuminated as the doors latched closed with a soft *whump*. The notice read simply, "This Briefing is Classified TOP SECRET."

"Thank you," the DD/CIA said to the assembly. "Take your seats. We have a lot of information to cover. Yesterday, the impossible happened, and it's our job to figure out both how and why. By now, all of you know that AllSouth Airlines Flight 482 disappeared east of Jacksonville, Florida. What most of you do not yet know is that Director Richard and Mrs. Heather Duncan were passengers on that flight. They were returning from Miami where, over the weekend, they attended the wedding of their youngest daughter, Julia."

Murmurs of shock and disbelief rustled roughly across the room. While the entire nation had been glued to the non-stop TV coverage of the missing airliner, most of those in attendance had not heard the closely held fact that the Director of the CIA had been aboard. The audible gasps from the gathered brain trust of the free world's most powerful intelligence agency testified to the true degree of surprise behind their professional, practiced poker faces.

"With all of the additional security measures implemented after the September 11th attacks, how a commercial airliner can disappear in mid-flight over the continental United States is a monumental concern for the entire nation from the President on down. Right now, you might feel relieved that you do not work for the TSA, but what started out as *their* problem is now *our* problem. It's *our* director who is missing, so you and your teams have one and only one priority for the foreseeable future—find the Duncans and get them both back safely!

"I don't want to color your views of what may or may not have happened this weekend, so I won't use words like *hijacked* or *crashed* or *terrorist*. It's up to you to figure that out. What I do want to do, however, is to give you the highlights of the events that occurred as we know the facts to be as of this moment. Then I'll turn the briefing over to others to provide you with more details and specific taskings.

"What we know for sure is this: Last Thursday afternoon, Director and Mrs. Duncan took an AllSouth Airlines flight from Washington Reagan airport to Miami International. Friday night, they hosted the rehearsal dinner and then attended Julia's wedding on Saturday afternoon. As far as we know, everything on the ground went well, and everything up to then went as planned. Sunday morning, the Duncans boarded Flight 482, also as planned. What was not planned, however, was that upon reaching a point off the coast of Jacksonville, the flight disappeared from the FAA's radar. Neither the two-man security detail accompanying them aboard the aircraft nor the larger contingent of SPOs that protected the director on the ground in Florida ever reported anything unusual or suspicious. So, we have very little to go on at this point.

"There are a few sketchy reports of a possible sighting of the aircraft in Bermuda a few hours later. I must emphasize that these are unconfirmed, and the wild speculation in the media last night about a 'Bermuda Triangle incident' is not at all helpful. They're causing a flood of calls from every nutjob out there to 9-1-1 emergency operators and FBI field offices across the country. For reasons that Steve Krauss will detail for you in a moment, the task forces for this incident are being led by the Europe and Eurasia Mission Center."

The General paused and looked from one end of the room to the other. She pointed her finger and swept it across the front row of executives. "Let me make one thing perfectly clear to each and every one of you right up front. You have no higher priority than this. All collection assets are in play to resolve this crisis. You will make available any and all analytic resources requested by the task forces being set up. You have no budget concerns anymore. You are to prioritize this above all other requirements. I'm on the phone with the White House three times a day and, understandably, the President wants answers from me—answers that I don't have, but *you* are going to get for me. Starting right now.

"I want to emphasize one more thing for you to think about long and hard today, tonight, and for the rest of time, and no, it has nothing to do with secrecy or security. It has to do with *you*. Look at the men and women sitting to your left and your right."

The assembled crowd glanced around the room and looked at colleagues they had known for ten, twenty, or in some cases thirty years. Brief smiles of recognition passed through the crowd among men and women they had trained with, deployed with on remote overseas assignments, fought protracted wars alongside, and in many cases waged acrimonious budget battles against in the safety of their plush headquarters offices.

"Ladies and gentlemen," the General continued, "this is the same team of experts that we would have brought together if it were *you* who were missing instead of the Duncans. This same collection of professionals would be asked to find *you* if it had been you and your husband or wife on that plane. We're going to find the director, not because he's the Director of the Central Intelligence Agency, but because he's one of *us*. As I look around this room, I realize that I may very well be the only one here who is not career CIA. In the military, we have a saying that we leave no one behind. I'm asking you to put the same level of dedication into your work over the coming days or weeks that you would if it were your best friend or your co-worker or your husband or your wife who were missing. I'm asking you to do that for the director, because that's exactly what I'd be asking everyone in this agency to do if it were you on Flight 482, instead."

The crowd sat still, silently absorbing the deputy director's entreaty. Several executives shifted in their seats uncomfortably as the magnitude of the task in front of them started to come into sharp relief. The shifting of one of the world's largest intelligence enterprises into a cohesive whole focused on a single task—finding a single man somewhere on the planet—had never been done before. Even the hunt for Usama bin Laden was a far more limited, focused effort. This, they began to realize, was going to be a pivot the likes of which their beloved agency had never seen.

"With that, let me turn the microphone over to Dr. Steven Kraus, the Europe and Eurasia Mission Center's Issues Coordinator. Steve?"

"Thank you, General," Steve said, taking his place at the podium in the center of the dais. "We have been tasked with leading the analytical effort for this incident. The reason for that is because of the airplane that landed unexpectedly in Bermuda and where it then headed after it took off again. As the deputy director mentioned, an unidentified flight landed yesterday at L. F. Wade, Bermuda's international airport. It has not yet been confirmed that it was AllSouth Flight 482. TSA, DHS, and the FBI are all going over the evidence, from radar tapes to runway surveillance video, and we should have something more definitive from them tomorrow.

"Reports from Bermuda are all pretty well aligned. What we've gathered so far is that an unscheduled airliner landed in Bermuda without identifying itself. After landing, a helicopter landed near the plane. Three or four people exited the aircraft, boarded the helo, and took off. After that, the airliner also took off. Although the jet was not transmitting a transponder signal on its outbound leg, the airport's radar received a few sporadic returns showing that the aircraft headed east-northeast. In effect, towards Europe. That's why this Mission Center been tasked as the lead for these task forces.

"We have established three task forces, and most of your interactions will be with those. The first will focus on the aircraft. Where did it come from, where did it go, and where is it now? We're expecting to get significant support from the Directorate of Science and Technology and outside agencies. That's being headed up by Chris King. The second task force, led by William Nowitzki, is focusing on the tradecraft. Whether the AllSouth flight crew took the plane themselves or there were third-party hijackers, how did they get personnel and equipment through airport security and subsequently seize control of an aircraft in flight? Third, the people. *Our* people. Find the director and his wife. That task force is under Evan VanStone.

"All assignments, schedules, and contact information are being posted on the task forces' intranet websites, so check online and contact the appropriate leads if you have any questions. For the foreseeable future, we will have daily stand-up briefings at 2 p.m. in this room. Today's briefing is Agency only. Starting tomorrow and continuing indefinitely, we will have liaisons present from the FBI—"

A few groans filtered throughout the EOC at Krauss's mention of the Bureau, showcasing what some viewed as a harmless interagency rivalry and others as well-earned CIA snobbery.

"—and DHS's Office of Intelligence and Analysis."

The groans aimed at the FBI turned into hearty laughter at the mention of DHS's ill-regarded intelligence shop. While CIA officers often lampoon "military intelligence" as an oxymoron, they consider "DHS intelligence" to be an outright impossibility.

"See you all tomorrow afternoon," Steve Krauss said, ending the briefing.

Michelle watched as the crowd slowly filtered out of the EOC. Steve remained on the dais answering questions posed by a line of executives that stretched up the auditorium's stairs.

As her boss ascended the stairs in her direction, Michelle patted the seat next to her. He took the offered seat.

"We'll do the debrief of your trip to Thailand tomorrow morning at our office," Michael said to her. "Then, it seems, we'll both be back here in the afternoon."

Michelle shrugged. "I don't know. Steven asked me to attend this one, but I don't know what I have to add."

"Hey, it's *your* week off. If you want to work, that's fine with me. Spend your free time however you'd like."

She smiled, silently condemning in her mind the thought that most of the people who had so recently occupied the padded leather seats around her would actually consider sitting through two short speeches to be work.

The pair of covert action operators watched as Dagmar Bhoti made her way to the dais and approached Krauss. The Chief of CIA's Counter Intelligence Mission Center, the CIMC, was an almost legendary figure in some CIA circles ever since she led the investigation that uncovered the traitor Aldrich Ames in the 1990s. Not having foreseen the disappearance of the Director of the CIA, however, promised to tarnish the otherwise sterling reputation of the CIMC's first female chief.

Michelle watched as Krauss and Bhoti stepped down from the dais and walked up the steps towards her. She thought back briefly to the time her own hair was as short as Bhoti's sandy crop — not much longer than a crew cut standing straight up in short, immovable spikes. By contrast, the front of Krauss's longer brown hair bounced as he ascended each stair.

Dagmar Bhoti was one of the few CIA employees who knew the true nature of the covert action missions that Michael's team performed. Shortly after his appointment as CIA Director, Richard Duncan had brought Dagmar into the fold before sending Michelle to Johannesburg, South Africa, to kill a Canadian intelligence officer who had been turned into a double agent by North Korea. Michelle was disappointed that Duncan let Bhoti in on the secret of their team that morning, but the decision was not hers to make.

As Krauss and Bhoti approached, Michelle smirked at the thought that both Steve and Dagmar knew the truth of her real job on Michael's team, yet neither of them knew that the other knew. Michelle thought that the coming conversation could be fun — watching both squirm as each tried to talk around the topic.

Michael spoke first, addressing his fellow senior executive. "Hello, Dagmar. How are you?"

Not even the copious amounts of Visine she continued to apply throughout the day could eradicate the redness from her eyes. "I was doing much better Saturday watching the Nationals beat the Atlanta Braves, that's for sure. Sunday, though? Not a good day for anyone. I haven't slept since the incident."

Dagmar looked at Michelle and paused before asking the covert operative, "Steve mentioned he asked you to sit in on this briefing."

"Yes," Michelle responded, tentatively. She knew that Steve stood a better chance of getting reprimanded for extending the invite to a non-executive than Michelle did in accepting it.

"She works in the Special Activities Center," Krauss interjected somewhat defensively. "I thought her experience might help our tradecraft task force understand how something like this might have happened. She has experience doing...."

Krauss searched for the right word—or euphemism—to describe what his girlfriend did for the Agency. His eyes darted from Michelle to Dagmar and back again.

He parsed his next few words carefully. "...things that you and I couldn't even dream about."

Bhoti nodded and looked quickly across the faces of the other three. "I imagine some of those dreams might seem more like nightmares."

Michelle's mind raced as she debated what response, if any, would be most appropriate. The rapid approach of a man in an open-collar shirt saved her from the short-lived dilemma.

"Dagmar," he said, slightly out of breath. He looked at the unknown faces in the group and chose his words carefully. There seemed to be a lot of that going on today.

He leaned in to speak with Bhoti, and said, "We got a hit."

A spark ignited behind Bhoti's tired eyes. Her throat pulsated as she swallowed hard. "Let's take this into one of the breakout rooms, Andy," she said to the newcomer.

Michael stood up. "Good to see you again, Dagmar. I'll leave you to it."

Michelle rose to follow her boss out of the room but was stopped by Dagmar.

"Eden, why don't you join us for this discussion?"

Without waiting for a response, Dagmar turned to follow Andy down the stairs.

As the others strode down the tile-clad steps, Steve shot his girlfriend a wide-eyed look they both understood: *She called you Eden!*

More an alter ego than a formal cover name, Steve knew Michelle's operational moniker and could barely contain himself upon discovering that the CIA's most senior counterintelligence officer also knew it. Until that moment, he would have sworn on a stack of bibles that someone in Dagmar's position would have been actively hunting Michelle, not inviting her into an obviously sensitive conversation.

Michelle gave her boyfriend a sweet, slightly seductive smile. Their secret about "her secret" was safe between them.

Chapter 9

Andrew Roselski looked across the conference table at Michelle Reagan and Steve Krauss as Dagmar Bhoti made introductions.

"Eden and Steve, this is Andy Roselski from the Office of Technical Collection in DS&T. Go ahead, Andy. Brief them. You can catch up on the security indoctrination paperwork later," Dagmar said.

"Okay. Well, umm, we got a hit on the director's location. Or, at least where he was yesterday."

Krauss's eyes went wide. "Are you *shitting* me? How did you do that? Where *is* he?"

"Well, at least yesterday, he was in Bermuda. Probably at the airport, but the geolocation accuracy isn't quite good enough to confirm that. But yeah, in reality, it had to be the airport."

Krauss leaned forward. "How do you know that?"

"It's a cooperative, satellite-based tracking system code named *Quadrature*. It's in the Tangled Web technology-protection control system. I'll give you the short version of the history and the technology so that you'll understand its limits. It's good, but it's not perfect."

Krauss sat back and laid his hands flat on the table. If the CIA had some means of tracking individuals anywhere in the world, it's no wonder the capability was so highly classified he had never heard of it.

"Over the past decade or so, one or two Presidents I'm sure I don't have to name have gotten rather good at giving the Secret Service the slip. Some nights, they'd get away from the White House grounds in a friend's car and go meet up with whatever woman they're having an affair with that month. Eventually, the Secret Service got so sick of it that they came to us quietly and asked if we had any tech they might be able to use to track them when they go AWOL.

"We didn't have anything suitable on the shelf, but the concept of tracking is not new. We did some R&D on the idea under the cover story that it'd be used for tracking terrorists in Asia or warlords in Africa, or whatever. We do that, too, by the way."

Steve and Michelle nodded in unison. While not familiar with the technology, both had experienced first-hand how tracking and targeting terrorists had become the Agency's fastest growing mission since 9/11.

"Anyway, we had the problem parameters of the token needing to be only semi-cooperative and non-powered. That means it couldn't have a battery."

Krauss furrowed his brow. "What's the *token*?"

"In this case, we had to figure out what kind of small device the Secret Service could give to a President to wear that we could track remotely. We watched a *lot* of videos of a number of Presidents and eventually saw what everyone else usually ignores. What we came up with in the end were specially crafted cufflinks and lapel pins. Everyone in DC wears lapel pins. They're so common that your eye just skips right over them. The Secret Service wears them for easy identification of agents on the protective detail. Members of Congress wear them to show which chamber they're in — the House or Senate. Contractors wear them to show off their company names and logos. Most VIP protective detail agents wear them, and, yes, even the Director of the CIA often wears one. Sometimes, Presidents wear pins with the Great Seal logo and sometimes just the American flag. From the video footage we watched, it seemed like some Presidents never take them off."

"Interesting," Krauss said, "but with no battery in something so small, what powers a signal that you can track?"

"That's the really clever part. The lapel pins and cufflinks don't need power since they're just reflectors. We fabricate them so they reflect the most common cellular communications frequencies. As long as the reflector's in range of a cell tower that broadcasts in one of the four most popular frequency ranges, the reflector will, well, reflect it. There are four layers in each reflector — one per frequency band. Each layer is coded with a unique serial number. The reflections are received by any one of a dozen US satellites that have the Quadrature receiver on board, and — "

Dagmar raised a finger, and asked, "Andy, that's good, but what are the limits of the technology?"

"Good question. It's not perfect. First, the token has to be outdoors. Cell site signals are just too weak to be detected from a reflector that's indoors. Second, a Quadrature-enabled satellite must be in the line of sight at the time. Between the Air Force and NRO, we only have about fourteen or fifteen currently active. We got the mission package down to only a pound-and-a-quarter, which is really good — "

"That's great," Krauss interrupted, not caring at all about the technical details, "but is it *reliable*? By that, I mean if we're going to narrow down a worldwide manhunt to only one island and ignore the rest of the world, we'd better be *damned* sure your system is working correctly, or we're all screwed. Remember, the director's life is on the line here."

"Yes, sir, I'm aware of that. The system does not give false negatives, but we're going to miss more reflections than we catch. The most significant limitation of this system is that the token has to be outdoors at the same time one of our enabled satellites is visible in the sky somewhere overhead. It doesn't have to be *right* overhead, just a couple of degrees above the horizon. Honestly, that may only be ten to fifteen percent of each day. The longer the token is outdoors, the greater the chance of successful detection."

Steve looked at Michelle and Dagmar to see if either had any questions.

Michelle cocked her head, and asked, "Andy, how did you get a token on Director Duncan?"

"Oh," Roselski replied, "that. Yeah, his protective detail briefed him on the program and gave him the choice of whether to wear one of our lapel pins or not. He agreed, so we gave him a variety of cufflinks and lapel pins with the CIA logo and an American flag to choose from. He knows all about it."

"Well," Michelle said, and shrugged, "I guess Bermuda is the place for you to start looking."

"Yeah," Krauss said, tapping his fingers on the tabletop. He looked at Michelle, and said, "We probably would have, anyway, but this pretty much seals the deal. I'd like you to go out there and see what you might notice that others don't."

"Is that really necessary, Steven?" Michelle asked. "The island's going to be swarming with case officers from the DO whose job it is to find all of that out. I'm not a Core Collector by trade or training, and I'm sure the FBI and DHS will also have their agents on the ground, as well."

"Yes, they will," he confirmed, "and they'll do the interviews, collect physical evidence, and ask all the usual questions. But when it comes to the most brazen snatch-and-grab job of all time, *you're* going to be looking for subtleties they might not think of. Law enforcement and intelligence collectors will look at the situation from their point of view. You'd look at it... well—" Krauss stumbled trying to finish his sentence.

With two others in the room, he realized that he had to tiptoe around implying the kind of work that Michelle did for the Agency. "—from the point of view of the aggressor. I mean... you guys in the SAC had your Extraordinary Rendition program for terrorists, right? So, you'd, you know, be able to look at it from that perspective."

"If you really want me to...." Michelle agreed, hesitantly.

"If it would make things easier," Dagmar offered, "I could provide you a position within the Counter Intelligence Mission Center as cover for your trip. Phil Thompson is my lead investigator on the ground in Bermuda. He can backstop you there."

"Fine," Michelle said, and shrugged. "Sure, why not. Tell Phil I can be there tomorrow."

Chapter 10

Michelle Reagan walked briskly to keep pace with Phil Thompson as they crossed the tarmac of Bermuda International Airport toward the open hangar door. Waves of heat rippled up from the black pavement of the aircraft parking apron. Michelle ran the back of her hand across her forehead, wiping the accumulating sweat from her face.

The tank-top was a good call, but I should not have worn a skirt and heels on this trip. What the hell was I thinking?

"The local authorities were nice enough to empty this aircraft hangar for us," the senior counter-intelligence officer told his newly arrived guest as they walked into the cavernous steel-lattice structure. "They let us set up camp in here, away from the media. TV crews have staked out their spots in front of the passenger terminal and around the perimeter of the airfield hoping to get a glimpse of anything that moves."

Phil chuckled and gestured to the two-dozen FBI special agents scurrying between folding tables set up along one wall of the hangar. "Can't miss Hoover's Heroes over there." Plastic evidence bags and laptop computers littered the tabletops. Most of the agents wore the famous FBI raid jacket, a dark blue windbreaker with *FBI* in large yellow letters emblazoned across the back. "Our offices are in the two secure mobile trailers, over there. Best part is, they're air conditioned."

The two CIA officers walked toward a pair of trailers parked against the wall opposite the FBI's encampment.

Inside, communications equipment and computer screens flashed as classified messages came and went through an encrypted satellite link. The cool air sent goosebumps up Michelle's bare arms.

Thompson sat down at the small conference table at the far end of the trailer, gestured for Michelle to join him, and got straight to the point. "Welcome to Bermuda, Eden. Dagmar asked me to provide you whatever assistance you need. I got here yesterday afternoon and had four CI officers out and about most of the night making contacts and asking questions, so we're not all that far ahead of you. We're relying on the FBI to gather and analyze the technical data—mostly radar and radio communications tapes. They also have the lead for eyewitness interviews and bagging-and-tagging the physical evidence. What little there is of it, anyway. Dagmar didn't say what you were going to be looking for, only that I should give you as much help as I could. What do you want to do first?"

"Phil, first, thank you so much for being accommodating. I'm sure you have real work to do and babysitting me is not high on your priority list. I want to get a close look at the end of the runway where the plane stopped and the helicopter landed."

"Are you an analyst? Dagmar didn't say what you do for the Company."

Michelle shook her head. "Special Activities Center." She didn't elaborate further.

Thompson nodded. "I suppose if anyone knows how to successfully kidnap someone, it'd be you folks. *Rendition*, is that what you guys call it?"

Michelle let the question go unanswered. Sometimes it's simply better to let the scent of mystery hang in the air.

"Well, anyway," Thompson continued, "that'll have to wait until tomorrow morning. The Bermudians said they'll close the runway for us for two hours each day, from 10 a.m. to noon. That's the least-active time for the airport and gives us plenty of daylight to work in. The FBI has the lead for that activity since they consider it a physical search for evidence. They're treating the area as a crime scene. We all brief in the hangar at nine and head out as soon as the tower says the last plane has arrived at the gate."

Phil pointed at Michelle's shoes. "You, umm, probably want to wear something made for walking. I mean, if you want to...."

"Yeah, I wore this to try to look like one of your counterintelligence officers. I've never used the cover of an investigator, before, but don't worry, I brought clothes for the field, too."

"Actually, here in the hangar today, you'll fit right in. So, why don't we go," Phil said, and rose from his chair, "and I'll introduce you to the FBI's lead guy. Assistant Special Agent in Charge Craig Marx runs the Washington Field Office's violent crime and major offender squads."

"'Assistant Special Agent in Charge'?" Michelle repeated. "That's an obnoxiously long title." With a grin, she asked, "They don't get pissed and try to shoot you if you simply call them *agent*, do they?"

Phil chuckled. "I call him Craig."

"Good. That's more my speed."

***

ASAC Craig Marx looked over the shoulder of a female agent entering data into her computer. "Yeah, that's good. Send it." He glanced up as the two CIA officers approached.

"Craig," Phil said, "this is Eden, one of my counter-intelligence officers."

"Pleased to meet you, Eden," ASAC Marx said, and extended his hand to the lovely CIA officer.

Michelle shook his hand firmly and returned the blond, athletic FBI agent's greeting. His tanned face and wide, bright smile contrasted with the crow's feet accenting the corners of his eyes. *Must be from too much squinting on stakeouts*, Michelle thought, looking over the handsome G-Man.

Michelle got right down to business. "I want to get a look at the end of the runway where the plane stopped and the helo landed. Phil says we have to wait until tomorrow morning."

"Right. We had our first shot at it this morning, and we'll go again tomorrow. We'll brief here as a group at nine sharp and then head out in a caravan. The locals have been very accommodating, and we're doing our best to not get in their way. Not that I would hesitate to push them harder, but so far, there hasn't been a need to. They've given us everything we've asked for. Practically rolled out the red carpet."

"Not that you haven't been asked this a million times already," Michelle said, "but do you have any idea who might have done this?"

"Considering how much money their hotels and restaurants are making off us and the media, I'm starting to think the Bermudians may have kidnapped the Duncans themselves. Just to boost tourism, you know?" He chuckled, and said, "I'm just kidding, but that's my way of saying that, no, at this point, we haven't got a clue."

"No ransom note? No phone call with demands?"

"Nope. Nothing that you'd expect to have in any other kidnapping case back home. No politically charged demands or terrorist groups taking credit. But nothing about this case is like any other I've ever seen. When somebody goes after a senior government official, it's usually to kill them out of revenge and not to kidnap him and his wife. Trying to safely kidnap someone in mid-air while he's being protected by two well-trained bodyguards would take a pair of balls the size of Texas. On top of that, there was an armed TSA Air Marshal on board. That hasn't hit the media, yet, by the way. What this all adds up to, I have no idea. *Yet.* But we will."

"And you're sure," Michelle asked, pointing at ASAC Marx, "that only three people from the plane exited and all three got onto the helicopter?"

"Yes, the video's not very clear, but it shows that much for sure. The runway surveillance video is low resolution and intended for keeping track of objects the size of airplanes — not people — but the angle is good. You can count the three as each slid down the emergency slide one at a time. If you go over to *that* table," Marx said, and pointed to a female FBI agent several tables away, "she can show you all of the video footage we have."

"Thanks," Michelle said, "I'll make that my next stop."

Chapter 11

Michelle Reagan stood at the edge of the runway in the morning sunshine on her second day in Bermuda. She watched attentively as four FBI agents made plaster casts of shoe prints in the grass adjacent to the temporarily quiet runway. As she looked across the empty expanse of the east end of L. F. Wade International Airport's Runway 12, a welcome onshore breeze gently tousled her ponytail from shoulder to shoulder.

For what seemed like the hundredth time that morning, she again studied the AllSouth Airlines plane in the runway surveillance photo in her hand. In her mind, she envisioned the aircraft sitting on the empty tract of runway that stretched out in front of her. The helicopter toward which the four specks in the picture ran stood motionless in the image—an instant frozen in time. The small helo in the photo sat centered in the triangle formed by the runway, a line of landing lights, and the airport's perimeter fence.

Michelle craned her neck to look at a cell phone tower adjacent to a maintenance hangar. From her years of training and practice with high-powered rifles, she estimated the distance to be just under a half-mile. *That's probably where the signal from the Tangled Web thingy came from.*

Off to her right and just off the airport property, she watched two motorcycles take practice laps around the sharp turns of a local racetrack. *The macadam aircraft parking apron between the runway and the racetrack would have made a perfect landing zone for the helo, but that would have required the hijackers to run their prisoners around the nose of the airliner and have to control them for another few hundred yards.*

She put herself mentally in the role of the aggressor, a role she was completely comfortable playing. The extra distance would have been difficult to cross while coaxing two prisoners forward. Quite likely, it would have been the difference between success and failure. *No, landing the helo right where they did was exactly what was necessary for this job. Whoever did this job planned it well. Damned well. Nothing was left to chance. They knew what they were doing, that's for sure.*

Begrudgingly, Michelle started to feel a measure of professional admiration for her adversary. Getting the Duncans back was not going to be easy. Or safe.

***

"Where did they find it?" Michelle asked Craig Marx once they were back in the hangar.

The seasoned FBI agent lifted the bloodstained blouse from the evidence table in front of him and continued describing the items his team was eagerly processing. "The Bermudian Coast Guard is recovering wreckage from a luxury yacht that burned and sunk about fifty miles southeast of here. No word, yet, on whether it was an accident or not. They haven't found any survivors, and no distress call went out, so it must have happened pretty quickly. The locals are bringing everything they recover here, and we're going through all of it, piece by piece. There's no guarantee that it's related to this case, but we're better off bagging and tagging it than not. Besides, the fact that there's blood on this shirt at least makes it appear that something bad happened."

"You mean other than the ship burned up and sank, eh? What makes you say it's a luxury yacht?"

Marx walked to a nearby table and turned over a circular life preserver resting on a plastic sheet. The ship's name, *Blue Ayes*, stood out in bold white letters against the bright orange flotation ring. "With the name handy, we simply looked it up in Lloyd's of London's online database. We'll follow up with subpoenas later, but for now, this is what we in the FBI call a clue."

Michelle laughed, put her hands on her hips, and chastised the FBI agent. "I call it cheating."

Chapter 12

The day after her return from Bermuda, Michelle Reagan sat opposite Steve Krauss and Dagmar Bhoti at the conference table in Steve's fourth-floor office in CIA Headquarters.

"The whole operation was obviously well planned and executed," Michelle said. "What struck me was the specific spot where the helicopter landed. Look at where the airliner sat in relation to the helo."

Michelle pointed two fingers to the satellite photo on the table. A CIA analyst had added graphic annotations to show where the helicopter and AllSouth jet met at the end of the runway. "The helo landed right in the middle of this grassy area and not over here on the large paved parking apron."

Krauss and Bhoti squinted at the areas Michelle indicated with her index fingers.

"On the one hand," Michelle continued, "I interpret that to mean that the helo pilot had good training and experience. *Good*, but not great. If he only had a little flying experience, he would most likely have had to put down on the large, wide-open, flat, paved area on the other side of the plane. But he didn't. Instead, he chose to land right in the line of sight from the airplane once its main cabin door opened. That made it a straight shot for the hijackers and hostages to run from the plane to the helo. It's much easier to control a couple of hostages running in a straight line compared to having to guide them around the nose of the airplane and then all the way over to the parking apron."

"So," Dagmar asked, "what makes you think that the pilot's training was only good?"

"If the pilot had the kind of training and experience that's common among military pilots, especially special forces pilots, he could have put the helo down much closer to the plane and made the getaway that much faster. Landing like that would have reduced the risk of them getting caught by the airport police, but he didn't. Instead, he made everyone run pretty far. I've been on a few helo insertions courtesy of both Army and Navy special forces pilots—"

"You have?" Steven asked, surprised. His girlfriend had never shared that particular tidbit with him. Michelle usually kept the operational details of her missions to herself, only letting her love in on the things she felt he absolutely had to know.

" — and those guys can land on a dime," Michelle continued. "They can put one landing skid down on a rooftop and let the tactical team off while the other skid is hanging in mid-air five stories above the street below. A pilot with that kind of training and experience would have landed the helo much closer to the plane, say, here." Michelle tapped a spot on the photo just off the end of the runway. "So, you're looking for someone at the low-to-middle end of the piloting skill range — a decent commercial pilot or maybe someone who had mainstream military training, but not too much active duty time.

"Another thing I've been trying to figure out is the number of hijackers. That's been *damned* hard to nail down. I've put the absolute low end at three. One flying the helo and two aboard the plane."

Krauss countered her theory. "The 9/11 hijackers had four or five terrorists per plane." He leaned back in his chair and interlaced his fingers behind his head — his preferred way to think, even if it did show everyone in the room an occasional underarm sweat stain. "The task force's working theory right now is that there were three or four aboard the plane and one flying the helo."

"I'm leaning towards the lower end," Michelle retorted. "I think that's the case because the helo has six seats — more than enough room. If it only had one pilot, then it can carry five passengers. If there were additional hijackers aboard the plane, I think at least one more of them would have accompanied the hostages aboard the helo to help control them. My assumption here is that the hostages were the most important part of this op and ensuring they made it to the helo quickly would have been the team's first priority. Besides, once everyone boarded the chopper, what would have happened if the prisoners started fighting back? One person has to fly while one other would have to deal with two unruly prisoners. No, I think if the hijackers had had a choice, they would have applied their manpower to controlling the prisoners all the way to their intended destination instead of leaving the additional man aboard the jet. Why would they even care about the jet afterwards, anyway?"

Krauss wagged his head slowly from side to side, unsure about Michelle's analysis. "Assuming that the plane was later crashed into the Atlantic, the task force thinks that Islamist terrorists wouldn't care that they'd end up dying or, as they say, 'being martyred.' So, there could have been three or four more onboard the jet just to keep the passengers from rising up."

"True, but what difference would it have made in the end if the passengers *had* actually retaken the aircraft? The FBI said the aircraft only had thirty minutes worth of fuel left when it left Bermuda, so it wouldn't have been possible to fly it anywhere they could actually land. With so little fuel left in the tanks, the point of no return was reached less than fifteen minutes after takeoff. Best possible case is... *what*? That if the passengers did take it back once airborne, and one of them happened to be a pilot, and somehow they could do it all within fifteen minutes, *then* they could have turned the plane around in time to land safely? How likely is that, really?"

"That would indeed be a long-shot," Dagmar said, in resignation. "And obviously, they didn't land back at the airport. You think they're all dead?"

Michelle nodded.

"We need to focus on the Duncans," Dagmar said softly. "We'll leave the search for wreckage to the Coast Guard."

Krauss did not like the thought that a hundred people may have died aboard the ill-fated AllSouth flight. With no reports of a wayward airliner having landed anywhere else in the world, the possibility of finding the jet intact shrank by the minute. Slowly, he said, "The Navy has the lead for that, now."

"Okay, whatever," Michelle said, shrugging. "They have more resources, I suppose. Speaking of wreckage, was anything useful found in the wreckage of the yacht the Bermudians found? Craig Marx showed me a blouse with what looked like a blood stain on it."

Krauss and Bhoti glanced nervously at each other. After a pause, Krauss nodded, and said, "Yes, but we're not releasing much info on that just yet. The DNA tests came back with a presumptive match for one of the Security Protective Officers on Director Duncan's detail."

Michelle's shoulders drooped. A DNA match meant only one thing to her: one of her fellow CIA officers had died in the line of duty. The few times a year she walked past the Memorial Wall in the lobby of CIA's Original Headquarters Building, she blew kisses to two stars engraved on its bottom row—one for each of the teammates she had lost in the line of duty. Michelle lowered her eyes to the photo on the table so Krauss and Bhoti wouldn't see her blink away the tears welling up.

Krauss paused uncomfortably before continuing. "We're waiting until the FBI completes the conclusive tests before we give information on the DNA match to the task forces. Key personnel already know, though. In the meantime, there's a full-court press ongoing to trace the yacht's position in the month before the incident and determine who rented it. The FBI has the lead for that so the information can eventually be used in court, if needed. Of course, we're pursuing it through intelligence channels, as well, which is almost always faster."

Michelle nodded silently. "What else can I do to help?"

Bhoti and Krauss sat silently.

After a moment, Bhoti broke the silence. "Just keep the Duncans in your prayers, I suppose. I get the feeling that this hunt is not going to be quick or easy."

Chapter 13

Steven Krauss walked through the condo's front door and dropped his worn leather briefcase down against the wall. The tan attaché landed with a resounding *thud*, which gave him little relief from the accumulated frustration he carried. Three short beeps from the disarmed alarm panel next to the door told him that Michelle had beaten him home—again. Knowing she was home and safe always made his homecomings sweeter.

"You're home early," Michelle called from the living room. "It's not midnight, yet," she added with a sarcastic tone.

Steve dropped down next to her on the sofa and loosened his tie. "Tomorrow will be one month since the hijacking. I just got fed up with it all and left early today." He looked at his wrist. The black-and-gold watch Michelle had bought him a few years earlier for his fortieth birthday showed 9:20 p.m. "*Early* being a relative term, I suppose."

"Well, I for one am glad you're home. You haven't taken any time off since the day of the incident, and you need to get a good night's sleep for once."

He stood up, walked to the sideboard in the dining room, and poured a glass of Jack Daniels into a short glass which bore the engraved initial *K*. "Do you want a drink?"

"No, thanks. I've got a hand-to-hand combat workout planned for tomorrow with Alex and a couple of paramilitary officers. Just about the entire Agency has been on no-notice recall orders for the last month. No travel. No training. No missions. Nothing. At least I get to work out a lot and enjoy yoga classes three times a week with Allison."

Michelle looked closely at her love. His face looked tired, but there was clearly more bothering him than he wanted to let on.

"Steven... what's really bugging you?"

Krauss threw back his head and downed his drink. With an overly exaggerated slow motion, he set the empty glass onto a cork-and-wood Columbia University coaster on the coffee table. His chest heaved, and he exhaled loudly.

"We've figured out damned-near everything about the hijacking but have no idea where the hell the Duncans are now. It took the FBI no time at all to find the four women who smuggled the weapons and explosives through airport security. Within a day of finding that blood-stained blouse and the other wreckage floating in the Atlantic, the FBI had watched all the airport surveillance videos from Miami and had no trouble identifying Evelyn O'Doherty. She wore the same blouse that morning at the Miami airport and made no effort whatsoever to hide her identity. She even purchased the first-class tickets for herself and her father with her own credit card, for Christ's sake! How much more blatant can you get? Her father was a career pilot for Aer Lingus, so we know who flew the plane once they'd seized control."

He threw his arms up in a gesture of frustration and shook his head.

"O'Doherty even chartered the *Blue Ayes* yacht under her own name," Krauss said, practically yelling. "It's as if they weren't trying to hide at all. Assuming they're not idiots — which they're obviously not — they knew we'd find all of this. What gets my goat is that they were so blatant about it all. It's like they don't care about being caught. Even the Unabomber hid his face with the hood of his sweatshirt, and then he went to live in a shack in the woods. But these two were right out there in the open like they didn't have a care in the world!"

Krauss yawned and shook his head. "By the way, the FBI's adding both of the O'Dohertys to their Top Ten Wanted list tomorrow."

"Maybe that'll help," Michelle said, trying to put a positive spin on the Bureau's chance of getting a good tip from the public. She didn't so much as believe it herself as she wanted to cheer her boyfriend up. "It'll put their photos out there for everyone to see. That should get them some good tips."

"It's going to light up their switchboard with a million false starts," Steve said, his grumpiness getting the best of him. He looked down at the empty glass and shrugged. "Maybe it will actually help. I don't know. At this point, it can't hurt. We know damned near everything there is to know about those two, except where the hell they are now."

"You do know *why*, don't you?" Michelle added. "Why they used their true names?"

Steve squinted at Michelle.

"They don't care if you know their identities."

"Yeah, so?" he asked as he stood to refill his glass.

"They're never going to use their real names again. They had new identities ready to go beforehand. Take it from me, some days I change identities more often than I change shoes. It goes with the job. The O'Dohertys prepared their escape—their *out*—well in advance of the mission. *Well* in advance."

"Yeah, the task forces have been going all over that with the Agency's cover experts," Steve said, reflecting on the extensive preparations his adversaries had made in preparation for their so-far successful endeavor. He refilled his glass and sipped it slowly. "Marx is coming over tomorrow to brief the task forces again. If you wanted to sit in... two o'clock, as usual."

Michelle nodded. "Okay. I'll come to headquarters after my workout. Remember, though, he knows me as Eden and thinks I work for Dagmar in counter-intel."

Steve nodded and polished off his second glass of whiskey, wondering if he should have a third drink or just take Michelle to bed. He did both.

Chapter 14

The next day, Michelle took what she had come to think of as her usual seat in the back row of Emergency Operations Center Two. After a short tongue-lashing of the audience by the General for the task forces' collective inabilities to locate Director Duncan, FBI Assistant Special Agent in Charge Craig Marx took the podium. He tilted the microphone up higher as he cleared his throat.

Marx briefed the assembly on the FBI's latest findings and analytical assessments. He related the confirmed match of the DNA found on Evelyn O'Doherty's silk blouse to one of the CIA's SPOs. CIA officers throughout the standing-room-only auditorium listened attentively as Marx presented recently collected information on the ties between O'Doherty's mother's family and Irish Republican Army cells across both Ireland and Northern Ireland.

"The FBI's intelligence analysts don't think there was direct IRA involvement in this matter," he explained. "There's growing suspicion that the Russians are behind this."

Soft murmurs of derision from the far-left end of the room turned increasingly hostile. "It was *not* the Russians. Damned FBI," one voice yelled from the crowd.

Marx explained the FBI analysts' theory about the Russians' intelligence agency. "Ever since the hijacking, the FSB has been buzzing like crazy. The increase in chatter has been significant."

The senior analyst from CIA's Russia Division rose and addressed ASAC Marx politely. "With all due respect to the FBI's intelligence analysts—" The executive ignored the resulting laughter from the audience. "—the Russians are crazy, but they're not insane. We have our sources, too. Moscow has been going crazy trying to find out what happened just like we are, but not because they're behind it. They don't know who took the director or where he is any more than we do. There's no *way* the Russians would do something like this and risk certain retaliation."

"I appreciate your thoughts," Marx continued. "We're not saying it was an authorized operation, only that they certainly have the resources to pull off something as audacious as this. And they have a long history of using expendable cut-outs like O'Doherty."

Comments of dismissal from the audience subsided slowly as the FBI agent wrapped up his presentation. Pointing to the Europe and Eurasia Mission Center's senior analyst, he said, "I'd be happy to put you in touch with the specific analyst at the Hoover building you should talk to."

At the conclusion of the briefing, the gathered crowd funneled rapidly out of the EOC. After answering a few questions from departing executives, Steven Krauss and ASAC Marx made their way up the stairs. Steven took a seat next to Michelle while Craig stood on the stairs trying to work away the sting of the harsh comments he'd received. He smiled ruefully at Michelle knowing that, sometimes, people have only the messenger to shoot.

"If not the Russians," Marx asked no one in particular, "then who?"

Chapter 15

Dagmar Bhoti's voice bellowed through the secure phone into Steven Krauss's ear. "We found him, Steve. Roselski got a hit!"

Krauss slammed down the mug containing his fifth cup of coffee of the day and jumped to his feet. "*Where*? *When*? Dagmar, it's been two months, and we've had a lot of false reports. Are you sure it's for real this time?"

"Roselski has been getting Quadrature hits for the past half-hour. I've had him triple-check the system. It's *real*. It's not a false alarm. The hits keep streaming in. Ever since the hijacking, Andy has had the system set for immediate reporting of every hit. We've seen nothing at all since Bermuda, not *one*. And now every—"

"Where the hell *is* he, Dagmar?" Krauss yelled, interrupting the counter-intelligence chief several grades his senior.

"You're not going to like it," she responded.

"I already don't like it. I haven't liked it for the past two months. Where is he?"

"Iran."

"*Iran*?"

"Iran. Meet me in Andy's office in ten minutes. He's pulling it all up on the map, then—"

Krauss didn't wait for her to finish her sentence. He slammed the telephone handset into the cradle and sprinted through his office door. His forgotten mug of coffee fell to the floor and shattered.

***

Andrew Roselski pointed to the map on the computer monitor with one hand and moved the mouse with his other. "We got nothing since Bermuda and then, all of a sudden, we got hits from three Quadrature-enable satellites within just a few minutes of each other. I ran a quick diagnostic, and it came back clean. These are real hits. The director is there. Right now. Or, at least his lapel pin is there. Remember, the system only finds—"

"Yeah, yeah, got it," Steve Krauss said impatiently. "Where in Iran? Show me."

Roselski tugged at the wheel in the center of the mouse with his index finger. The map zoomed in on the Persian Gulf. "Bandar Abbas Naval Base. Right smack in the middle of the Strait of Hormuz. *Here*," he said, pointing to the map. "It's probably the most heavily defended part of Iran. Maybe other than Tehran. You'll have to ask the folks in Persia House about that."

"What time is it over there?" Krauss asked.

"Middle of the night. Let me check." Roselski clicked through a few windows on his computer. "They're eight-and-a-half hours ahead of us."

"Eight-and-a-half? A-*half*? Seriously?"

"It's Iran. What can I say? Who knows why they do what they do?"

Krauss picked up the secure phone from Roselski's desk and dialed one of the task force leads. Evan VanStone answered on the second ring.

"Evan, Steve. Call the imagery analysts over at NGA supporting your task force and have them pull *everything* they have from the Bandar Abbas Naval Base in Iran for the past six months. I want to know the timeline of every ship's deployments and returns, every bit of new construction or heavy maintenance, and anything else that looks out of the ordinary. And I need it done yesterday. Tell them to work all night if they have to, and I'm sure they'll have to. I want an initial report by video teleconference two hours from now and a full briefing in person in EOC Two at ten o'clock tonight. Tell them to have a rep at the 2 p.m. briefing tomorrow ready to present to the General, as well."

"All right, Steve, will do, but why? Did you get a source report or something?" he asked, a sense of hope tinting his voice.

"Yes, it's a reliable Agency source, but don't tell *them* that. In fact, don't tell *anyone* that. *Now* we finally have somewhere to look, but I'm not convinced, yet. Not by a long shot. We need confirmation. A shitload of confirmation. Tell NGA to ramp up collection and immediate exploitation and reporting of all new imagery at top speed. It's a full-court press for them. I want every possible image taken by every satellite on every orbit. *No* exceptions. All birds are in play, here. Every damned one of them. We can't let anything get by us on this, got it?"

Steve hung up the phone before VanStone could answer. He put his hands on his hips, looked at Roselski and Bhoti, and took a deep breath.

"If this turns out to be real," Krauss said barely above a whisper while staring at the small circles of Quadrature hits dotting the map of the Iranian coast displayed on Roselski's computer screen, "the hardest part hasn't even started."

Krauss straightened his tie and looked at Roselski. "Give me a printout of that map with the Quadrature hit marks on it. Confirmed or not, I have to tell the General."

***

Michelle woke up and looked over as Steve dropped roughly into their bed. "I'm glad you're finally home," she said wearily. "What time is it?"

"Four-something."

Michelle groaned and rolled onto her side. "Good job finding the director, babe. I've barely seen you in the last couple of days. Please sleep in tomorrow. You need it."

"Can't. I'm meeting with the General after she returns from the White House. They're discussing options for getting the Duncans out."

"Good," Michelle said softly. "I can't imagine how they'll do that. Trying to sneak into a naval base in the middle of Iran is a fool's errand. I wonder what kind of chumps they'll find for that mission?"

Chapter 16

"Eden, we need you go to into Iran." General Barbara Folson gauged Michelle Reagan's reaction from across the polished mahogany conference table in the office suite the deputy director shared with the CIA Director and his senior staff on the seventh floor of the Agency's Original Headquarters Building.

Oh, fuck me, Michelle thought as she stole a glance across the table at Dagmar Bhoti. *I wonder if this is her doing. Things have been so nice and quiet the last few months. I should have known it wouldn't last.*

"You'll be part of the extraction team sent in to rescue Director Duncan and his wife," the deputy director continued. Her sallow complexion was the result of more than two months of crushing stress and endlessly long days. "The President has authorized a military extraction of the Duncans. The Air Force will be pummeling the hell out of the Iranians with just about every B-1 and B-2 bomber in our inventory. He's also taking this opportunity to use the B-2s to destroy the Iranian's nuclear weapons development capabilities at a dozen-and-a-half deep underground facilities. The ground assault to rescue the Duncans will be led by Navy SEALs out of Virginia Beach. You'll be assigned to them with the cover of an Agency liaison from the Special Activities Center. That part is actually true."

Michelle nodded. "I've trained with them before." *If that's the true part, what's the rest of the story, here? Why does she want me on this mission? The SAC has plenty of paramilitary operators who are specifically trained for straight-up combat missions. What's really going on?*

Michelle looked around the small, crowded table. She knew her team lead, Michael, and Dagmar from the CIMC, but she didn't recognize the silent black man in the three-piece suit. He sat next to Folson wordlessly, holding a manila envelope on the table in front of him. The anxiety washing across his face in waves led him to press the envelope under his hand harder than he intended, as if he might unintentionally force it into the polished wood of the table itself.

"Dagmar tells me," the General continued, "that you're the right person for this particular job. Not too many field officers have met the director, or more importantly, are someone he would recognize as a friendly face."

"We only met once," Michelle countered, certain that there had to be someone else better suited for the mission ahead.

"It was not a meeting the director will ever forget," Dagmar interjected. "I'm confident you're the right choice for this mission." Her insistence made it clear that no one else would even be considered.

Michelle wondered if this might be Dagmar's way of getting rid of her. If Michelle did not survive the incursion into Iran, there would be one less person left alive who knew about Dagmar's involvement in Michelle's mission to South Africa. *She may be able to put me in harm's way, but she'll have a much more difficult time getting rid of Michael. Bhoti's not off the hook, yet.*

"We all hope and fully expect the extraction mission to be successful," General Folson said, clearly forcing into her voice an upbeat tone that she was not truly feeling. "But it's obvious that the Iranians are expecting us to attempt a rescue of some sort. Satellite imagery of Bandar Abbas shows increased levels of preparedness and the reinforcement of some defensive structures. If things don't go as planned—" The D/Dir's voice cracked slightly.

She cleared her throat, and said, "If things don't go well... and if an extraction becomes impossible, but you're able to get close to the director, then you have a different mission." The General turned to the silent man seated to her left. "Show her. Eden, this is DeWayne Washington, the Agency's General Counsel."

Michelle kept her expression completely neutral, a tradecraft skill quickly perfected by all undercover officers who wanted to be successful in their career—or on occasion, just live through the day. Reinforced at the Farm through endless months of mentally exhausting training, the expertise came at a cost, but paid dividends throughout every field officer's years in the field. Michelle concealed her surprise that the Agency's top lawyer was being brought into a conversation that had anything even remotely to do with what she did on Michael's team. For Michelle, the day was getting stranger by the minute.

"Pleased to meet you, Eden," Washington said, his Brooklyn accent in full bloom. "I wish it were under more pleasant circumstances. There are only two copies of this document," the attorney said, and removed a single sheet of paper from the unmarked envelope.

Michelle recognized the colorful official seal of the CIA adorning the top of the piece of Agency stationary.

"I keep this copy in my office safe, and the other copy is retained by the director in his. The memos are not classified, however, discussion of them is strictly limited to those with an absolute need to know. As of today, you now have the need to know. This document is called Directive One.

"The first Directive One was signed by Major General William Donovan during World War II before one of his trips into the Pacific Theater of operations. He traveled overseas frequently to confer with allied nations and, in two or three cases, went behind enemy lines himself—against the advice of, well, pretty much everyone. I guess that's why they called him *Wild* Bill. Anyway, before his second such trip, he authored and left behind in his office a letter stating that if he were to be captured, he authorized the Office of Strategic Services or the Department of War—as the DoD was called back then—to attempt to rescue him, if possible. If an extraction were deemed to not be practical, then he authorized any agent of the US Government to kill him to prevent his knowledge of the Allies' forces, capabilities, or plans from falling into enemy hands. He knew full well that no one can withstand interrogation over the long run. Everyone has his limits. He did not want what he knew about our war plans and intelligence sources to become known to the Japanese or Germans. Director Duncan signed his own Directive One letter on his third day in office as CIA Director."

Michelle looked around the table, an expression of shock edged its way out of her practiced stoic countenance. Her astonishment at the very concept that anyone might so much as suggest that the CIA would kill its own Director got the upper hand in her attempt to suppress her feelings in front of the executives sitting around the table.

Her rapid-fire retort came out quicker than she would have liked. "The entire Intelligence Community just spent the past two months executing the world's most extensive manhunt in history—quite successfully, I might add—and now you seriously expect me to waltz into Iran and—"

"This is only for the worst-case scenario, Eden," General Folson interrupted. "I felt the same sense of revulsion at the idea. I only learned about Directive One after the hijacking. It's not what we usually think of, and it's definitely *not* our first option. Not by a long shot. We want the director, Mrs. Duncan, and every member of the extraction team, back home safe and sound. Only as an absolute last resort, if you're able to get *in* but cannot get *out*, only *then* would this even be something to consider. I also need to stress to you that this is not an assassination. The Agency does not do that anymore, thank God."

Michelle sat silently for a moment and gathered her thoughts. She looked at Dagmar Bhoti and recalled the early morning meeting that they had had several years before in which Dagmar, Michael, Richard Duncan, and she had sat at the conference table in the director's office, just a few doors down the hall. The mission to South Africa on which Director Duncan had sent Michelle to kill the Canadian intelligence service's Chief of Station in Johannesburg was most certainly what Folson insisted this was not: an assassination.

"Eden," Michael said, speaking for the first time. Her team lead's tone was uncharacteristically soft. "As integral to my team as you are— as you've always been—you are still a civil service employee. Unlike military personnel, you have the right to say no, or even to walk away from it all if you felt you needed to. But if you choose to go, I know you'll find the inner strength to do what needs to be done."

A native Texan, his usual cadence was far more brash. Michelle recognized her mentor's subtle way of sending her a signal the others would not catch. For the first time since she joined his team, Michael was telling her that this was a mission she should seriously consider declining.

"In the military," the deputy director said, reflecting, "ordering troops into combat comes with the job. This is not the same. Mike's right, I can't order you to go. You could say *no* or simply resign if you wanted to—"

Michelle shifted uncomfortably in her seat, uncrossed her legs, and recrossed them. Her poker face was long gone. "I understand, General, but I also see the Agency's need here. You probably didn't see me in the EOC when you first announced the director had been kidnapped. Your passion and speech about how the manhunt would have been the same if it had been anyone else in the room really touched me. I understand the gravity of the situation here and the damage that could be done with the information in Director Duncan's head. I hate to think about what they'll do to him during an interrogation. I get it, General, and to be honest, I'm not okay with the concept of this mission, but... I get it. So, I can do it."

Heads around the table nodded and DeWayne Washington slipped the single sheet of stationary back into its envelope.

"Just one question." Michelle looked Deputy Director Folson directly in her steel-grey eyes. "If that outcome *does* become necessary, what am I to do about Mrs. Duncan?"

Chapter 17

Five days later, Eden sat against a side wall of the Squadron Assembly Room—the SAR—that occupied the east end of the third floor of the Navy SEAL commander's office suite. The SAR was a veritable museum of successful Naval Special Warfare operations.

To her left hung a photo of four snipers from Dagger Squadron with the captain of the Maersk Alabama after his rescue from Somali Pirates. On the opposite wall hung a photo of six operators from multiple squadrons in Osama bin Laden's bedroom, kneeling around his corpse. Under the photo and engraved plaque hung the decommissioned AKM-47 that his son, Khalid, had carried on the night the SEALs raided their compound in Abbottabad, Pakistan. The rifle that bin Laden himself held the night he was killed had been presented long ago to the Director of the CIA after the FBI had finished examining it for fingerprints and DNA.

Commander Neal Towns stood at the podium preparing his briefing materials as Navy personnel filtered into the SAR. SEAL operators, special warfare boat crewmen, and assorted intelligence specialists entered and lingered, talking amongst the gathering of the world's most celebrated fighting force.

Two women dressed in pressed khaki uniforms entered the SAR and looked around excitedly. They spotted Michelle and made a beeline for her side of the room.

"You must be Eden," the taller of the two Lieutenants said with a broad smile. "We heard you were going to be here for the briefing. I'm Tamara Cruikshank, but everyone calls me Banshee. This is Valkyrie."

"Hi," the blonde Lieutenant said, thrusting her hand forward to shake Eden's. "I'm Valerie Sheppard. Or Valkyrie. Either works. It's great to meet you!"

Eden rose and shook each of their hands. With a frown, she replied, "Well, you've already figured out who I am. So much for my cover."

The naval officers' demeanors fell quickly from one of joy at meeting another female Operations professional to one of surprise and concern at having unknowingly outed an undercover officer—a cardinal sin in their business.

Eden broke into a wide grin. "I'm kidding! Good to meet you, too."

"Oh, whew," Valkyrie said, recovering from the shock and allowing herself a smile. "You had me going for a minute, there."

"I can see that," Eden said. "I can also see how you got the nickname *Valkyrie* from Valerie, but how did you get the nickname *Banshee*? I can think of a few ways, but I don't know you well enough to want to imply anything quite so, umm, personal?"

"No, no, I get asked that all the time," LT Cruikshank replied. "I was going through the Army's Airborne course at Ft. Benning, Georgia. You know, jump school? Anyway, one of the Army NCOs said that on my first jump I screamed like a banshee as I exited the C-130. Personally, I think half of the guys screamed, too, but, well, you know, the name stuck."

Eden nodded as she watched her host, Master Chief Petty Officer Mitchell Dombrovsky, approach the three women. A muscular SEAL operator in tan fatigues followed close behind the khaki-clad senior NCO. Eden marveled at how well the exceptionally tall man filled out his uniform. His skin was darker than any she could recall seeing in person. Fluorescent lights reflected brightly off his bald head, contrasting his smooth complexion.

Dombrovsky spoke first. "Eden, I'm teaming you up with Senior Chief Petty Officer Reginald White for the duration of the mission. Everyone calls him Timber. I would say that you should stick to him like white on rice for this operation, but it'd come out too corny. So, I'll just leave you two to get acquainted. Timber will guide you through equipment issue, mission workup, and be with you every step of the way, both to and from the objective."

Eden thanked the Master Chief and introduced herself to Timber. With a firm handshake of her own, she nearly winced at what would be a crushing grip if he had chosen to squeeze just a little bit harder.

Timber spoke in a low, gravelly voice. "Pleased to meet you, Eden. Banshee, Valkyrie, and I are in Ghost Squadron. We work mostly intelligence and special surveillance missions. Then when something out of the ordinary comes along, they give us the odd jobs, as well."

Eden smiled. "I definitely qualify as an *odd* job. I'm sure you have better things to do than babysit me."

"It's not babysitting by any stretch of the imagination. There'll be rounds inbound and it'll be my pleasure to guide you through safely. If even half of what the Master Chief told me about you is true, you're no shrinking violet yourself, so I'll be happy to have you watching my back, as well."

The resounding voice of Commander Towns bellowed from the front of the SAR. "Dagger Squadron take your seats so we can get this briefing over, and you can all get one last roll in the hay before we go wheels-up tomorrow morning. First, let me introduce our liaison from the CIA, Eden."

Eden waved briefly to the group.

"She's an Agency operator out of their Special Activities Center and will be teamed up with Timber from Ghost Squadron for the duration of this op. Most of you have worked with SAC folks before—"

Someone on the far end of the room let out a low-pitched "boo."

"Damn, Pete," Towns said critically, "who pissed in your Cheerios this morning?"

Eden sensed an opportunity to stand up for her Agency against the alpha male of the testosterone-fueled group. Loudly, she responded, "*Oooh*, I didn't know we were taking turns. I'll sign up for Thursday!"

Laughter erupted across the SAR. Valkyrie's hand shot up to cover her mouth, delighted and in disbelief at the newcomer's aggressiveness. It took Commander Towns almost a full minute to regain control of the room.

"In all seriousness, people, we have a mission to execute." Towns briefed the assembly on the background of the mission to rescue CIA Director Richard Duncan, codenamed *George*, and his wife, Heather, codenamed *Martha*.

"The Bandar Abbas Naval Base is shaped like a trident," Towns said. "The one area of particular interest to us is the eastern-most section you can see on this satellite image to the right, *here*." The commander pointed to a photo projected on the large TV screen behind him. "The Air Force will be pummeling the shit out of the western and central areas. That includes both the quays and the dockyard facilities. You do *not* want to be anywhere near those areas—the flyboys are going to leave nothing standing. Every ship in port will have multiple five-hundred and two-thousand-pound bombs dropped on her, taking each and every one of them out of service permanently. That includes all three of the Iranians' Russian-built Kilo-class attack subs. The surface warfare boys want the Air Force to make absolutely sure those boats can't put to sea and pose a threat to the carrier group off of which we're launching. The first strike by B-2 stealth bombers will occur at 0345 hours. You'll never see or hear them, but the ordnance they deliver will wake the dead. Their first-round targets will be the Iranian air defenses, Silkworm anti-ship missiles, coastal defenses on a couple of islands in the Gulf, Naval Infantry barracks on shore, and all ships in port. After that, B-1 low-altitude penetrating bombers will clear the decks of anyone and anything on the surface throughout the center and western areas of the base. They guarantee us it'll be an inferno that even the Devil will envy."

Pointed comments of derision at what an Air Force 'guarantee' was worth rippled through the gathering of Navy personnel.

Towns continued his presentation describing the approach to the shore by rigid hull inflatable boats, the initial assault of the shore, and the placement of sniper teams. "We'll have four teams of snipers operating as two combined troops. One will take up firing positions on the east-end of the Navy base. The other will be here," he said pointing to the image projected on the screen behind him, "on top of this warehouse where they'll have a good view of our area of operation."

The commander answered a few questions from the snipers and clicked the computer to the next image. "Intel informs us that this building is the Iranian version of a Shore Patrol headquarters. In civilian-speak for our CIA friend, that's the police station. This building is designated as Objective *Hotel*. Intelligence believes that one or both of the Duncans are being held here. It makes sense — that's where they'd have cells in which to lock people up. I don't know if you can quite make it out on this image, but Intel says the Iranians have put a machine gun nest on the roof and surrounded it with sandbags. The sniper teams will take out anyone on the roof. After that, assault teams one and two will make entry. Banshee from Ghost Squadron is assigned to this team."

The next image in Towns's briefing showed a less-well-defended building. "This building is farther north and is assigned to assault teams three and four. Intel's not sure if this is where the Duncans are being kept or if it's just used for interrogations. Either way, we're going to take it down. If you find that it's used for interrogations and there's anything of obvious intelligence value, grab it quickly, but don't stick around just for that. Get in and get out. I'm assigning Valkyrie, Timber, and Eden to follow teams three and four to this building, designated Objective *Sierra*."

Towns continued the briefing until he'd answered all of the audience's questions. He wrapped up by describing the logistics preparations for the teams' load-ins the next morning on Air Force C-17 transports, and the ferrying of personnel and equipment out to the aircraft carrier *USS George Washington* from which they'd stage for the insertion into Iran.

After the briefing, team members filtered out of the SAR in small groups. Banshee and Valkyrie hung back to talk to Eden.

"Have you inserted by helo, before?" Banshee asked the CIA officer.

"Yes, a few times. I typically operate in small teams or solo, so being part of a larger assault like this will be new for me."

"Oh, it'll be fine, Eden," Valkyrie added. "The assault teams will take the beach before we land, so it'll be a breeze for you and me."

A big smile came across Banshee's face. "I'm going in with the two Dagger Squadron assault teams to Objective Hotel, so I'll be crashing through the waves with them. It's going to be insane!"

Under her breath, Eden agreed. "That's what I'm afraid of."

Chapter 18

Eden leaned against the railing of the USS *George Washington* and looked out across the cerulean blue waters of the Persian Gulf. Her Navy hosts would have politely corrected her had they heard her say *the* before the name of a ship, but Eden didn't care much for naval etiquette. Calling bathrooms "heads" and stairs "ladders" never resonated with her. She would have been perfectly satisfied to keep her feet on dry land.

"The water always looks beautiful at the beginning of a cruise," Timber said, "for about a week. After that, it starts to look like a desert you can't cross. After six months at sea on a float, as we call them, most sailors agree it looks like a set of horizontal prison bars which stretch as far as the eye can see."

Eden looked down at the white frothy sea spray as the floating city steamed southeast. "I can only imagine. I don't think I'd do very well cooped up onboard for that long."

"We deploy from a lot of types of ships—mostly surface, but submarines too, sometimes. And I'll tell ya, there's one thing that makes aircraft carriers the best."

"What's that?"

"The food! With over 6,000 men aboard, they have more flavors of ice cream than you can throw a flash-bang at. Well... 6,000 men and women, I mean. I have to get used to saying that nowadays."

"How long have you been in the Navy, Timber?"

"Twenty-one glorious years," the tall, bald man said with a wide smile and bubbling pride.

"So, in all that time and in all seriousness," Eden asked with her lips drawn tightly, "what's the best flavor of ice cream?"

"Pistachio, by far!"

"Seriously?"

"My favorite, hands down. You'll love it, trust me."

"Not something with chocolate?"

"Not for me. We usually load up on a big lunch the day before an op. Some of the guys carbo load, but not me. I Pistachio-ice-cream load!"

"I usually go for chocolate chip cookie dough, myself."

"Suit yourself. I always treat myself to a triple scoop. I figure that I'll burn the calories off on the mission, anyway. And if the op goes badly and it's just not my night, well, then at least I didn't deny myself any of the pleasures I deserve on the day before I meet my maker."

"I definitely see the logic in that. Okay, I'm in. Let's go find the others and head to lunch. Lead the way, Senior Chief."

Chapter 19

The US Air Force B-2A *Spirit of Pennsylvania* stealth bomber soared through smooth air high above the Gulf of Oman. It headed northwest, towards the Iranian naval base at Bandar Abbas. At forty-five thousand feet above the calm sea, the bomber's black skin blended into the night sky with a degree of perfection made possible by the multi-billion-dollar research budget the Air Force expended over two decades to develop the world's most invisible aircraft.

The electronic message from Global Strike Command's underground bunker on Offutt Air Force Base outside of Omaha, Nebraska, was relayed over a pair of Air Force MILSTAR communications satellites in geosynchronous orbits above the equator. Received by the SATCOM antenna atop of the B-2's fuselage, the missive was decrypted by the communications system located a dozen feet below the cockpit. The plaintext message blinked into view on the display of the flat-panel communications screen situated between the bomber's two pilots. The electronic trip across the world took less than one-and-a-quarter seconds from the time a Staff Sergeant at Offutt pressed the send key and when it appeared for the flight crew to read.

In the twelve hours they'd been aloft, all previous messages the aircraft commander, Colonel Peter W. Tolliver IV, read were routine status reports. Most did little more than inform the two-person crew that the decision on whether to continue or abort the mission was still being decided by the National Command Authority. No doubt, Tolliver reasoned, a decision of this magnitude would be made by the President himself. In the second-plus that it took for this particular message to bounce off two satellites and cross the globe, Tolliver's world changed.

The night-vision-friendly red text scrolled across the cockpit's communications display screen. Tolliver and his co-pilot, Captain Amy Lawrence, read the message simultaneously. "Slipstream One... Slipstream One... Code Yankee Bravo... Repeat... Code Yankee Bravo."

"Commander, Pilot," Lawrence said, using the crew members' roles instead of ranks in the military's usual order of addressing radio messages 'to *you*, from *me*.' She enunciated each word of the rest of her message especially clearly. "I have validated Command's message with code Yankee Bravo. I repeat. My code is Yankee Bravo. My mission briefing package says this is a *Go* code for the primary target bombing run, as briefed. Please confirm, sir."

Tolliver noted the captain's adherence to protocol. Although this was the colonel's last combat mission before he pinned on his Brigadier General's star and left the cockpit forever, it was his new co-pilot's first combat mission—in the B-2, anyway. The formality followed by the two-person crew served partly as a safety measure for the positive control of nuclear weapons—the B-2's *raison d'etre*—and partly because of the recordings made of all voice and data communications for later mission replay, auditing, and post-mission training.

"Pilot, Commander," Tolliver replied. "I confirm receiving code Yankee Bravo. My mission package agrees with yours. We are *Go* for our primary target. We have valid war orders, Amy. Begin your electronic threat and countermeasures checklist. I'll execute the aircraft-status checklist."

"Copy, Colonel."

Peter looked out the small window to his left and thought about the crew of Slipstream Two. Somewhere, fifty miles off in that direction, he knew, the crew of the mission's second B-2 just received and confirmed their own 'Go' codes to execute their assigned bombing run against the Iranian naval port at Bandar Abbas. While Tolliver's Slipstream One would drop its complement of five-hundred and two-thousand-pound bombs on radar sites, anti-aircraft batteries, and the barracks of the local Naval Infantry battalion, Slipstream Two would drop its own mixture of smart weaponry on every ship in port, including, perhaps especially, the Kilo-class submarines the Iranians had purchased decades earlier from Russia. An underway submarine would be almost impossible for a B-2 to attack successfully. In port, alongside the pier, however, it's the very definition of a sitting duck.

"Commander, Pilot. Checklist complete. All electronic systems are functioning nominally. Enemy search radars are active, but no threat to us at this distance. I do not recommend any countermeasure at this time."

"Airframe systems all check out as nominal," Colonel Tolliver advised the captain. "Key the auto-pilot to begin the approach run to the primary target. We're seventy-five miles from bomb-bay door opening. That's about ten minutes. We're right on time. Amy, how many combat missions did you have in the A-10?"

"Seventy-four, sir. Mostly close air support. Just a couple of fixed-site targets like this mission," she replied.

"No, not like this mission, Amy. Not like this one at all," the colonel said softly. "Close Air Support against troops in the field is one thing. They can at least try to shoot back at you. Tonight, we're going to kill 650 or so sleeping soldiers and sailors in their bunks. Not that they could shoot down a B-2 even if they tried—and they may very well try—but this afternoon, when you go to sleep safe in your own bed, you'll remember that they went to sleep last night feeling safe in theirs, too."

"Yes, sir, but we don't go around kidnapping their senior government officials, either," the captain responded respectfully. "They're a legitimate target in my book. Fifty miles to open doors, colonel."

"Oh, I'm not arguing against the mission, Amy. I volunteered for this one so that someone else wouldn't have to lead it. This is my last-ever combat mission while it's your first—in this airframe, I mean. A good juxtaposition, don't you think?"

"Yes, sir, and I'm honored to be flying it with you. You're kind of a legend in the wing."

"Oh, lord. You're supposed to be an ass-*kicker*, not an ass-*kisser*," the colonel said, and laughed into his oxygen mask.

Circles began radiating from a point on the display screen between the two pilots. The image on the screen zoomed in to show the enhanced night-vision view of the port just a few miles in front of the aircraft. Two red digits in the upper right-hand corner started to count backwards from sixty.

"One minute to target," Amy advised calmly. "Continuing approach to bombing run. Weapons release in five-one seconds."

Colonel Tolliver raised the red safety latch on the console below the monitor between the two pilots. With a practiced hand, he flicked the switch underneath the protective cover upwards. "Bomb-bay doors open. We're vulnerable."

"No change in search radar pulse repetition frequencies," Amy reported as she looked across her threat-warning receivers. "No threat from any search or acquisition radars. They don't see us, sir."

"In ten seconds they won't need to see us," Tolliver said quietly. "They'll be able to feel us."

Peter Tolliver released the safety interlock, making the trigger on the yolk in his hands live. *An odd choice of words*, live, he thought.

Exactly the opposite of the purpose of the weapons the trigger he was about to press would release. The weapons were *live,* but soon their targets would be *dead.*

Peter looked at the photograph taped above the cockpit window to his left. He put two fingers to where his lips were pursed beneath his facemask and touched them to the picture of his wife—his angel.

He looked down at the targeting screen and studied the enhanced image of the naval facility his B-2A Spirit approached. With a motion he had performed a thousand times both in training and on previous combat missions, the colonel squeezed the weapons-release trigger on his control yolk.

With a thought of the Iranian troops sleeping in their barracks nine miles below, he intoned his parting words to them, as much for his own benefit as for theirs. "May God have mercy upon your souls."

Chapter 20

Eden watched with rapt attention throughout the helicopter's approach as a forest of thick black smoke plumes bellowed from the Bandar Abbas Naval Base. Columns of toxic residue climbed vertically from their burning targets in the windless night. The black plumes rose straight up, only to be bent at a forty-five-degree angle by an on-shore breeze at altitude. The wind pushed the smells of burning ships, petroleum, and incinerated sailors inland and away from the invaders approaching the shore.

The SEAL assault team destined for Objective Sierra huddled in the nylon web seating of their Sikorsky SH-60 Seahawk helicopter as it flew barely two-dozen feet over the waves of the Persian Gulf. With precision honed through years flying special operations insertion and extraction missions, the Warrant Officers at its helm landed their chopper and its precious cargo in an empty field in the southeastern extreme of the naval base.

As the chopper's skids came to rest on the gravel, Eden followed immediately behind Timber and Valkyrie as the team jumped through the helo's large, rectangular side door. Distant echoes of gunfire and secondary explosions from fuel tanks and an ammunition depot rumbled across the flat ground. Not far to the west of their landing zone, sharp reports of SEAL's sniper rifles made their characteristic and unmistakable sonic dents in the air. Having successfully discharged its passengers, the Seahawk lifted its unburdened frame into the air and headed out to relative safety over the Gulf.

A dozen Dagger Squadron SEALs queued up single file in their assault formation. As the combined team had rehearsed days earlier in Virginia, Eden took her place behind Valkyrie near the end of the queue. Lieutenant Commander Burton "Bugsy" Thomas led the combined force from the front of the stack. Timber brought up the rear as the lethal procession of fifteen Navy and CIA special operators jogged north towards their objective.

The green glow of a small cluster of buildings in front of the team grew larger in Eden's night-vision goggles. The assortment of squat storage shacks and a maintenance yard with a few high-bay buildings proved to be empty, exactly as expected at 4 a.m. The team maneuvered north to cover the three hundred yards to their target in as little time as possible.

The Air Force's aerial assault had caught the Iranians completely by surprise. However, everyone knew reinforcements—sailors living off base, local police, and Iranian army units—would all be called upon to respond to the ground assault. Whether the attack could be successfully repelled or not, all involved fully expected the Iranians to do everything in their power to cause maximum casualties to any invading force.

Eden heard the reports of suppressed rifle shots in front of her before she heard the SEAL's warning, "Contact, right!" A football field's length to her right, two Iranians, one with a pistol in hand, fell from the short volley of SEALs' rifle shots. From her fleeting view of the two men, Eden thought that they were likely just two very unlucky sailors—possibly Shore Patrol officers—and not part of any kind of organized defense. Whatever real resistance the team would encounter was still somewhere in front of them.

The formation wound its way north. Bugsy halted the stack against the exterior wall of a dining hall. Pointing at Eden, he gave a thumb's up. Eden returned the gesture, assuring him she was keeping up just fine.

Bugsy visually confirmed that all team members were accounted for. As he turned back towards the head of the stack, he stopped short. He turned back to face Eden and pushed his radio headset more securely against his ear. He listened intently to an announcement on the command channel.

"Teams one and two have entered Objective Hotel, the Shore Patrol building," Bugsy relayed to Eden, whose radio was only tuned to her team's encrypted channel.

"The snipers took out the machine gun crew on the roof," Timber added for Eden's benefit. As did Bugsy, he had two radios. He listened in his left ear to the command channel and to Bugsy's team channel in his right.

"They're inside and are engaging hostiles," Bugsy announced to his team. "They're receiving heavy resistance but are making quick work of it." He paused to listen to the radioed reports on the command channel. "Positive contact. They've found Martha! She's alive."

Eden's heart leapt. After all the mystery surrounding the hijacking and kidnapping, the CIA's conclusion—indeed Steven Krauss's career-risking gamble—that the Duncans had indeed been spirited away to Iran was finally paying off. The last of her lingering uncertainty about the Tangled Web signals and whether the director and his wife would even be alive once the rescue force arrived evaporated.

Bugsy relayed the messages from the command net. "Martha's locked inside a—"

The brilliance of the explosion caught Eden and the SEALs off-guard. The blinding flash of light crossed the half-mile distance from the Shore Patrol headquarters in an instant. The two-second delay until the roar of the blast reached Eden seemed like an eternity. Her view of the rising inferno that engulfed the Shore Patrol facility was unobstructed. Her jaw dropped, as did her stomach. The CIA officer ripped the NVGs from her head and looked at the plume of red, yellow, and black fire and smoke rising to the heavens west of her position. "What the hell?" she muttered in astonishment.

"What the hell just happened?" Eden demanded of Bugsy.

"Stand by. Stand by...."

Eden looked directly at Bugsy. She disliked not being able to read the naval officer's expression clearly. She felt cut off from him by the camouflage paint and night-vision goggles concealing most of his face. Judging by the way his thin lips were drawn back tightly, she feared it could not possibly be good news.

"Command has lost contact with teams one and two. Stand by...." Bugsy announced. He held his left earpiece against his head tightly, as if easing up on it might allow his brain escape through his ear.

The SEAL team leader looked up and down the file of men and women, all of whom were concerned with the fate of their brothers-in-arms—their comrades, neighbors, teammates, and friends. "Command has no contact with either team. Snipers and spotters report that the entire building has been cratered. It.... Command is speculating that it was booby-trapped. Stand by...."

Bugsy read the serious expressions on the faces of the men and women standing in front of him. "Command thinks the building was rigged to explode and someone—maybe a SEAL—tripped the detonator. It might have been wired to the door of Martha's cell. They don't know."

Bugsy paused to listen to the last of the radio reports and looked again at his team. "Okay, men, we still have a job to do. George is still out here somewhere, and we're still 'Go' for Objective Sierra. We need to double-time it, and when we get there, everyone triple-check every hallway and door for tripwires. We'll mourn our friends and drink a beer in their honor when we get back. Right now, we have a mission to complete. On *me*. Let's move!"

Bugsy led the formation forward at a flat-out sprint. The stack ran from building to building using each as cover for their advance until they reached their target—Objective Sierra.

Bullets sprayed into the dirt and walls around the formation. The sharp clatter of the Russian-made combat rifles juxtaposed against the dull and distant rumbling of burning ships and occasional secondary explosions. Three Iranian troops continued firing at the SEALs, more waving AK-47 rifles in the air than actually aiming. Four SEALs returned fire and the Iranians dropped to the ground, dead.

"I'm hit," a SEAL officer in the middle of the formation said.

"I'm on it," Doc, team four's medic, replied immediately as he withdrew his first aid kit from a pack on his left thigh.

"Beard and Gramps," Bugsy ordered, "you two take the Lieutenant back to the landing zone and secure it for the chopper's return. I'll take the rest forward."

"Check," the two SEALs said in unison.

"Moving," Bugsy said, as much as commanding the team as advising them. The reduced formation of twelve operators followed closely behind, sprinting from building to building. The acrid smell of burning ships and buildings hung in the air and stuck in the noses of the assault team. Distant explosions became fewer and softer. The majority of what could be blown up had already been destroyed.

"Command, team three. We've arrived at Objective Sierra," LCDR Thomas reported over his radio. "Making entry now."

Bugsy gave deployment orders to the team. "Dagger Three on me for the entry. Dagger Four and Ghost Squadron, remain here to cover our exit or until I call for you."

Replies of "Check, sir," echoed from the SEALs.

"I'm coming with you," Eden stated flatly. If she were to only get one chance to either rescue Director Duncan or take one shot at him, she knew she had to be inside the building with the assault team.

Bugsy's slight pause gave her all the evidence she needed to discern his dislike for the idea. Eden, however, would not back down— not when she was so close to her objective.

"I'll pull up the rear of the stack," she said, knowing that would be where Bugsy would want her, anyway.

"Fine," the commander reluctantly agreed. "Let's move. Breacher, door handle."

The second SEAL in the stack unholstered a shotgun from across his back. He placed the muzzle of the weapon halfway between the door handle and the wall and fired two quick shots of one-inch slugs into the door's lock.

Eden covered her eyes instinctively, banging a hand against her night-vision goggles.

The twin shotgun blasts sent fragments of wood and metal flying.

Calls of "Clear" and "Moving" echoed along the stack of operators as they advanced from room to room. Gunshots from Iranians defending their prize echoed through the confined spaces of the single-story office building. Suppressed return fire from SEALs quickly eliminated the threats.

"Heavy door ahead," Bugsy advised his team. "Explosive breach this time, Pete."

The breacher removed a prefabricated block of explosives and reached into a pocket on his body armor for a detonator.

"Who's out there?" The team froze upon hearing a shaky voice speaking in English from beyond the door.

Bugsy looked for Eden who was pushing her way to the front of the stack.

Bugsy whispered, "Is that him?"

"I'm not sure," she whispered back. "I'll have to ask him a question to confirm it. You okay with that?"

Bugsy stared at her blankly for several heartbeats. Silently, he pointed to SEALs and gave orders with hand signals. His operators dispersed along the hallway and took up positions to cover both the heavy door in front of them and the door behind them through which they would be making their exit. Once all movement ended, the team lead felt he was as best prepared to both attack any threat in front and defend his vital avenue of escape as he could be, under the circumstances. Satisfied with the tactical setup, he pointed to Eden with an umpire's "play ball" hand signal and nodded.

The CIA officer knelt to the left side of the door and replied to the disembodied voice. "Director Duncan, my name is Eden. Do you remember me? You and I met for an hour in your office about two months after you first took office. Do you remember that?"

The voice responded tentatively. "Eden? Yes, yes, I think I remember you."

"Good, sir, but I need you to confirm it for me. After our meeting, you sent me on a mission. It was the first mission of that kind you'd ever ordered. I need you to tell me which country you sent me to. Which country was it, sir?"

The silence from beyond the door stretched for seconds which seemed like hours. One by one, Eden ticked off the passing seconds in her head. One. Two. Three. *Damn, it must not be him.* Her heart raced, fearing what she heard next would be bullets ripping through the door and the wall, all aimed at her. Four. Five. Six. *Damn, it's not –*

"It was South Africa. Johannesburg, South Africa. But I thought we agreed that morning to never talk about it again," the voice reported.

Eden could have sworn she heard him chuckle. She looked at Bugsy and gave him a thumb's up. Only those in the director's office that winter morning knew about her mission to kill the Canadian Chief of Station in Johannesburg. Eden was certain—the Director of the Central Intelligence Agency was behind the door in front of her.

Bugsy joined Eden at the door.

"Are you alone in there, sir?" Eden asked.

"Yes, I am. Just like you and I were in my office that morning."

"Good, he's alone," Bugsy whispered, turning to order the beaching of the door.

Eden tugged on Bugsy's arm and shook her head.

Mouthing the word "No" silently, she held up two fingers. "There are two others in there. Guards," she whispered.

"He said he's alone," the SEAL commander replied.

"Trust me. There were four of us in his office that morning. So that means there are two guards in there with him now," Eden whispered. "Blow the door, then we'll make entry. You go in high. I'll go low. I'll take whichever guard is farther to the right," she said quietly, motioning the positions with her hands.

Assigning herself the guard farthest to the right was a tactical decision she made for her benefit. If things went sideways upon entering the room, she might only get one shot at the guard—or at the director. She knew she was gambling that the guard to the right would be closer to the director, but time was of the essence. By allocating the left-most guard to the SEAL team lead, she gave herself the maneuvering room she would need if it came down to having to carry out Directive One.

Bugsy nodded his agreement with Eden's plan. The breacher took his position at the door and completed wrapping the U-shaped explosive assembly around its handle. He held the detonator up over his head, the visual queue for which his teammates waited. Each operator prepared for the imminent blast by covering the lenses of their night-vision goggles and opening their mouths. That way, the pressure of the explosion in a closed space wouldn't rupture their eardrums.

The detonation of the C-4 explosive sent fragments of wood, metal, and drywall spewing into the room beyond. The heavy metal door flew inward, arching into the sidewall. It came to rest at an untenable angle, hanging by a single hinge.

Bugsy quick-stepped into the room and spun to his left. The SEAL commander found his target holding his hands to his face. The surprise of the detonation had overwhelmed the Iranian guard. The infrared laser dot from Bugsy's suppressed M-4 rifle traced its way across the Iranian's chest. With a single squeeze of the trigger, the commando's rifle spat three 5.56-millimeter rounds in quick succession. All of them found purchase in their target's upper chest.

Eden rotated through the doorway and scanned the room quickly. Her eyes swept past the cage imprisoning Director Duncan and found her target. The guard's forearm covered his face as a shield against the blast. The camouflage-clad figure had anticipated the dynamic entry and lowered his rifle at the intruder kneeling just inside the doorway.

Eden shifted her Sig Sauer .45-caliber pistol toward the guard, aimed along the sights atop its barrel, and loosed a pair of suppressed rounds in rapid succession into the belly of her target. The Iranian non-commissioned officer staggered back two steps. Eden adjusted her aim and put her third round of the night into the man's right eye. Through her night-vision goggles, she watched the green-tinted spray of blood splash against the wall behind him. His body slumped against the metal bars of the prison cell and came to rest in a heap.

Eden approached the cell and addressed Director Duncan. "Are you all right, sir?"

Duncan's ears rang like church bells from the detonation of explosive his rescuers used to open the door. "I think so," he yelled. "What the hell is going on out there?"

"Hell is right," Eden said off-handedly. She looked at the door of the cell, stepped back, waved her hand at Bugsy, and said, "Breach it." The statement came out as more of a command than she intended, but she didn't mind.

"No, wait!" Duncan urged. He absolutely did not want to suffer through another explosion going off even closer to him than the last one had. He jabbed his finger in the direction of the guard Bugsy killed. "The key is in *that* guard's shirt pocket. He opens the cell with it to take me to the bathroom down the hall."

Eden, amused by the thought that it could be so easy, scrunched her face and mumbled, "*Humph.*" Nothing ever worked out quite *that* easily for her in the field.

Eden found the key right where the director said it would be. She approached the cell's door to unlock it. Bugsy slapped the CIA officer's hand away from the lock and gripped her wrist tightly.

"What the—?" Eden spat out.

"Wait a second, Eden." Bugsy eased his grip on his guest's hand and turned to speak with his teammate. "Pete. Check the cage's lock and door for tripwires."

A perplexed look encroached on Director Duncan's face. "Tripwires?"

Eden lowered her hand and stepped back to allow Peter Belinsky to inspect the cage. In her haste to free Richard Duncan, she realized that she risked walking into the same trap that had killed his wife. His wife, yes, and probably most or all of Dagger Squadron's first two assault teams. Eden stepped aside to let the SEALs find and disarm any awaiting traps.

Belinsky traced his flashlight across all four edges of the door. He inspected the lock using a mirror to get a peek inside the mechanism itself.

The SEAL stepped back and compared notes with his commander. Neither had found anything to indicate the Iranians had rigged the lock. Bugsy nodded at Eden.

She stepped to the door and raised the key to the lock. "I'll open it. Everyone, stand back." With a twist of her wrist, she gave the lock on the door a quarter-turn counter-clockwise. The dark metallic box securing the cell door let out a pleasing click. In less than ninety seconds from the time she had stepped into the room, the CIA officer had freed the director of her agency from the confinement his Iranian captors had subjected him to for over two months.

"All right, let's go," Bugsy said loudly. "We have a chopper to catch."

Richard Duncan's face was drawn taught. "Wait, what about my wife?"

Without skipping a beat, Eden grabbed his upper arm with her left hand and urged him towards the door. "Another assault team was sent to get her at the Shore Patrol station. We're going to rendezvous with them back at the landing zone. We don't have much time. Let's go, sir."

Eden pulled Duncan forward and gave him clear instructions. "Stay immediately behind me at all times, do you understand? Stay right on my ass, and I'll keep you alive. Got it?" She didn't wait for an answer as she pulled him into the middle of the line of SEALs as the team retraced its steps through the building.

Once outside, the assault team rejoined the half-strength remnants of assault team Dagger Three, as well as Timber and Valkyrie from Ghost Squadron.

"We got George," Bugsy advised the anxious SEALs who had been covering Dagger Four's flank. "Let's get the hell out of here."

Lieutenant Commander Burton Thomas led the formation south. As he maneuvered his team along the outskirts of the naval base, broadcasts on the command channel advised of incoming reinforcements. Commander Towns announced to all team leads that Naval Intelligence reported that aerial surveillance assets were tracking reinforcements arriving in everything from pickup trucks ferrying armed sailors to police cars from neighboring towns.

"Stay left," Bugsy ordered, "and keep eyes on our six. Intel reports —"

The *cracks* of automatic weapons fire interrupted the lieutenant commander mid-sentence. Dirt danced as bullets impacted the ground a dozen feet from the stack of SEALs. The commandos turned to return fire and saw a pickup truck with a mounted machine gun drive around the corner of a building across a small parking lot.

Volleys of bullets flew in both directions. The sounds of the mounted PKM heavy machine gun resounded across the field and were answered by the suppressed shots of the SEAL operators returning fire.

"Take cover," Bugsy ordered. He quickly assessed the advance of a small Iranian Naval Infantry unit. The veteran commando figured that these poorly organized and unevenly equipped Iranian sailors had likely as not grabbed what equipment and weapons were already at hand and sped to the naval base in haste with whatever and whoever they could.

Wood chips sprung from the outside walls of the cafeteria as bullets ripped a line above Eden's head. "Down!" she shouted to Duncan. "Get back!"

Behind Eden, Valkyrie spun and raised her M-4 rifle. Two hostiles on the roof of a building across the street strafed AK-47 rounds towards the invaders. Bullets ventilated a diagonal line through the wall a few feet from Timber. Val sighted her rifle's optics on the rooftop threat and squeezed the trigger. A three-round burst dropped the taller of the two hostiles, and he tumbled off the roof. The head of the second Iranian exploded from the shots of another SEAL, and the Iranian's body fell straight back and out of view. Val watched as a spray of green mist—as viewed through her NVGs—hung briefly in the air behind where the dead man's head had been.

AK-47 rounds impacted around the SEALs. Screams of pain and cries of "I'm hit," rose from two operators. Eden looked at the green-tinted Iranian troops advancing on their position and instinctively pushed Richard Duncan down and against the wall. Eden was armed with a pair of her favored type of pistol—.45 caliber Sig Sauers—and concluded, rightly so, that the advancing troops were still too far away for her handguns to be effective. She had no intention of waiting for the enemy troops to close the distance enough for her weapons to be of use. She pushed Duncan farther away from the advancing troops to let the SEALs cover her retreat.

"On me," Eden commanded her director. "Timber, Val, let's go around the east end of this building. Then we can sprint back to those maintenance sheds and make it to the landing zone from there." Eden didn't wait for an answer. She trusted that Timber would follow immediately behind.

At the corner of the wood and steel building, Eden stopped to ensure her charge was still close. A quick peek around the corner told her what she needed to know—the coast was clear.

"She's hit," Timber said loudly.

Eden looked back at the tall SEAL. Timber held Valkyrie up with his left hand. His right shined with the blood that soaked the side of the young woman's uniform. "She took a round in her side."

"I have George," Eden said with no delay. "You'll have to help her."

"Who's *George*?" Duncan asked, quizzically.

Eden spat the answer out mechanically. "You are. The code names for you and your wife are *George* and *Martha*. Very easy to remember."

"Where is she? Where's my wife?"

"She's either on one of those helicopters *way* over there at the landing zone or already in the air," Eden said, knowing full-well that, almost certainly, neither statement was true. Eden felt certain in her heart that Heather Duncan had been in her cell when the Shore Patrol headquarters exploded. Her body would never be found or returned to her family. If Richard Duncan successfully made it home to his family alive, he and his daughters would have nothing but their tears to bury.

Eden glanced back around the corner. She was working feverishly to avoid having the same fate Martha met befall George and the remaining members of the rescue team.

"Let's move," Eden ordered everyone in general and no one in particular. "Stay behind me." She led the group of four along the east wall of the cafeteria and into the open field beyond as they headed back towards the maintenance sheds. Bullets continued to zing through the air as the firefight between the remaining SEALs of Dagger Three and Four and a small squad of Iranians raged a few dozen yards off to her right.

In the distance to the south, Eden eyed her goal—two Seahawk helos in the landing zone, their rotors spinning wildly. "*That's* our objective," she said to the group, as much for self-confidence as to align her mental compass.

Cracks of AK-47 fire rose from the distance. The sharp sounds were joined by the whizzing of bullets overhead. Each sounded like a series of long metal cables someone had *twanged*. Advancing Iranian troops on her right angled towards her and her small group while firing at the SEALs arrayed at the other end of the cafeteria.

"Back!" she ordered. "Get back. Back. *Back!*"

She ran to the corner of the cafeteria, crouched, and looked over at Timber. "Iranian troops. The reinforcements have arrived. We can't go that way. Not without taking heavy fire."

A series of three back-to-back explosions joined the rising crescendo of gunfire.

"Grenades," Timber announced. "Probably Iranian hand grenades. Russian-made, of course."

"*Great,*" Eden said with as much disdain as she could hang from a single word.

"The fence," Timber said, and pointed to the east. Uttered as a statement, he made it as much suggestion as question. "We can cut the chain link and maneuver south through that parking lot using the cars as both cover and concealment."

Eden looked at the fence fifty yards away and scanned the parking lot beyond it for signs of activity. Not seeing anything moving, she peeked around the corner again. She pulled her head back quickly before the Iranian troops could see her and immediately agreed with Timber. "Right. The fence it is."

Eden grabbed Duncan's sleeve firmly. She ran hard for the fence line, pulling him along whether he wanted to go or not. Failing to get her objective out of the country was not an option for her. The price of failure was unthinkable.

Timber lumbered to a stop at against the chain-link fence and placed Val Sheppard on the ground as gently as he could in his haste to deal with the metal barrier blocking the team's escape.

Valkyrie stifled a moan through gritted teeth as her impact with the ground sent a ripple of pain through her abdomen.

Timber reached into his vest, removed a folded multi-tool, and handed it to Eden.

Eden extracted the wire-cutter heads and attacked the links of the fence with gusto.

Behind her, Timber scanned the open field they had just crossed. He held the scope of his M-4 rifle to his eye, ready to answer any threat.

"Okay, I'm through," Eden said, and deposited the tool into a pocket on the front of her body armor vest. She pushed Duncan through the newly cut gap and scrambled after him. Eden pulled the opening wider and Timber squeezed through with Valkyrie in tow.

The wounded lieutenant grunted in pain as she was manhandled through the opening in the fence, half in Timber's arms and half over his shoulder.

"Let's go," Eden said. She led the team between rows of cars which sat silently in the parking lot outside the naval base.

A distant rumble of Iranian vehicles joined the echoing clatter of firearms spewing their deadly rounds. Eden's view of the steady southerly progression of the haphazard assortment of counterattacking vehicles sent a sinking feeling through her gut. *If the Iranian reinforcements have already made it to Dagger Three and Four at the cafeteria, there's little other than a few SEAL snipers to stop the advancing troops from converging on the landing zone – our only way home.*

"Hurry up," Eden said, renewing her purchase on Duncan's arm. "We have to run." She pulled her charge forward and prodded him between successive rows of parked cars.

"Shit, "Timber muttered. "Look." He pointed to the roof of a building in the distance.

"The snipers," Eden said exasperated. "They're—"

"Bugging out," Timber said, completing her thought. "That's bad. That's *real* bad."

Eden could feel the worry reverberating through Timber's voice. "They're supposed to cover our retreat. The heat must really be on, and we're nowhere close to the LZ."

Timber, Duncan, and Eden watched from behind a ten-year-old Toyota sedan as additional Iranian reinforcements arrived. Three pickup trucks and a jeep with a dual-barreled mounted machine gun rained heavy firepower towards the retreating SEAL snipers and the helicopters behind them. Dismounted infantry — or armed sailors doing a good imitation of it — advanced south towards the two remaining helos in the landing zone. The head of a machine gunner in the bed of a pickup truck disintegrated into a fine mist, courtesy of a SEAL sniper.

"We'll never get past those vehicles to the south and to the LZ," Timber lamented. He looked back towards the cafeteria where familiar outlines of AK-47s and Iranian sailors wielding them ran in every direction.

"We need to do something," Director Duncan said, more to himself than his protectors. "Can't go that way," he said, pointing in the direction of the helicopters, "and can't go back that way, either." He nodded his head in the direction of the cafeteria and the office building that had served as his home for most of the past week.

Eden looked to the only two other ways they could go and assessed their tactical options. To the team's east was a small bay at the north end of the Strait of Hormuz. In the other direction, winding its way north and arcing east, a narrow access road led off base and into the city of Bandar Abbas.

"We can take this car," Eden said, thinking aloud, "and drive around the bay to the east. From there, we can radio the Navy for a pickup somewhere on the far side."

Timber and Duncan looked across the water and up along the access road. Duncan could make out only a few features in the dark. Timber scanned the flat expanse of the bay with his night-vision goggles and then ran his eyes quickly along the empty roadway.

"If I were alone, I'd just jump in the water and swim south," Timber said. "SEALs always retreat into the water. It's where we're safest."

"If we did that, you'd have to leave Valerie behind. Do you really want to do that?" Eden asked.

"No," Timber said, "of course not."

Eden drew one of her two Sigs from its holster and smashed the driver's window of the Toyota with the butt of the pistol. She reached inside, unlocked the door, got in, and opened the other doors. While the team piled into the sedan, Eden reached under the dashboard and yanked a tangle of wires into view.

To hotwire the car, she needed to see the colors of the individual ignition and battery wires. She removed her night-vision goggles and withdrew a small flashlight from her tactical vest. The CIA covert action specialist identified two of the dark green battery wires and quickly tied the ends together. After separating the third green battery wire from the tangled mess hanging from beneath the dashboard, she located the light-green ignition wire and the lone red battery wire. In a smooth, practiced motion, she tied their bare ends together. Finally, holding the final pair of green and red wires in her hands, she brushed the bare ends together several times, sending sparks into the dark night.

On her fourth attempt, the Toyota's engine turned over. With a brief smile at having found a modicum of good fortune that evening, she pulled the door closed, backed the car out of the parking spot, and drove north — the opposite direction from everything she considered to be the right way home.

Chapter 21

Eden kept the headlights of the Toyota off and drove by night-vision goggles. She navigated along the dirt road to the far end of the small inlet in the bay adjacent to Iran's smoldering naval base. Across the small body of water, a series of decrepit warehouses and abandoned industrial facilities ringed the inlet.

She piloted the sedan to the end of the road. With crumbling industrial skeletons on one side and an empty field on the other, she angled the car to give her a clear view to her west, across the inlet where the conflagration at the Iranian naval base continued unabated and shifted the transmission into park. Having come to the end of the road — both literally and figuratively — she stared straight ahead into the blackness of the Strait of Hormuz.

"Okay, Timber, try your radio on the command net. Let 'em know we're about a kilometer east of the base."

"Check," the tall SEAL said, and exited the vehicle.

Eden listened through the space formerly occupied by the car window she had shattered minutes earlier. "Trident Forge actual, Timber. Trident Forge actual, this is Timber, over."

He paused to listen and then repeated his radio call.

"Trident Forge actual, this is Timber, transmitting in the blind. We have George. Repeat, we have George and are located one click east of Objective Sierra. I say again, four survivors, one click east of the objective."

Silence. Except for Valkyrie's soft moans from the back seat.

"How ya doin', girlfriend?" Eden asked quietly. She removed her NVGs and tilted the rearview mirror so she could see Val's face. The mixture of green camo paint and red streaks of blood across her jaw rippled slowly by contortions of pain that flowed across the wounded SEAL's face. "We'll get you some help really soon, Val, just hang in there, okay?"

"*Mmm hmm,*" came the pained reply.

Timber knelt next to the open window and addressed Eden. "Nothing. No reply at all."

"Okay, let's give it ten minutes and see what happens."

Eden craned her neck to get a better view of the naval base across the inlet. She squinted as she peered into the inky distance, only able to see the headlights of a few vehicles scurrying about.

"Timber, take up a defensive position at the back of the car. Let me know if you can see anything with your rifle's magnified scope."

"Check."

Timber laid his rifle across the sedan's trunk and scanned the scene across the inlet with the eye of an experienced reconnaissance specialist. Like a commentator plying his trade during a championship tennis match, he quietly narrated for the vehicle's occupants the activity at the increasingly busy military base across the narrow waterway.

Iranian trucks and personnel converged on the SEALs' landing zone which had previously held all the team's hopes for escape—hopes which now faded further into the distance with each throbbing heartbeat.

Richard Duncan wrapped his arms around himself and shuddered. His hands shook and the skin on his face quivered. He bent forward and, if his seatbelt hadn't stopped him, he would have curled into a fetal position in the Toyota's front seat. "I'm not feeling well," he said. "Something's wrong."

Eden looked at her Agency's director. "I didn't think you got shot. Did you?"

Duncan shook his head. "No. It doesn't hurt, but it feels—" He rubbed his arms to keep the trembling under control.

Eden removed one of her gloves and felt Duncan's forehead for a fever. She felt nothing out of the ordinary, other than his quivering. She unzipped a pocket on the front of her tactical vest and removed two granola bars. She offered the oats-and-almonds snacks to Duncan. "You've got the adrenaline shakes. It's normal. Eat these. I brought the ones with chocolate chips this time."

Duncan looked at her wide-eyed. "You brought *junk* food on a *military* assault?" He snatched the two bars and tore the wrapper off the first before Eden could answer.

Eden smiled. "Yeah, but only because bananas tend to get mushy."

"*Bananas*? Are you seri—"

Eden giggled. "No, no, I'm kidding, I'm *kidding*. But eat both of those just the same. You need it more than I do right now, and it's the fastest way to stop shaking when you're coming down from an adrenaline high. Your adrenal glands have been squirting out adrenaline all night, what with all the explosions and running we've been doing. Not to mention getting shot at. Adrenaline is a 'fight or flight' hormone that tells your liver to release a bunch of the glucose — blood sugar — it stores because your muscles need the energy to get you away from danger. With all our running and the overall stress of the evening, your muscles have been burning both their stored energy and whatever they got from your liver at a frightful rate. The shakes happen when your body runs out of its easiest-to-get fuel. So, you can either suffer while waiting until your body pulls more sugar out of your fat cells, which happens slowly, or you can replace it immediately with a snack. Personally, I prefer chocolate, so, there you have it. Your first practical lesson in tonight's Combat Stress 101 class."

Duncan stared at the covert-action officer almost without blinking.

Timber's voice came through the open window at Eden's elbow. "Police cars are expanding their patrol radius. I think we need to find a safer foxhole to crawl into."

"Yeah," Eden said, and glanced at her watch. "It's been eight minutes, but I agree. Get in. I'll find us somewhere safe so we can go to ground for the rest of the day."

Timber returned to the car, careful to lift Valerie's head onto his lap gently.

Eden made a U-turn and coaxed the stolen vehicle down the access road and along the edge of the run-down industrial complex. Once out of line of sight of the naval base, she turned on the car's headlights and passed a series of hulking warehouses, a few of which seemed to have more holes than walls.

The CIA officer drove slowly along the barely paved access road. She passed a small housing development, continued along a secondary road, and turned the Toyota into the next housing development she came to. Eden estimated she'd gone three or four miles from the parking lot outside the naval base and decided it was as far as she dared drive that night.

She pulled into the neighborhood slowly and steered the sedan methodically up one street and down the next. Rows of small, boxy single-family houses lined the streets. After five minutes of driving, she found what she was looking for.

Eden brought the car to a stop at the curb and turned off the headlights, but left the engine running. "Stay here and stay out of sight. I'll be back in ten minutes. Twenty at most. Timber, use your NVGs to watch out for trouble."

"Check."

Eden set off at a jog into the night, leaving her three companions behind.

"What do you think she's looking for?" Duncan asked, barely above a whisper.

"An empty house, I'm guessing," Timber replied.

The two men sat silently. Valerie Sheppard lay across the rear seat of the car, her head resting on Timber's lap. The enlisted SEAL gently stroked a wayward strand of hair out of the wounded officer's face. While under other circumstances Timber's act might have been interpreted as fraternization—a forbidden romantic gesture between the two—there in the car, stuck behind enemy lines in an undeclared military action, it served purely as an of compassion for a wounded teammate.

Timber busied himself comforting Valkyrie. To Duncan, the wait seemed interminable.

The spy agency's director jumped an inch out of his seat when Eden's voice surprised him.

"Okay, I've got a house for us," the Special Activities Center operator announced.

Eden drove the car onto the adjacent block, slow enough so as not to rev the engine and risk disturbing the quiet neighborhood. She pulled into the driveway of a single-story house at the end of a cul-de-sac and parked the car in the open one-bay garage. She separated two of the wires of her jury-rigged ignition bypass, and the engine of the purloined Toyota sputtered to a stop.

Eden exited the vehicle first, pulled the garage door down fully, and helped Timber maneuver Valerie Sheppard onto the bed in one of the house's three small bedrooms.

"Don't go into the room at the end of the hall—the one with the closed door," Eden ordered. "Director, draw all of the shades and curtains."

"Will do," he replied, glad to finally be of use and able to participate productively in his own rescue.

Eden dragged two dining room chairs a dozen feet into the living room and set them facing the couch. She laid down on the sofa, taking up its full length by herself.

"How is she," Eden asked Timber as he walked into the room.

"Valerie is more comfortable now, but in a lot of pain. I double-checked her bandages and gave her a shot of morphine. She needs medical attention soon."

Eden nodded.

Duncan took a seat in front of the sofa. "Have you heard anything on your radio, yet, Timber?"

"No." The muscular SEAL grunted as he lowered himself onto the chair next to Duncan.

"Best to turn off the radio for a while," Eden advised. "If they haven't answered by now, they must not have received the transmission. Save the battery for later."

Without a word, the SEAL turned the volume dial on the radio in his vest until it clicked off. He sighed and stretched his legs out in front of him. With a long look at Eden, he asked the question on everyone's mind. "Now what?"

"I assume there's a Plan B," Director Duncan said hopefully. "An alternate rendezvous point or something?"

"The first helicopter was Plan A," Eden replied, trying to keep the sarcasm in her voice to a minimum. "The second helo was Plan B. We didn't think we'd need a Plan C. We'll stay here for the day, rest up, and hideout during daylight. In the meantime, we'll put our heads together and come up with a great idea, I'm sure."

"Any preliminary thoughts on that?" Duncan asked, sounding every bit the manger that Eden routinely decried.

"Not at the moment," Eden said shortly.

"What if we can't figure a way out?" he asked ruefully.

Eden looked into the eyes of the man she came to rescue. "Directive One," she said soberly.

Duncan's throat went dry. He could only stare at Eden, wordlessly.

The silence hung uncomfortably in the air between them.

Timber squinted as he looked from Eden to Duncan and back again. "What's Directive One?"

"Nothing," Richard Duncan rasped, barely able to get the word out of his mouth.

Chapter 22

Timber rose from his chair, and said, "I'm going to check on Val."

Eden nodded.

Richard Duncan looked at Eden as she lay on her back across the length of the sofa. Once Timber was out of earshot, he asked, "How many sailors did the Navy send in tonight?"

"About seventy, total. Thirty SEAL assault operators and snipers give or take, a couple of explosives experts, two-dozen small boat specialists, and four helicopter crews. And that doesn't even count the Air Force."

"Air Force?"

"Yeah, B-1s and B-2s," Eden confirmed. "A couple of B-2s opened the door for our choppers and small assault boats by taking out the Iranians' coastal anti-air and anti-ship defenses. The B-2s were followed in by B-1s flying at damned near the speed of sound. All told, they took out the ships in port and laid waste to most of the rest of the navy base."

"Between the explosions, sirens, and screaming going on outside, I couldn't figure out what was happening."

"The SEALs weren't told the next part, but it'll be all over the news by now...." Eden looked down the empty hall to see if Timber were listening. It didn't matter to her whether he was or not. "The President knew there'd be no way to keep this operation a secret, so he used it as the excuse he needed to send the rest of the Air Force's B-2 stealth bomber fleet to take out the Iranian deep underground nuclear weapons research facilities. General Folson said the President figured that if we were wrong about you being here, he might as well use this opportunity to do some good. If it cost him his job, then at least he'd leave office having set Iran's nuclear weapons development program back a decade or more."

Duncan leaned back in his seat. "That may be the first noble thing that SOB's ever done," he said smiling, clearly not a fan of the Commander in Chief. "And that begs the question... just how *did* you find me?"

"Oh, that. Yeah. It's a technical thingy that DS&T put into your lapel pin. It's a reflector of some sort that—"

Eden sat bolt upright and pointed at the director. "Where is it?" she asked louder than she intended. "Do you have the pin with you? From your jacket! Where is it?"

"My lapel pin? No, the admiral took it from me."

Eden's face fell. "Admiral? What admiral?"

"The one in charge of the Iranian naval fleet based here. As soon as our sub arrived, he took it off my sport coat as a souvenir. We hadn't even gotten off the sub, yet. He had a shit-eating grin across his face as he pinned it inside his uniform hat to keep as a reminder of how he had beaten the 'Great Satan.' His translator wasn't very good, but I got the gist of what he meant."

Eden's shoulders drooped forward. "So much for Plan C," she mumbled. "That explains why DS&T saw it moving around so much," Eden said thinking back to the map plots over which Andy Roselski and Steven Krauss had obsessed.

"I don't understand," Duncan admitted.

"The reflector—called the Tangled Web—had four clusters of hits on the map. One was over the Shore Patrol building. One was on the building where we found you. Another was all around the fleet headquarters building, and a last one was in a VIP residential area. That must be where the admiral lives. Or lived."

Timber appeared in the hallway.

Eden looked up from her perch on the sofa. "How is she?"

"Sleeping now. She's lost a lot of blood. I changed her bandages again and am going to wash up."

Eden nodded.

Duncan turned his attention back to Eden. "*Tangled Web* is not a technology. It's actually the classification control system which DS&T uses to protect highly sensitive-technol—"

"Oh, God!" Timber's excited utterance from the far end of the hall startled both Eden and Duncan.

In a single movement, Eden launched herself off the sofa, drew the Sig Sauer .45 from the tactical holster on her right thigh, and sprinted down the hall.

She stopped short of the bedroom doorway in which Timber stood. Towering a foot above her, the sailor looked intently at the bloody sheets half-covering the two corpses lying in the bed of the master bedroom.

"Did you—?"

"I *told* you," Eden interrupted, "*not* to open the door at the end of the hallway." She pulled the door shut firmly and pointed to the hallway bathroom. "Wash up in there," she ordered the man who was easily twice her size.

"Did you kill them?" he asked in a pained voice.

"Kill who?" Director Duncan asked as he arrived at the end of the hallway.

"Nobody. Go back to the living room."

"She killed the owners of the house. In their own bed. That's—"

"*You*," Eden said pointing at the Naval Special Warfare operator, "go wash up in the hallway bathroom. And *you*," she continued rapidly while shifting her index finger towards Richard Duncan's chest, "come with me."

Eden led her director by his elbow back to the living room and gently pushed him down into his chair. Timber washed his hands and rejoined the pair who silently watched his approach.

Timber spoke first. "Did you have to do that?"

Director Richard Duncan rubbed his chin, nervously. He wasn't sure he wanted to know the answer to that question.

"Yes," Eden said simply. Even though she did not want to have a conversation on this particular topic, her companions were both professionals and deserved to know the truth if they were to be able to work together and escape from the Islamic Republic.

The career Navy man shook his head. "That's well outside the Rules of Engagement, Eden."

"Timber, when the Agency sends me into the field to do a job, it's not because they *want* to, but because they *have* to. I don't do what I do out of convenience, only out of necessity. Everybody loves to send you SEALs in to tackle the hard jobs. You're everyone's darlings. But me? I'm nobody's first choice. Quite the contrary, actually. I'm the director's option of last resort. So, I have only one Rule of Engagement when I'm in the field."

"What's that?" the SEAL asked.

"Don't get caught."

"How has that been working out for you?" Timber asked, intending it to sound funnier than it came out.

"Actually, pretty damned well until now," Eden said, and chuckled.

"So now what?" Duncan asked to change the topic and diffuse the tension in the room.

Eden took a deep breath and followed the director's lead, turning the conversation to a more productive direction. "He's right. Let's start talking about our options. It'll get your minds off of... other things. We have, what, five options?" She ticked the options off on her fingers. "North. South. East. West. And staying right here. I'll skip the option of turning ourselves into the Iranians for the moment."

"Yeah, that would not be at the top of my list, either," Timber agreed.

"Okay, well," Eden said, "let's take them one at a time. First, we have north. We can steal a new car each night and leapfrog our way to the border with Turkmenistan. We cross the border and make our way to the capital, Ashgabat. It's not far from the border. I stayed there once on a mission, many years ago. Nice place, actually. We get there and drive right to the US Embassy and we're home free."

"How do we get across the border?" Timber asked.

Eden looked at him. "I didn't say it would be easy. I have three pairs of passports sealed in plastic under the back Kevlar lining of my body armor. One pair is American, one Canadian, and one Mexican. Three have my picture and three have Director Duncan's. All have forged Iranian entry stamps, but they should be good enough to get us out through a land crossing. They're not backstopped enough to get us through the international airport in Tehran, though."

"'*Should be* good enough'?" Duncan asked.

"Hey, pal," Eden said, and grinned, "DS&T works for *you*, not for me."

"Only passports for the two of you?" Timber interjected.

Eden nodded. "It was intended as a last-ditch option. Quite the Hail Mary. As for you, I didn't even know about you until I got to Virginia Beach for the mission briefing. Sorry, no passport for Valerie, either."

Timber leaned back in silence.

"But, on the plus side, Timber, you're an experienced SEAL and well trained to evade a pursing enemy, right? We can drop you off a mile or so from the border, you can get safely across on your own, and we'll all meet up a mile past the checkpoint."

Timber contemplated Eden's plan. "What about Val?"

Eden paused to think. "Well, we can't have a severely wounded woman with no passport in the car with us at the border. That's a non-starter. Assuming she won't be able to walk, I guess you'll have to carry her across."

The three sat still for a moment, knowing full well that such a plan would be highly unlikely to enable all four Americans to successfully penetrate a well-guarded national border. No one wanted to be the one to admit that, in her condition, Valerie was a significant liability in any scenario that included an attempted border crossing.

"What about east and west?" Duncan asked. "Iraq is west and Pakistan is east. We have military forces and Agency officers in both countries. Maybe we could get close to the border and call for a Special Forces helicopter to pick us up just inside Iran? That way, we can all get across the border safely. Together."

"Sure," Eden said with an edge to her voice, "that could work. Did you happen to bring a cell phone that has the US Air Force on speed dial?"

Duncan stewed in his seat. He did not like the sarcasm spewed at him by a woman who was supposed to be working *for* him. "Obviously not, and I don't appreciate the tone."

"Sorry, that's just my usual defense mechanism when I'm trapped behind enemy lines with a country's combined military and national police forces trying to hunt me down, so they can put me in front of a kangaroo court. All of which would be followed by a very public and likely quite brutal hanging or beheading or whatever the hell they do here to agents of the Great Satan. So, forgive me. I'm under just a *little* bit of pressure here."

"East and west," Timber said, changing the subject in hopes of lifting the tone of the conversation, "have the same issues as going north. Getting across the border is going to be a problem."

"Hell, just getting *to* the border is going to be a problem," Eden said. "Do either of you happen to know how to speak Farsi? I don't. Odds are we couldn't even buy a tank of gas without being reported to the police."

The group let those thoughts simmer. Each of the three noodled through variations on the theme to find ways they might overcome the obvious tactical and logistical flaws.

"I know we tried it already," Duncan offered, "but what about radioing for the Navy again?"

"They didn't answer us the first time when they were only a few miles away. What makes you think they'd answer us this time?" Eden asked. "And besides, assuming the Iranians aren't idiots, they would probably have recovered at least one usable radio from a dead SEAL on the base by now, so they'd know which frequency to listen on. Every military has direction-finding equipment, so we'd be leading the bad guys right to us at the same time we're trying to vector the good guys to our position."

"Yes," Duncan admitted diplomatically, "there's truth to what you're saying. I wasn't thinking that we'd try it now. In fact, we'd need to wait until nightfall when we're ready to move, anyway."

"I don't understand," Eden said, puzzled.

The director continued. "What I'm thinking is that the US Navy knows what frequency and encryption system is used on their radios. That's a given. So, if they're still looking for us, and I'm sure they are, they'll have surveillance aircraft from their carriers monitoring those specific frequencies. They might even coordinate with the NRO to have our satellites listening for transmissions, as well. Although I emphasize the word *might*."

"So," Eden asked, careful to sound serious and not flippant, "you want us to wait until nightfall, radio pickup coordinates to them, abandon our safe haven here, and push all of our chips in on a bet that the Navy *might* be lucky enough to receive Timber's transmission. Is that what you're suggesting?"

"Do you have a better plan?" Duncan asked.

"We could go south," Timber offered.

"Sure, who's up for a swim? The assault boats are long gone by now." Eden did not conceal her disdain for the idea at all. "And what about Val?"

Timber leaned forward, pointing at Eden. "You talked about stealing cars and driving north. We could steal a boat and sail south, instead."

Duncan considered the concept and offered his voice in support. "Could work, I guess."

"I don't know anything about boats, especially not how to steal one," Eden said.

"Small boats," Timber said, "just have pull starters on outboard motors. Larger boats have diesel engines with an ignition system. For my first tour in the Navy, I was a junior rating on a patrol boat. That was before I tried out for the teams and went to BUDS. I'm sure we can figure it out."

"I can sail small craft, as well," Duncan said, eager to contribute to the planning. "I do a lot of sailing. I admit, they're mostly civilian sport craft of thirty feet or less, but even something that size would get us where we need to go."

Eden thought back to the hour she had spent in the director's office in CIA's Original Headquarters Building early that morning all those years ago when he ordered her to South Africa—on the mission she swore to herself she would forever erase from her mind. The nautical theme to his office, model boats, and photos all attested to his reputation around the Agency as an avid sailor and sport fisherman. "And where do we go if we *are* able to steal a boat? I don't like it," she said, clearly not on board with the concept so enticing to her compatriots.

"We sail south," Timber offered. "Or south-southwest, I think. What's across the strait? Dubai? Saudi Arabia? Maybe Oman, depending on which way we go?"

"It's the United Arab Emirates," Duncan corrected. "That's the country. Dubai is a city in the UAE."

"Okay, sir, the UAE, then. Whatever. Right now, I'd be happy ending up in either, frankly."

"Stealing a boat sounds crazy," Eden said, dismissively. "Isn't our best bet heading north to the border of Turkmenistan? I know how to steal cars. We can find a new house to hide in each day and drive only at night."

Timber answered, barely able to conceal his sneer. "You mean find a house like this and murder the owners again? *Again* and *again* every night? How long do you think it'll be until the Iranian cops see the pattern of a serial killer marching due north and we get caught at a roadblock or highway inspection checkpoint? If nothing else, they'll see we're making a beeline for their northern border and will be waiting for us there. No, I'd rather take my chances on the open ocean. That's the *Navy* way."

"Eden," Duncan said in a smooth tone intended to lower the temperature of the conversation from near boiling to a mild simmer. "We know our Navy is still operating somewhere south of us. I think the idea of using a boat to sail south has merit. If we don't end up making contact with them along the way, then we'll make landfall on the opposite side of the strait in one friendly country or another. At least one that's a good sight friendlier than this one. This is a good plan."

"*Mmmmmmmmmm,*" Eden mumbled as the logic of their argument started to sink in.

Timber pressed to make his point. "Eden, I think you already know that all four of us would not make it across any of the land borders. It's a real longshot that we'd even make it as far as the border itself, regardless of whether we go north, east, or west. From where we sit right now, we're only a mile or two from the water. We can wait the day out here in the house and get some shut eye. Around midnight or so, we head to the commercial marina east of here that Commander Towns showed on the satellite photos during his briefing back in Virginia. At the marina, we'll steal a fishing boat and sail south under the cover of darkness. We can navigate by night-vision goggles and keep the boat's running lights off."

Timber paused to let the CIA officer consider the merits of the plan. "It's the best plan, and the only one that keeps us all together. It *can* work."

Eden sat up and rubbed her neck. She didn't want to admit it, but Timber's idea was starting to appeal to her. "I'll sleep on it. We can talk more about it later." She stood up and walked slowly towards the hallway bathroom. She gazed into the bedroom at Valerie and stopped to look at the lieutenant whom she had come to respect.

Eden looked back towards the living room. "Timber, I'm sorry."

Timber turned around and looked down the hallway towards Eden.

Eden nodded her head towards Val's motionless body. The CIA officer stood still as Timber joined her in the doorway. They both looked mournfully at Valerie Sheppard, whose lifeless eyes stared blankly at the bedroom ceiling of a house none of them was ever meant to be in.

"Oh, man," Timber said softly. His breath filtered out of his lungs in a wheeze. "Not Val...."

"I'm so sorry," Eden said, slowly reaching her hand up and giving Timber's muscular arm a soft squeeze. "That's going to complicate our planning, but we'll figure out a way to get us all home."

Chapter 23

The following night, Eden eased the stolen car into the dirt lot across the street from Bandar Abbas's commercial marina. She shut off the engine of the Peugeot sedan she "borrowed" from the recently deceased occupants of the house she'd commandeered the previous night. This one, though, was the easier theft—the car keys sat on the hallway table in the house. Silence returned to the air as the last of the engine noise floated away into the still night.

She had readied herself for the pungent odor of rotting fish to permeate the marina, although she would have been perfectly happy if she'd been wrong about that. The strong stench of diesel fumes was not, however, something she had prepared herself for.

The CIA officer scanned the small harbor across the street. She slowly looked along each dock, at the array of boats, and peered intently at each of the nearby buildings.

"I see one armed guard walking patrol," she reported to Timber and Duncan, "and a building with lights on inside. That one's on the right-hand of the two docks." Eden handed her night-vision goggles to Richard Duncan. She didn't think he would spot anything she missed, but giving him a small role to play in the evening's activities would at least keep him occupied while she and Timber—the professionals—decided what to do next.

Timber focused his goggles on the distant building. "That'll be the harbormaster's office. I don't see anyone there, but odds are there's at least one man on duty. Maybe two."

"Which one do you want?" Eden asked. "It's your choice."

Timber sat silently for a moment. "There has to be another way. Some way that we don't end up killing civilians."

"We talked about this," Eden answered calmly. "Now that you're here and can see the lay of the land, what's your better idea? Remember, we need to be quiet and quick."

Timber had obsessed over this part of the plan since they first debated it the previous afternoon. The situation, now that he was able to reconnoiter the harbor with his own two eyes, was not all that different from what he expected to find in a commercial fishing marina after midnight: a guard, a staff member or two, and dozens of empty fishing boats.

"I still think," Timber said in his mild Arkansas accent, "we can get the jump on them and tie them up." He rubbed his hand along his smooth scalp, his nervousness giving away his own lack of conviction that such a plan would be as successful as the alternative.

Eden shook her head. "That's not a very practical idea. It's not that I disagree with the sentiment, Timber, but our entire escape plan hinges on us getting at least a three-hour head start on anyone who might come after us. Considering that they can radio from here to the Iranian Navy's patrols out near any of their naval bases on the islands in the Gulf to search for and intercept us, we need as much of a head start as possible. Anyone who stumbles upon a tied-up guard is going to immediately find out from him what happened, and then we're completely screwed. If—actually, when—they find a couple of dead bodies, it'll still take them a few more hours to figure out that it wasn't a robbery and that a boat is missing. We *need* that additional time. The way I see it, our entire plan—and our lives—depend on it."

Timber wanted to stand his ground, but as uncomfortable as he felt about the plan, it was hard to argue with her logic.

"Timber, I understand your hesitancy," Richard Duncan said softly, "but I think in this case... well... it may not be desirable, but it does seem necessary."

Timber nodded, acknowledging that he lost the same argument for the second time in less than a day. "The guard," he said, resigning his last measure of resistance. "At least he's armed."

"Okay," Eden said, nodding slightly. "I'll make my way to the harbormaster's office. You take up a position somewhere over there on the right by those steps. You'll be able to see the docks below and still keep an eye on the car. Director, you stay out of sight here in the car for ten minutes. When we're ready, Timber will come back for you and—" Eden hesitated to complete the rest of the thought about what was in the vehicle's trunk. "—Valerie's body."

Eden and Timber sprinted across the empty street and slipped into the marina unseen. Timber took up a firing position part way down a concrete stairway separating the street-level sidewalk from the quay below.

Eden maneuvered deftly between rows of boats and supply crates stacked along the wooden dock. Using the many shadows in the sparsely lit marina to her advantage, she worked her way down the quay's length to the harbormaster's office—hardly larger than a two-room shack.

Timber aimed his suppressed M-4 assault rifle along the dock, alternating between tracking the patrolling guard and following Eden's progress. The senior chief petty officer threw the occasional glance over his left shoulder to ensure no passers-by approached the Peugeot behind him. The last thing he wanted was to have some drunken fisherman stumble across Duncan in the car and scuttle their escape plan. He would not be the one who lost "the package" at this late stage of the mission—a mission that cost the lives of too many of his friends. Not on his watch.

He followed Eden's progress down the length of the pier and admired her skill. For someone not as trained or experienced as a SEAL at the silent-movement techniques the Navy's teams have perfected over the decades, she was doing a remarkable job. In the green glow of his night-vision scope, he watched her steal through the harbor like a pro. Even at the hundred-yard distance, he could clearly see her moving through the shadows from cover to concealment, pistol in hand, as she approached the harbormaster's office. He clicked the knob on his rifle's scope twice to zoom in further. The elongated silhouette of the Sig Sauer .45 and the suppressor mated to it hung in her hand alongside her right thigh. *Even from this distance, it's still clear how those pants hug her curves like—*

Snap out of it, Reggie! Timber reprimanded himself. *Come on, sailor, focus on the guard!*

Timber shook his head and repositioned his night-vision scope towards the far end of the right-hand dock the guard had been patrolling. Earlier, the guard had been making his rounds along the rows of the sixty or so boats in the harbor. Timber surveyed the wooden docks, past the slowly bobbing trawlers and swaying rope lines mooring each in place. *No guard at that end of the dock.* The boats gently knocked tire bumpers into the sides of the docks as they shifted in their berths. *Hmmm, no guard in the next row, either.*

Timber shifted his rifle's scope along the central stone quay from which the two wooden wharfs extended. No guard in the middle. *Where the hell did he go?*

Timber's index finger tapped along the side of the rifle's steel receiver, safely away from the trigger. He scoured the harbor's farthest reaches for any sign of the guard. If he let an armed guard sneak up on

Eden, it would sink their entire escape plan in a heartbeat. He had chosen to eliminate the guard while Eden had the more difficult job of evading detection as she snuck through the harbor. He would never live down a mission failure because he was engrossed by the curves of her butt, if he even lived through the night.

He slewed the rifle frantically searching up and down the waterway. From boat to dock to central quay, he sped up his search. His inhales came as gulps, each breath leaving his lungs as a strained wheeze. Timber sat up straighter and searched for Eden. *Had the guard found her?*

Through the night-vision scope, Timber saw Eden kneeling outside the harbormaster's office. No guard in sight there. He watched the CIA operative tilt her head to the left and lift her right eye just barely above the bottom of the window to peek inside. With her head angled that way, she exposed the minimum amount of her forehead and face to anyone inside the building. *Perfect tactical technique. She's good. Really good.*

A soft metallic sound—almost a buzz—sent a shiver up Timber's spine. He spun the rifle to his right and aimed it towards the second row of fishing boats. A dark figure walked into his line of sight from behind a sixty-foot fishing boat. The guard finished pulling the zipper of his pants up and wiped his hands on the back of his shirt.

Damn, so that's where he went. He was taking a leak.

With a practiced motion, Timber slowly exhaled the stress that had been growing in his chest like a cancer. *Oh, man.*

The Naval Special Warfare operator knelt on the concrete steps and brought his rifle up for the shot he hated having to take. Positioning himself for a better sight line, he rotated the rifle down and farther to his right, aligning the reticle in his scope with his target's ear.

The loud scraping sound surprised both men. Timber's dragging his rifle's magazine against the formed-concrete railing of the stairway broke the silence of the night like nails being drawn against a chalkboard. Unsure of what had made the noise in the dead of the night, the guard spun toward Timber and looked up to the street above. The harbor's late-night protector listened intently for a car or truck that might have been driving by, or perhaps a door scraping roughly against the ground as it was pulled open.

Timber lifted the M-4 over the railing. The weight of the foot-long suppressor kept the rifle barrel low, though it was easily handled by the strong sailor's practiced grip. The bright glow of the guard's eyes shining in the rifle's night-vision scope contrasted the dull green of the rest of Timber's view. The thin red crosshairs bobbed over the guard's face as the patrolman squinted, trying to identify the source of the sound. Timber's gentle squeeze of the trigger sent the rifle recoiling in his hands. The *tink* of the ejected brass round ricocheting off a concrete step was followed by a *plink* of the shell casing falling into the water. Timber reacquired the guard in his sights and saw the man's lifeless body lying on the wooden dock, one arm wrapped around a metal cleat.

He hung his head low, flipped the switch on his rifle to "safe," and lowered the weapon.

Dull thuds from along the dock perked the SEAL's attention. Eden sprinted along the dock and up the stairs. After arriving at the top, she knelt to confer with her teammate.

"All done at the office. I saw the guard fall, too," she said. "Good job."

"If you say so," Timber answered, his voice faint.

"Yes, it was," Eden added, gently taking the rifle from Timber's hand. "Go get George and Val. I'll wait here and cover you." Eden patted the big man's shoulder, knowing full-well how difficult it was for him to make that "pull," as operators called it.

Without a word, Timber stood, looked up and down the empty street, and crossed to the parked Peugeot. With little fanfare, the SEAL lifted a bloodstained bedsheet and its precious contents from the car's trunk.

Eden cracked a smile as Richard Duncan ran across the street in a half-crouch. If anyone had been looking down the street, his novice attempt at avoiding notice would have been an immediate giveaway.

As Timber joined Duncan and Eden, she motioned for the duo to follow her to the bottom of the concrete stairs.

"Stop here for a minute," Eden said. "You two decide which of these boats looks the best to steal. I have no idea. You're the sailors, so you're on your own deciding that. I'm going to go push the guard's body into the water. Have it figured out by the time I get back."

Eden jogged off at a brisk pace, restraining herself from the full-out run she wanted to break into. Her training overcame her almost overwhelming feelings of needing to get the hell out of the harbor. And the country.

"Any of them will probably do," Duncan offered, as he looked around the nearest row of fishing vessels. A sport fisherman, he was at a loss in a commercial harbor. His sailing experience was limited to smaller pleasure craft, not the sixty- to eighty-foot sea-going vessels that sat like silent sentinels along the aged wooden docks.

Timber looked along the rows of boats nearest them and then down the quay, past the harbormaster's office. "Let's go down towards the end. There are some larger boats, and it'll be easier to navigate them out of the harbor if we're already near the mouth."

Duncan nodded his ascent.

Timber hefted Valerie Shepherd's limp body over his shoulder in a fireman's carry. He nudged Duncan gently forward, prodding his charge along the quay.

Eden caught up to them at the second row of boats, and Timber explained the plan. She shrugged and nodded her agreement.

The trio walked swiftly along the quay and past the open doorway of the harbormaster's office. Duncan and Timber were unable to pass the door without sneaking a look inside. The floor of the office was bare, save for an overturned lunch pail against the far wall and the glimmering of a fresh bloodstain in the middle of the floor.

The silence of the night was unbroken, save for the occasional thudding of a moored vessel against the rubber tires used as boat fenders preventing hulls from colliding with docks. The team walked the final fifty yards of the quay looking intently at each of their potential escape options. The larger boats at the far end bobbed gently in their parking slips. They were spaced further apart than were the smaller vessels at the rear of the harbor. Larger fishing trawlers are harder to turn and are given wider berths to ease the tasks of docking and off-loading the crafts' cargo. At the second-to-last row, Timber stopped the group and pointed to a seventy-foot fishing boat on the end.

"This one," he said confidently.

"Why that one?" Eden asked.

"It's not so big that three of us can't handle the lines and, best of all, it's on the end, so it's a straight shot to get out of the harbor."

"Director?" Eden asked, if only to validate Timber's choice.

The CIA Director beamed at being included in the decision-making.

"Yes, I agree. It'll be easier to sail that one away from the dock and right through the mouth of the harbor. It's a big boat, so the fewer turns we have to make the less chance of us grounding it or colliding with something in the dark."

"Fine," Eden said. "Let's do it."

Timber boarded first and placed Valerie's body against the steel transom at the stern. The trio of escapees climbed the ladder to the boat's wheelhouse and gathered in front of the control panel. Timber shone his flashlight along the steering wheel and located the ignition switch.

Timber ran his finger over the wording above the keyhole, and asked, "Can anyone read this?"

Duncan shook his head.

"No," Eden said. "The top labels look homemade, so they must be Farsi. The pre-printed ones below those look like Chinese. Could be that's where the boat was made, I don't know. Doesn't matter what language they are, we just need to figure out how to start it."

"Can you hotwire it or pick the lock?" Duncan asked.

"I've never picked a boat ignition or anything like that, before, but it looks like a regular pin-tumbler lock, so, sure, I'll give it a try. We just need to know what the four groups of words mean. I assume the switch is in the *off* position now, facing twelve o'clock, so that's easy. One of the others must be *start*. Probably the fourth one at the three o'clock position, here." Eden stabbed the boat's dashboard with her finger to indicate the spot. "What about the others?"

"The one at *one* o'clock will be the *on* position," Duncan offered.

"Of course," Eden said. "That makes sense. And the last one? Some kind of accessory or electrical setting? Like in a car to just keep the radio on?" As the group worked to decipher the ignition system, Eden lifted a small black leather pouch of lock picks from her vest pocket.

Timber shook his head. "No, that's not right. These are diesel boats. Diesel engines don't have spark plugs; they have glow plugs. To start 'em, the glow plug pre-heats the fuel so the starter can ignite it. *Start* will be the third position—here at about two o'clock. The first is the glow plug position. Probably, anyway. Try picking the lock over one notch."

Eden made quick work of the ignition switch and left the cylinder rotated one position. The control panel remained lifeless. "Now what?"

"I don't know," Duncan said. "I would have thought that would have at least done something. Timber?"

"I'm not sure," Timber said. He looked at the sides of the panel and shrugged. "The boats I worked on in the Navy didn't use keys. They just had push-button starters. Maybe try it again?"

Eden stood silently for a moment, contemplating his suggestion. She answered Timber's gesture with a shrug of her own and returned the ignition lock to its original position at twelve o'clock. She picked the lock one click again, but the panel remained dark.

"We must be missing something," she said. "Or the battery's dead...."

"Maybe that's it," Timber said.

"A dead battery?" Eden asked, not happy with the prospect of having to board another boat that would be riskier to navigate out of the harbor.

Timber motioned Eden away from the control panel. "Or a disconnect switch to prevent it from going dead if someone leaves a light on below deck." Timber ran his flashlight over the control panel and brought his fingers to rest on top of two switches topped with red safety covers. "Maybe these—"

"Do you actually know what you're doing?" Eden asked, her voice rising.

"Sure," Timber answered. "Mostly."

With two fingers of his left hand, he flicked the safety covers up and out of the way. Putting his fingers under the pair of switches, he warned his companions, "Here goes nothing...." Timber snapped both switches to the up position.

A yellow light illuminated in the upper-right-hand corner of the panel. "I assume that's a good thing?" Eden half-said and half-asked, not at all confident.

"Unless," Timber said, "the order of the ignition switch was actually 'Off, On, Detonate'."

"*Detonate?*" Richard Duncan asked loudly.

"He's kidding! Relax," Eden said, and gave a short laugh.

"Sorry, sir." Timber said, and smiled. "SEAL humor."

Duncan shook his head. Three pairs of eyes shot to the panel as the yellow light turned green.

"Green is definitely good," Eden said. "I like green."

"Now," Timber instructed her, "turn the cylinder all the way to the right and hold it until the engine turns over."

Eden picked the simple lock again and held the tension wrench hard over, keeping the ignition switch in the three o'clock *start* position until the engine roared to life.

"You did it!" Duncan said, smiling from ear to ear.

Eden released the ignition cylinder and the spring-loaded switch snapped back to two o'clock, which she hoped was the 'get the hell out of Iran' position.

"Sir," Timber instructed, "show Eden how to cast off the lines. We're getting the fuck out of here, pardon my Farsi."

"Gladly!"

Duncan and Eden untied the ropes securing the boat to the dock and threw each overboard. At the helm of the largest boat he had ever captained, Timber navigated the craft by night-vision goggles. Its owners would never have sailed their prized possession without running lights. Timber's green-hued view of the water and nighttime seascape gave him an advantage that the boat's regular captain never had. The SEAL would see any approaching boat miles before it could see him, just the way he liked it.

Chapter 24

Timber volunteered to take the first watch. Neither Eden nor Richard Duncan could have piloted the boat out of the harbor as well as he could. The career Navy man steamed his stolen craft southwest for three hours during which he saw no other vessels daring to set out to sea. The devastation the United States' military caused at Bandar Abbas scared away even the hardiest Iranian military and civilian sailors. Those already ashore stayed there, and those who had been at sea when the bombing started sailed as far away from the maelstrom as they had fuel to take them.

The speed gauge on the instrument panel showed Timber was making just over sixteen kilometers per hour—about ten knots. He did some quick mental math and calculated that heading southwest for four hours and then turning due south would put them on course for the other side of the Strait of Hormuz. After all, south is south—eventually they'd find land not owned by the Islamic Republic. The SEAL sailed without navigational charts but figured that even if their course didn't tack precisely to the UAE, they should end up in Oman, or close to it. The operative word being *should*.

He guided *Octopus*—as he had decided to name his purloined fishing trawler—by visual navigation between three islands off the southern coast of Iran. The glow of fires still burning on two of the islands brightened the dark horizons on either side of the *Octopus*. Anti-air and anti-ship missile batteries smoldered on Hormuz Island to his east. A raging blaze burned wildly, consuming fuel depots outside both the Qeshm airport and the island's power plant to *Octopus's* west. The lack of firefighting equipment fitting for the massive conflagrations— and no chance of getting additional manpower or equipment from the mainland anytime soon—would leave the petroleum tanks burning for the remainder of the week and billowing thick black smoke skyward.

From the helm, Timber watched Eden as she stared into the wind on *Octopus's* bow. Her brown hair looked green through his NVGs and fluttered behind her in the salty breeze streaming across the bow. At first, Timber thought she was keeping watch. Richard Duncan clarified that she was staying upwind of the nauseating stenches of diesel fuel and rotting fish. *She's a land-lubber at heart. But good people, just the same.*

Timber glanced at his watch and took a best guess at their position based on little more information than dead-reckoning made possible by wristwatch and speed gauge. It was time. Timber gently pointed *Octopus's* bow southward. Her bow rotated slowly across the horizon; the diesel engines having been designed more for hauling fish than sprinting to freedom. Timber watched his boat's magnetic compass bob and rotate slowly in its cradle until it pointed exactly the way he wanted to go — directly away from Iran.

Eden felt the change in direction and took the cue to join the two men in the deckhouse.

"Timber," she asked, "why don't you let the director drive and you go up top? Time for you to make a Hail Mary radio broadcast."

The two men switched places and Timber gently pushed the radio's soft-plastic earpiece into his ear. "All right, my friends. Here goes nothing." Timber stopped and thought for a moment. "On the other hand, maybe it's more like 'Here goes everything.'"

Eden followed Timber up the ladder to the open deck above the pilothouse. She greatly preferred to stay where the air was far less saturated with the nauseating odors of the fishing profession.

"United States Navy, United States Navy, this is Senior Chief Petty Officer Reginald White calling any station. Come in." Timber paused for a reply he was convinced would not come.

"United States Navy, this is Senior Chief Petty Officer Reginald White transmitting in the blind. I have secured the mission objective and am sailing south from the area of operations in a civilian fishing vessel that we, uhh, borrowed."

Eden giggled at Timber's euphemism for their midnight raid on the commercial fishing harbor and liberation of what she had come to think of as the slowest getaway vehicle on the planet. Timber snort-chuckled, more in surprise at Eden's reaction than in self-appreciation of his own choice of words. His reaction caught Eden off-guard, leading her into in a fit of laughter. She knew he was trying to act professionally on the radio while still concealing as much information as might be useful to an enemy that could intercept the radio broadcast. With the stresses of the past two days behind them, sharing a laugh turned out to be good medicine.

Timber recovered his composure and repeated the radio call. "United States Navy, this is Senior Chief Petty Officer Reginald White transmitting in the blind. I have secured the mission objective at this location and am sailing south. Requesting a ride home, if you please, sir!"

Eden nodded her whole-hearted agreement with the sentiment.

Timber tapped his palm on the railing. "I'll repeat the transmission every five minutes or so. George can handle the controls, I'm sure. All he has to do is keep us pointed south."

"Yeah, I'm sure he can handle that. Back home he has a reputation as a sport sailor and fisherman. Of course, he's ridiculed mercilessly behind his back by the rest of us grunts, but what the hell, right? It's not like we can all hang out at his expensive yacht club in Annapolis or wherever. I'm sure he's used to having GPS and an autopilot on whatever boat he owns back home, but—oh, *shit!*"

"What?" Timber asked, spinning around to locate the threat. He raised his rifle and searched the horizon.

Eden thrust her night-vision goggles to her face and scanned the sea around the boat.

"Whew," she said. "I just realized that I left him steering the boat by compass, but neither of us gave him a pair of NVGs! He's completely blind down there. I totally forgot about that and just had a horrific vision of us running into something out here. We could sail right into an island, and he'd never see it coming."

"Sorry, my fault. I should have given him mine."

"No, no problem. I'll go downstairs to keep him company and act as the lookout. You keep making the radio calls. If that doesn't work and you end up seeing a friendly mermaid, maybe you can sweet talk her into putting in a good word for us, eh?"

"Yeah, sure. I'll do just that."

Eden climbed down the ladder and rejoined Richard Duncan in the pilothouse. With one eye on the green-tinted seascape and her other on the compass, she admired his being able to maintain their course so well with minimal lighting from the instruments as his only guiding light.

"You know," Eden said, "I never asked you... how did the Iranians get you here from Bermuda? No one at the Agency could figure that part out. The yacht was blown up, but where were you by then? The leading theory is that you were taken on another yacht to Africa, and then by aircraft to Iran."

"The yacht was destroyed?" Duncan asked.

"Yes, somewhere southeast of Bermuda. Only about fifty miles out or so. You didn't know?"

"No, that's too bad. We were only aboard the yacht for twenty minutes or so. I'm not really sure. It all happened so fast. Things from that day are a bit of a blur."

"I can certainly understand that. So, where did they take you?"

"To a submarine. One of the Iranian's diesel-electric Kilo-class subs. Ugly, smelly boats. *Ugh.*" Duncan shivered from the memories.

"Um hmmm. The possibility that they'd use one of the three Kilos they bought from the Russians way back was discussed by the analysts a lot during the two months you were gone. But they always discounted that theory saying that those subs have less than one-third of the operational range needed to make that long a trip. So, they were sure it had to be something else—like an aircraft."

"Yes, those subs do indeed have a limited range. The captain told us all about that. He was quite open in telling us what was going on throughout the trip. Even if we escaped from the cell, it's not like Heather or I could go anywhere or call for help. The captain was the only one on board who spoke any English and even that is being generous. But he liked to practice it. Or maybe he was just showing off, I don't know. Of course, as limited as it was, it's still better than my Farsi. They kept us in a stateroom they'd converted into a holding cell by welding a jail door to the frame—bars and all with a horizontal slot at the bottom to pass food through. The captain would come down—or up, I don't know—once a day just to gloat about how smart they are that they could pull something this big over on the Great Satan and we never knew it was going to happen. I felt like crap for the first couple of weeks each time he'd do that. Although, after we figured out he wasn't going to hurt us, well, then I just tried to keep him talking to get as much information out of him as I could. He liked to practice his English."

"Hey," Eden said with a smile, "we'll make a collector out of you, yet!" She gave him a friendly tap on the shoulder. "Not that I know much about collecting, myself. Not really my thing, you know?" She smiled again. Duncan knew exactly what she meant.

"The captain explained some of what they did to make the trip possible," Duncan said, adjusting the wheel to keep the boat tacking south. "They used a commercial freighter to pre-position six fuel bladders along the sub's route between Iran and Bermuda. The sub needed to use a minimum of three and ended up using four. One must have floated away—they never found it, he told us. And they didn't need the sixth one. The captain was rather proud of that fact, for whatever reason. Maybe he just needed someone to brag to. Heather and I had little choice but to listen.

"Speaking of Heather," Duncan looked at Eden.

Out of politeness, she lifted the NVGs away from her face. She knew what question was coming.

"Do you think she was aboard one of the Navy helicopters we saw yesterday? Do you think she might have gotten out of there?"

"If I knew, I'd be the first to tell you. Honestly, I don't know one way or another. I was with you the whole time, remember? I truly hope she did, but I can't know for sure." That, as far as it went, was the truth. "There were two assault elements, and obviously I was on the one that happened to find you. Just like we ran into a lot of resistance, I *do* know that the other team did, as well. Beyond that, though, we just have to hope for the best."

Richard Duncan nodded silently, afraid to press her for more details. Eden slipped the NVGs back over her eyes and resumed her lookout duties. The dour tenor of the discussion of his wife's fate put an early end to their conversation.

Octopus bobbed and surged through the surging waters of the Strait of Hormuz. The trawler's powerful diesel engines easily moved it through the four-foot seas. Time passed slowly as one nautical mile of green-tinted seawater stretched into the next.

Eden looked at Director Duncan. "I'm going to head back up to talk to Timber. Just keep us heading south, and I'll yell down to let you know if there's a buoy or boat or something we need to avoid."

"Sure thing. I'm glad I can finally contribute in a meaningful way to our escape. This trawler is larger than what I normally sail back home, but I can keep it heading south without a problem. I'll yell if I need you."

Eden nodded and joined Timber on deck.

Timber pointed to twin glows on the horizon on each side of *Octopus*.

"Look over there," he said to Eden. "The Iranians have naval bases on a couple of the islands offshore, protecting Bandar Abbas. Or they were supposed to, anyway. Our Tomahawk cruise missiles struck the air defenses and Silkworm anti-ship batteries in the first strike last night."

"Oh, right," Eden said. "I remember that from the briefing. Then the Air Force bombers came through and bombed the shit out of everything else."

"Yeah," Timber replied, "but the Navy struck first!"

Eden laughed. "Yes, you got the first punch in. That's true." She scanned from horizon to horizon and marveled at the reflections the orange glows made against the scattered clouds. Considering the intense pounding the Iranian Navy took the previous night, she hoped it unlikely they had anything left to patrol with, assuming any of their sailors even had the gumption to leave port.

"Hey, Timber," Eden asked, "how did you get that nickname?"

Timber grunted and gave a half-laugh. "Oh, that was a long time ago. Do you really want to hear that story?"

"I *was* just making conversation before, but *now*? Yeah, you bet."

"Okay, well, I was about three months into Green Team training. That's like a nine-month-long try-out for DEVGRU. Anyway, we were doing Close-Quarter-Battle training, and I screwed up on a target-selection drill. The usual punishment was to send SEALs to go climb these huge cargo nets that are near the shooting house."

"I've been there for CQB training," Eden said, as she scanned the horizon with her NVGs, keeping an eye out for boats or hazards to navigation. "I know exactly where you're talking about."

"Right," Timber continued. "I messed up, so I went and climbed the nets. I admit it—I was tired. That's no excuse, but it's the truth. I got about half-way up the net and was too far over to the right. I had trouble keeping my balance but, *man*, I fought it with everything I had left. I did *not* want to fall off and have to climb them three more times if I ended up hitting the deck. Anyway, I was trying to keep my balance and shaking the whole net something fierce. At some point, I leaned over too far and just couldn't pull myself back. It was clear to me and the instructors on the ground that I was going overboard and there was nothing I could do about it. I tipped over in slow motion. One instructor laughed hysterically while another yelled out, 'Tim-*ber!*' as I fell off and landed square on my beautiful black ass."

Eden laughed. "Sorry, I'm sure it didn't make you look good to the instructors, but it *is* kind of funny."

"Yeah, I guess so. Time has eased the pain of the moment. Anyway, the name stuck."

"It could be a lot worse. It's a good nickname. I like it."

***

For the next few hours, the pair continued to watch the barely changing seascape as they sailed slowly south.

After a while, Eden returned to the pilot house to keep Richard Duncan company. The monotony of the voyage reminded her of the many missions on which she had waited endless hours for her target to emerge. That, she reckoned, was an apt description of her entire career: hours of mind-numbing boredom punctuated by moments of sheer terror.

Without warning, twin daggers of pain stabbed Eden in her eyes. She ripped the light-amplifying goggles from her face with her right hand and threw her left arm up to protect her eyes. A brief cry of pain echoed from Timber on the upper deck, equally blinded by the brilliance of the high-intensity light that appeared out of the black of the night, directly in front of *Octopus*.

"What is *that*?" Duncan yelled, almost rhetorically.

Eden raised her arm slightly, using it as a sun visor. Unable to see through the blinding whiteness, she tried to focus on whatever must be carrying the light. Something was out there, but what? That they were in danger was obvious — but what kind of danger, she had no idea. She dropped her right hand almost reflexively and slowly drew her .45 from its holster on her thigh.

The bright white light turned the scene on the bow of the trawler into daylight. Eden squinted to make out the source of the illumination. The hairs on the back of her neck stood up. Her instincts for survival all screamed in unison: "This is it!" But what particular *it* they were warning of, she had no idea.

Almost unconsciously, Eden raised the Sig Sauer and pointed it squarely between Richard Duncan's shoulder blades. If this was going to be it, she knew she wouldn't have time for more than a single squeeze of the trigger. *What the hell is that light?* Eden strained hard to make out any forms in the darkness in front of her. Pulling the trigger would be one decision she could never take back. There'd be no way to un-ring that bell if she were wrong.

The impact from behind her sent Eden tumbling to the steel deck. Her head bounced off the red-painted floor plate. What felt like a thousand-pound weight landed in the small of her back. Her breath flew out of her chest, expelled violently by the impact and came out in a raspy rush. Her right shoulder erupted in pain as her arm was pulled behind her and torqued outward roughly. The Sig Sauer was torn from her grip by unseen hands. Eden would have screamed in agony, if she still had the breath to do so. Her empty lungs burned for air, but the tremendous weight pinning her to the cold metal deck made breathing impossible. Faster than she even realized it was being done, her hands were yanked behind her and bound. She tried to squirm free but could not move more than an inch in any direction.

Stunned from her fall, the world spun in her head. Screams echoed throughout the deckhouse. They registered in her mind but seemed impossibly far away. She tried to place the voice—not Director Duncan's voice, that much she could tell. The voices were deeper, more like Timber's but... not.

Soon, the spinning slowed and the packed-cotton feeling in her head eased. The pressure on her back let up enough to allow for her to take several shallow breaths. The air tasted sweet, and for once, she didn't mind the hints of diesel fuel and rotten fish.

Eden began to recognize the words being yelled. In English, she marveled.

"Get down, down, *down*! On the deck!"

"Drop the gun!"

"US Navy!"

"Command, we have George—"

"Unidentified armed female—"

"Confirmed, we have the senior chief, too."

"She's with me. Don't hurt her!" That voice Eden knew. That was Richard Duncan. The other voices she had never heard before.

Eden's head continued to swim, but not as bad as at first, but she still couldn't move. What felt like a hundred hands patted, probed, and pulled at every part of her body. *Every* part. Magazines of ammunition were jerked from her belt and sent clattering across the deck. An unseen hand ripped her backup Sig Sauer from its holster under her left shoulder, almost taking the shoulder with it. Lock picks and her last remaining granola bar flew from her vest pockets as if they had wings of their own.

"Let... me...." she tried to say.

The invisible hands were having none of it. They lifted—practically levitated—her from the deck as if she were just a rag doll. Her hands and feet remained bound and useless. She had a close-up view of the legs that carried her out of the deckhouse, over the side of the trawler, and deposited her roughly in a small speedboat.

"Let... me... up...." Eden managed to eke out between bounces and pushes. The invisible hands remained as firm as vice grips. She winced as her face was abruptly mashed into the corner of the boat's floor where it met the sidewall.

A soft electric hum whined behind her. Her face was pressed firmly into the sidewall of the new boat as it turned and accelerated like a sportscar. Accelerated to where, though, she had no idea.

"Creeper Two," a voice behind her said, "this is Gauntlet. We're clear. Blow the charges."

"Copy," the distorted voice said through the radio speaker.

"Can't you let her up?" Duncan's voice said from somewhere behind Eden.

"No. We know who you and Senior Chief White are, but not her. We were expecting two of you, not three. We'll sort it out when we get you back to the—"

The bouncing boat surged and leaned to one side as the blast from behind it interrupted the nameless voice and shook the speedboat. Eden's face dug further into the hard deck and rubber sidewall. She snorted in a decidedly unladylike manner, which she regretted only momentarily. She resolved to do whatever the situation required to keep the accumulating water on the floor out of her nose. She snorted again and a solution of seawater and mucus flew from her nose.

Timber's voice, tinged with a measure of regret, carried forward from somewhere far behind Eden. "Well, there goes my *Octopus*."

Settling in for the remainder of the bumpy ride, Eden began to accept that she was overpowered, and the trip was not going to get any more comfortable. *This is either going to be a very long ride, or a very short one.*

Chapter 25

Eden scraped the last of the frozen green delicacy from the bottom of her bowl and smiled. She heaped it into her mouth and savored the delightful aftertaste of the Pistachio ice cream. She pointed her spoon at Timber across the large dining table in the officers' Wardroom and smiled. "You're right. No sense denying yourself the good stuff. This might just start to rival chocolate chip cookie dough, but it's a close call. For me, there's just something special about chocolate, you know?"

Timber, Bugsy Thomas, and two officers from SEAL Team Four chuckled. Eden rubbed her shoulder, still sore from the rough handling she'd received at the hands of the Team Four commandos who had pulled her from the fishing trawler and brought her, Director Duncan, Timber, and Valerie Shepherd's remains safely back aboard the aircraft carrier *USS George Washington*.

"So," Eden said to her rescuers, "you call that surprise maneuver an *underway*?"

The SEAL Team Four officer nodded. "First, we surrounded your fishing boat with our faster assault boats. Then, it's just like a magician at a kid's birthday party—make you look one way with a bright light while we sneak aboard behind you. Simple in concept, but like anything else, it takes a lot of practice to get right."

"Well, you certainly got it right," the CIA officer agreed.

A deep voice bellowed from the doorway—a bit too loudly, Eden thought, for such a small room. "Attention on deck!"

The SEALs sprang from their chairs and stood ramrod straight. Eden rose last, out of politeness for her comrades more than any reverence for military protocol.

"As you were," another voice answered dryly.

Richard Duncan followed a uniformed naval officer into the room. The pair of senior executives were flanked by four young Marines armed with holstered sidearms and cautious eyes. It occurred to Eden just how damned good Marines look in their crisp blue-and-khaki uniforms.

"Eden," Richard Duncan said, "this is Calvin Nguyen, Captain of the *USS George Washington*."

Eden extended her hand towards her host. "Glad to meet you, Captain. Thank you for your hospitality. A girl could get used to this."

"We're happy to have you all safely back aboard," Captain Nguyen said. "I hope the food is to your liking. Having you all remain sequestered here in the Wardroom until we can complete the initial debriefing and travel planning to get you back stateside has at least enabled you to enjoy breakfast while you wait." The captain peered at Eden's bowl with the telltale green remnants of her ice cream on the table. "You seem to have a different idea of what breakfast is than I do, but, hey, to each his own. Or her own, as the case may be."

Eden shrugged and smiled. "I've been cooped up in far worse places, believe me." She turned to Director Duncan, and asked, "Is everything returning to normal back home?"

"I just got off a video teleconference with the President, the Chairman of the Joint Chiefs, and General Folson. I'd say that things back in DC are just as screwed up as they were two months ago. So, yes, back to normal."

Eden chuckled, as did a few of the men around the dining table. Captain Nguyen smiled politely.

"They're sending an Air Force jet from Germany to take me home," Duncan continued. "I do want to ask you something, though. I would like you to be on my security detail for the return trip. I'd feel more comfortable with someone I know and trust at my side. Would you do that?"

"Nope, not a chance. No offense, but I'm a non-official-cover employee, and if I ever want to do fieldwork again, I can't be seen with you. Sorry, but I have enough trouble traveling sometimes, and I don't need the extra scrutiny. Nothing personal. And besides," Eden said, raising her voice and turning her head to speak over her shoulder, "*someone* threw my two favorite pistols into the ocean." Eden cast an evil eye at one of her rescuers from Team Four.

The SEAL officer broke into the smile of a Cheshire cat and raised his hands in an exaggerated shrug.

Eden grinned and went on. "I'm probably going to catch a commercial flight home in the next day or so. I'm sure I'll see you back home during a debriefing session or two... or ten."

"Yeah," Duncan said with a grin. "I'm sure we'll both have quite a few of those."

"Oh, and also, I hadn't gotten to see you since I heard the news, but I'm so sorry to hear about your wife. I never knew Heather, but, well... I'm very sorry for your loss."

"Thank you," Duncan said. Slowly he added, "I'm not sure what I'm going to tell our girls about how she died. I—" His voice cracked. Slowly, he wiped the start of a tear from one eye.

Eden put her hand on the CIA Director's shoulder, and said, "I'm so sorry."

She gave his shoulder a squeeze, and Richard Duncan nodded his appreciation.

Chapter 26

Michelle Reagan pushed the large pine-veneer hospital room door open slowly.

Steven Krauss sat upright in bed finishing his lunch, or what passed for lunch in Arlington Memorial Hospital. He was pretty sure he'd live through what put him in the hospital in the first place, but much less confident that he'd survive what the nurses euphemistically referred to as food.

"Hi, hon," Michelle said quietly, peering through the partially opened door. "How are you feeling? Are you okay?"

"Oh, thank God you're home safe!" Krauss practically yelled. He dropped his fork, which landed on the plastic tray with a *clang*. "I thought I'd lost you! Don't you *ever* do that to me again!"

"I know, I know. I'm *sorry*," Michelle said, pulling the door closed behind her. As Steve started to push up out of the bed, Michelle placed her hands on his shoulders. "No, no. Stay in bed." She ran her fingers through Steve's graying brown hair as they kissed. "I love you. Are you feeling better?"

"When you didn't make it back to the carrier...." he said, and enveloped Michelle with both arms.

"I know, I know, but it's okay now."

"I thought that it finally happened, and you weren't coming home. I—"

"*Shhhh*, honey. I'm back. When your secretary told me you'd been hospitalized for exhaustion, I felt terrible. Now I know how you felt those times you've had to pick me up at the Portsmouth Naval hospital when I was injured. What happened to you?"

Steve put the lunch tray on the rolling cart next to his bed. He grasped both of Michelle's hands in his and held them tightly to his chest. "Oh, it was nothing."

"You're in a *hospital*. It wasn't *nothing*."

"Well, it's more embarrassing than anything else. I was already working long hours for the last couple of months—you know that already. When you deployed, I packed a suitcase and just lived out of my office. I showered at the gym and just kept working to make sure that the task forces had analyzed every report, planned for every contingency, and were leaving nothing to chance. We were all in the EOC watching live feeds beamed back from Bandar Abbas via reconnaissance aircraft orbiting overhead. We also got to listen to some of the radio transmissions the Navy piped back stateside for us. The General was in the White House Situation Room watching the same feeds with the President and the Secretaries of Defense and State."

"Wow, I didn't realize we became international TV stars," Michelle said, grinning.

"Yeah, well, it started to look more like a tragedy than a sitcom. We couldn't hear anything from the ground itself. Someone in a Navy plane overhead narrated what they were seeing, so we got some play-by-play commentating. When the Shore Patrol building exploded, the EOC went completely silent. Everyone was so still that all you could hear was someone's shoe squeaking as they shifted from one foot to the other. No one so much as breathed. We had no idea what just happened. It caught the Navy guys by surprise as well. Whoever was narrating from the air started cursing like a sailor, to coin a phrase. Someone realized that the White House was listening and cut the audio off for a while. No one moved, and we were afraid to even talk to each other. When the audio came back on and the Navy reported the loss of essentially the entire assault team, we were devastated. I had no idea if you were in that group or not. My heart stopped."

"We were shocked, too, "Michelle said. "Both by the force of the explosion itself and also what it meant. It seemed like it took a full minute for our team to process what we'd just seen and heard and continue to move forward. In combat, confusion reigns supreme, and a minute is forever when you're in the thick of it. *Hey*," She interrupted herself as a thought occurred to her. "Were you able to see us? Could you see *me*?"

"No. We had a wide view of the whole area from the aircraft high above. We couldn't identify individual people or tell who was who. I think the Navy had other aircraft and drones in the air that probably could, but they weren't sending those video feeds back to us. I'm sure they don't want the White House or some admiral micro-managing combat in real time from the comfort of a padded chair back in DC. I can understand that. So, it was obvious from what we were able to see that the Iranians brought in reinforcements faster than anyone had expected. We could easily see the heat signatures of the vehicles as they were driving in. Later, once the Navy's choppers left the scene, phone calls were flying furiously to find out who had made it back to the choppers. The helos had to take off, but three small SEAL assault boats waited for stragglers. They were shooting up everything on shore with those powerful Gatling cannons they have. We watched streams of tracer rounds raking everything onshore. We heard that a half-dozen SEALs had to swim out to meet the boats just offshore. It took the Navy a few hours to determine who made it out in a helo or on one of the small boats. At that point, no one knew where you or the director were. The fear was widespread that you'd all been killed or captured. The worst part was not knowing. We had to start planning for any number of worst-case scenarios."

"Obviously, we never made it to back to the landing zone," Michelle said, filling in the gaps. "Four of us got separated from the rest of the assault team. Some of that team died and some made it back to the small assault boats you mentioned. Throughout the entire flight home, I kept trying to think of what might have happened if the four of us had stayed with that group. I just don't know. Maybe we would have been shot along the way or maybe we would have made it out safely. I honestly doubt the director could have swum out to rendezvous with an assault boat. Think about it—swimming through the surf, wearing street clothes, panicking about where his wife was and whether she was okay or not, and trying to make it out to a boat you can't see while bullets are whizzing overhead in both directions. I seriously doubt he would have made it, but who knows. When the adrenaline is pumping, people can do the impossible. Personally, I think he would have frozen in panic and drowned."

Steve stroked Michelle's hand. "When we heard that you had not been recovered with the rest of the SEALs, I went nuts. I had NGA analyzing every frame of every image from every asset a dozen times each. I drove down to Springfield and started looking over the imagery myself. Turns out that imagery analysis is *far* harder than it looks, and I'm terrible at it. I'm glad we have those guys to do that kind work for us. I went back to headquarters completely dejected. After that, everything's a blur. It turns out that I didn't sleep for about three days. I looked for you and had absolutely everyone looking for all of you non-stop. I just worked until I collapsed. I got brought here by ambulance. They won't let me leave, although that's probably my fault. I've been telling anyone who would listen—and even those who wouldn't—that I had to get back to work. They've been sedating me at night, probably to ensure I don't escape." Steve smiled at Michelle. "I'm pretty sure I would have tried, although I don't know how far I might have gotten." He squeezed Michelle's hand firmly. "You're obviously far better at that than I am. But, I'm fine now that you're back by my side."

Steve took a deep breath and let it out slowly. "I can finally relax." He lifted and kissed both of Michelle's hands.

"Well, now you don't have to escape," she said. "I'll drive you home this afternoon. But we may have to wait to celebrate my homecoming until you have your energy back. I'd hate to put you right back in the hospital because I tuckered you out, umm, celebrating. You'd never live that down!"

"Yeah, but it'd be a hell of a way to go! Well, now, so, tell me. Where did you go after you got separated from the main group? We never figured that out."

"Right," Michelle said, feeling guilty that she was the reason that her group separated from the others. "After we found the director and headed back to the helicopter landing zone, *then* the real shooting started. The SEALs engaged the Iranians and a few of us moved around the other side of what I think was a cafeteria to keep the director out of the line of fire. Then we got cut off from the rest and there were too many troops between us and the helos for us to be able to make it out that way. We saw the helos lift off, so I ended up stealing a car. We spent the next day in some random house in a nearby neighborhood."

"Stole a car?" Steve asked in disbelief.

"Yup. Bet you didn't know I could hotwire a Toyota, did you?"

"*Hmm.* The next time I lose my keys, I guess I can skip calling triple-A."

Michelle described the rest of the escape, leaving out the messy details she knew Steve would not want to hear. From experience, she knew he had only so much tolerance for the killing that so often occurred in her line of work.

Michelle sat on the side of the bed holding Steve's hands in hers.

Steve went on. "I'm so glad you're home. You have no idea —"

"Okay, lover boy," a woman's voice said as the door flew open. "Time to —" Allison DeMott marched into the hospital room as if she owned it. The cartoon characters on her colorful scrubs jumped with her for joy as she saw Michelle. "Hey, *hey*! The prodigal daughter returns."

"Hey, Alli. Nice scrubs. New?" From her perch on the bed, Michelle reached for her friend, and the women hugged.

"So," Allison said, looking at her friends sharing the hospital bed, "you know how much I'd love to join you two in that bed, but I have to drop this off and get over to Georgetown." Allison placed a bag of M&M's on Steve's lunch tray and winked at him. She billowed her shirt out and looked at the colorful figures as she answered Michelle. "Yeah, I'm covering shifts on the pediatric ward for a nurse who's out on maternity leave. I saw these super-cute ones in the store, so I bought 'em. Beats the plain green I always wear in the ER. So, girlfriend, you're back? Where were you this time?"

"Yup, I'm back," Michelle said with a large grin. She and Steve had been friends with Allison for the better part of a decade. Michelle still kept up the veneer of her saleswoman cover with her BFF and appreciated that Allison had stopped asking her the hard questions. Allison had long ago given up pointing out the various holes in Michelle's cover stories. Michelle was sure that Allison knew she was really a CIA employee and not a sales rep for a catering supply company, but never confirmed her suspicion. Some questions are simply best left unasked.

"Since Steven was working so much, I decided it would be safe for me to go visit some customers in Florida and Texas for a week or so, and he'd never miss me. I figured 'how much trouble could he get himself into,' right? Well, silly me. Now I know."

"I missed you in yoga class, too, so... hopefully you'll be home for a while? Maybe?"

"Yes, I'm not going anywhere."

"Good, good, good. Well, gotta run, kids. The traffic in DC sucks, and I'm working extra hours this week. But not as many hours as lover boy here. Rest up and drink lots of fluids, okay, Steve? Seriously. And not the kind made from grapes or hops, you hear?"

"Yes, ma'am," Krauss said with a smile and threw her a mock salute.

Allison smiled and gave each of them a kiss on her way out of the room.

Chapter 27

The conference table in the CIA Director's office suite was a battlefield. Maps and satellite images fought for supremacy while avoiding the landmines of coffee mugs and bottles of water. The smiles and laughs contrasted sharply in Michelle Reagan's mind with the last time she sat in Richard Duncan's office.

Duncan, Dagmar Bhoti, General Folson, Michelle, and her team lead, Michael, crowded around the table for a final recap of the rescue mission.

"As much as I don't agree with their methods," Folson said, leaning back in her chair, "I have to give the Iranians a modicum of credit for having the *cojones* to even attempt something like this, much less pull it off successfully. Their modus operandi has always been to finance a proxy to do their dirty work. Even though they paid the O'Dohertys to effect the actual kidnapping, they deployed their own submarine in a rather creative manner for the long-haul transportation."

Duncan nodded. "Even though Secretary of State Bauer doesn't agree with me, I still believe Foreign Minister Ansari's denial that the regime was behind this. I think this was an off-the-books operation. Or whatever they would call it. From my conversations with Admiral Shaaro in Bandar Abbas, I got the distinct impression that this was all a backroom agreement he made with his cousin who runs the security apparatus for their nuclear research facilities. As I told the debriefers at least a dozen times, I think this was something the two of them cooked up between themselves. One cousin had the need and the other, the means."

"Sir," Dagmar Bhoti said, "I want to make sure we're consistent in what disinformation we put out to the Iranians and Russians on what we know about Iran's nuclear program. Or, at least what little is left of it. You said earlier that you admitted to knowing about the eighteenth site. But that's it? Not the other two?"

"Yes," Duncan confirmed. "As we suspected, they already knew that we knew about the eighteenth site dug into the mountain near

Alam-Kuh. I didn't have to admit to that for a while and denied any knowledge of any others. They never got rough with me, but were starting to play good-cop, bad-cop. That's why they moved me out of the jail building but kept Heather there. They wanted to use my uncertainty and fear of what was going to happen to her against me. They didn't bring in what I'd term a professional interrogator. Admiral Shaaro did most of the questioning himself. Through an interpreter, I mean. His cousin, Fazel Shaaro, was present for the questioning a few times, too. They kept saying the quicker I answered all of their questions, the sooner I'd get to take Heather home."

"You do realize, sir," Eden said, "that they were never going to let you go. I'm sure they *claimed* they would, but if things were as you said, and this was a private deal made between one Navy admiral and the intelligence agency's chief of security, they couldn't afford to ever let you go. When they were done questioning you, they would have killed both you and your wife. And probably the interpreter, too."

"I didn't think that was the case at the time. I thought they were sincere, but...." Duncan hesitated, not wanting to believe that he never even had a chance to see his wife again. "Your assessment does make sense when looking at it from a distance. At the time, though, I didn't want to think that they would do such a thing. I wanted to hold onto any chance that Heather and I could end up safe and just forget any of it ever happened. I needed to believe that was at least a possibility. It—"

"Yes, sir," Michael agreed. "That's pretty much Interrogation 101 — give the subject a path forward. But it's the path forward that *they* wanted you to take, not what was going to get you released. I agree with Eden that there was never any chance of that. Had the word gotten out afterwards that the Iranian Navy was behind your kidnapping, it's very likely that the admiral would have been the one locked up in a Tehran cell much smaller than the one he kept you in."

"I hate to admit it," Duncan said, reflecting on the events that cost his wife her life, "but while it's all going on around you... while you're in the middle of it all... you *want* to believe what they tell you. At least I did. Sometimes I feel ashamed about it. Other times... I'm glad I didn't let on about the other facilities we know about."

"Don't blame yourself," Eden said sympathetically. "Everyone has their limits. Given enough time, you would have told them everything. It sounds like they hadn't even started the rough stuff with you, yet. Eventually, you would have told them, and there's no shame in that. Maybe the worst wouldn't have been what they did to you, but what they might have done to your wife while you had to watch it happen right in front of you. That's—"

General Folson interrupted. "I think he gets the idea. It certainly would have been a horrible experience. We're glad that you didn't have to go through any of that, sir." Turning her attention to Eden, the General continued. "Eden, by all accounts, you were quite the heroine on this mission. From making a dynamic combat entry into the holding cell, to hotwiring a car, to stealing a fishing boat. Your quick thinking and tactical skills were really put to the test. I'm sure that your experiences in this operation can inform our operations training classes at the Farm and elsewhere. I would like you to put together a list and maybe a description of what kind of training worked well for you, and what you would have liked to have known more about before you went in-country. We can use that to update the curriculum for operations trainees."

"Sure," Eden responded. *As long as they don't make me teach the whelps. Going into Iran was bad enough. Having to teach newbies might just be what makes me quit.* "I'll email a list to you."

"Thank you all," Director Duncan said to dismiss the gathered executives.

As the group stood to leave, Duncan turned to Michelle. "Eden, would you mind staying behind for a minute?"

She nodded silently.

After the rest had left, Duncan closed the door and returned to the table to address Michelle.

"I just wanted to thank you for what you did for me. And what you didn't do *to* me." Duncan drew his lips back. Not into a smile, but Michelle understood the reference and his pained look.

"Sir, I understood the severity of the situation. You didn't get to hear it, but I was really moved by a speech the deputy director gave in the EOC during one of the early briefings. She reminded the senior executives present that this would be the same group assembled to search for and rescue any of them if they had been the one kidnapped. I realized that she was right. That's such a great thing about the people in this agency. We really do look out for each other no matter the cost and that's what made it important for me to do whatever I could to help."

"Well, I appreciate that. I truly do. Now that we're back, I wanted to ask you one question. After you got me out of the cell, I asked you about Heather. I know what you said then, but did you actually know at that point that she was already dead?"

"No, I did not," Michelle answered honestly. "We knew that the Shore Patrol building exploded, but we had no way of knowing who was still in it or who might have gotten out. I know I was intentionally vague that night, but, well... I had to keep you moving forward. I had to put you on the path *I* wanted you to take. There was absolutely nothing that any of us could have done for her at that point, so I just had to focus on getting you out safely."

"That's pretty much what I thought, but I wasn't sure. Would you have told me if you had actually known?"

"At the time, to be frank, I'm sure I would have told you anything I needed to in order to get you moving towards the helicopters. If I had to lie my ass off to do it, then, yes, I would have lied. The psychology of the situation being what it was, my best choice would have been to tell you whatever you needed to hear to get you to put all your energy into going where I told you to go. That's just the way it had to be."

Duncan nodded slowly. "I know. I knew it then, too. I just had to hear it for myself. Thank you for your honesty."

"Again, I'm very sorry about your wife."

"Thank you," Duncan said, rising to indicate the conversation was ending. "I do appreciate everything that you did to get me out of there. And for *not* shooting me." Duncan chuckled. "You really would have done it, right? If you had to?"

Michelle ducked the question. "Hey, sir, *you're* the one who signed that piece of paper in the first place, remember? Maybe the next time a lawyer sticks something under your nose, you'll want to read the fine print more closely."

They both laughed as Michelle headed for the office door.

Chapter 28

The Navy chaplain closed his prayer book and looked at the coffin. "Earth to earth, ashes to ashes, dust to dust. The Lord bless her and keep her, the Lord make his face to shine upon her and be gracious unto her, the Lord lift up his countenance upon her and give her peace. Amen."

From a ridgetop forty yards away, a bugler blew Taps which echoed among the curved white headstones of Arlington National Cemetery.

A tear streamed from Michelle's left eye. The memory of Valkyrie's face—fixed in a wide smile as she stood alongside Banshee at the pre-mission briefing—hung foremost in her mind.

Two Honor Guard sailors approached opposite ends of Valerie Shephard's casket and lifted the American flag draped over the dark wood cover. They pulled the flag taught from its four corners and folded it tightly. Val's parents sat sobbing under the blue canopy protecting the seated mourners from the hot summer sun. Jamie Shepherd, Valerie's younger sister, sat next to her parents and quivered uncontrollably. The Navy Petty Officer leading the funeral detail presented the flag with crisp military precision to John and Marie Shepherd. Valerie's mother's hands shook as she accepted the flag offered in honor of her daughter's service and sacrifice.

A solemn procession of uniformed Naval Special Warfare operators formed to approach the casket. One by one, operators placed a SEAL Trident pin—the golden uniform badge of a Naval Special Warfare operator—onto the dark wooden top of Valkyrie's casket. With a clenched fist, each drove their tribute into the brown wood, and the line of insignia grew from one end of her casket to the other.

After the final pin had been emplaced, the SEALs stood at attention. A staff member of the Arlington National Cemetery's grounds crew slowly dipped his hand out of sight and pressed the green button on a concealed control panel. With a faint electric hum, the casket descended slowly. What had been a silent lamenting of the gathered mourners grew louder in waves of sobs and cries.

As her sister's casket disappeared from view, Jamie Shepherd's silent cries broke into a howl from deep within. Her mother reached around her only remaining child and hugged her tightly. Both women shuddered as the casket came to a stop at the bottom of the grave.

One by one, Valerie's friends and relatives took turns placing a shovelful of dirt onto the casket. Symbolic of their love and support for her in this life, each played his or her part in helping Valerie Mary Shepherd move on to the next.

After the ceremony, Lieutenant Tamara Cruikshank approached Michelle and gave her a hug.

"I'm so sorry for your loss, Banshee. I didn't get to know Val very well, but she was a great woman."

Timber approached the women and shook Michelle's hand. Military etiquette precluded an enlisted man from shaking an officer's hand. Protocol for funerals also barred the senior NCO from saluting the Lieutenant. As a compromise, the colleagues exchanged smiles and nods.

"Hey, Master Chief."

"Hey, yourself, L-T." Timber's southern accent caused the letters to hang in the still air.

"*Master* Chief?" Michelle asked, puzzled. "I thought you were a *Senior* Chief. Master is higher than Senior, right?"

"Sure is," Banshee confirmed with the small amount of glee she could muster under the circumstances. "You're looking at the Navy's newest Master Chief Petty Officer. He certainly earned it."

"Yes, he definitely did. If it weren't for him, I might not be here today." Michelle glanced at Timber and continued. "I didn't know you were up for promotion. Congratulations!"

"Thank you. And I wasn't. But one letter of appreciation from your director to the Chief of Naval Operations, and boom. Before you can say 'Rescue Mission,' I get ordered to the admiral's office for an ambush promotion ceremony. My captain had gone behind my back and brought my wife into the office, so when I got into the Command Conference Room, I thought it was going to be some kind of intervention or something! I was completely surprised. But it was great."

Banshee explained. "The CNO can promote enlisted sailors essentially any time he wants. It doesn't work that way for officers. That takes an act of Congress. Literally. An act of *Congress*! Rumor has it that Lieutenant Commander Towns is going to make Commander below the zone, now. And Bugsy, too. Probably."

"That's great," Michelle replied. "I was really curious as to how the whole mission was going to be viewed by the brass. I mean, since so many operators died—that was terrible. I was afraid the folks on the raid would get blamed for it not all going perfectly."

"Yeah," Banshee said. "There was a lot of concern among the officers about whether the Pentagon would be looking for scapegoats or not. In the end, the Navy realized this was not a mission that realistically could have happened without casualties. That makes sense if you think about it, at least in hindsight. Not that everything the Navy does always makes sense."

Timber concurred. "Invading a country's premier naval base is something better suited for a battalion of Marines conducting an amphibious assault. This was not a straightforward snatch-and-grab rescue mission. The Air Force devastated most of the base, sure, but if we had actually sent in the Marines, my view is that we probably would have lost fifty to a hundred troops, and not just a dozen. It was bad enough, believe you me, but making this a full-scale invasion would have really made the losses mount."

Banshee shifted her gaze to the CIA officer. "Eden, are you going to be back down in our neck of the woods anytime soon?"

"I don't have any immediate plans right now, but I make it down that way every now and then."

Banshee tried to be upbeat. "You'll have to let us know the next time you come down our way. We'll all go out and raise a glass in Valkyrie's honor."

Michelle smiled, and agreed. "That would be a great way to remember her. It's a date."

Chapter 29

Michelle walked into the headquarters auditorium a few minutes after the Agency-wide gathering had begun. General Folson was finishing up her opening remarks. Employees filled the igloo-shaped conference center—the Bubble, as it's affectionately called by CIA headquarters employees—to standing-room-only capacity for the director's first address to employees since his return.

Michelle stood against the back wall of the Bubble directly under the small circular government-issue clock that hung just above and to the left of the main entrance. The domed ceiling arched high overhead. Ten-foot-wide circular sound-absorbing disks adorned the ceiling. Seats cascaded down the auditorium towards the stage, giving Michelle a bird's-eye view of the entire assembly.

The gathering of analysts, administrators, executives, and collectors—spies of every shape and sort—gave their director a standing ovation as he took the stage. As he approached the podium, Richard Duncan walked past three empty chairs occupying center stage.

Michelle was excited to see her boyfriend publicly presented with one of the Agency's most prestigious awards. She beamed with pride at his accomplishments in leading the task forces that had made the director's rescue possible.

"Thank you," Duncan said, waving to the crowd as he ascended the stairs to the stage. "Thank you very much for that warm welcome." The applause died down as the employees took their seats. "It's so wonderful to be back home. I can't tell you just how much seeing all the cards and emails many of you sent to my office over the past few weeks have meant. Thank you."

A short round of applause rippled through the crowd.

"The Director of National Intelligence did not send me a card, though. He had other ideas. He told me that I'd missed nine of his senior staff meetings while I was gone, and I was late on over two dozen reports due to the Senate Select Committee on Intelligence." The audience laughed at the reality that government meetings and paperwork are truly unending.

"So, I figured, two can play that game. I sent the DNI my travel voucher for two months of TDY at sea. He sent back a handwritten note denying my expense claim. He said that all meals and transportation had been provided free of charge by the host government."

Laughter erupted across the room.

"In all seriousness, though, I dislike making light of such a somber series of events as has occurred this summer. I know that many, many people put themselves in harm's way to effect my rescue and, tragically, a number of them were injured or killed. To me, those events are not just words on a report or segments of drone videos watched on computer monitors. All of the losses have been tremendously personal for me. I had not seen my wife for the final two or three days before she was killed during the rescue operation. I will always regret that I never got to say goodbye to her."

Duncan paused to collect himself.

"One of the others who died was a female naval officer whom I had never met before that night. She was wounded by gunfire during the rescue and ended up with a small group of us who got separated from the main force of SEALs. I can't go into all the details of the operation, but I'll never forget the bravery and commitment of that young woman as she struggled to keep up with us and, although she was in tremendous pain the entire time, never complained once. She died that night and—I don't think I'm giving away anything I shouldn't be—she was the first female member of any SEAL Team to have died in combat. I didn't get to speak with her much that night, but I did have the opportunity to try to comfort her during parts of our escape. Later, I helped carry her remains as we made our surreptitious departure from Iran."

The audience sat silently, watching Richard Duncan wipe the start of a tear from the corner of his eye.

"It made a real impact on me, as you can probably tell. The other day, I was walking out of a Senate hearing and it struck me just how insignificant some of the things we think of as important really are. Later that afternoon as I was returning to my office from the Hill, I walked past the Memorial Wall in the lobby of the Original Headquarters Building just as I've done a thousand times before. I've spoken in front of that wall at every annual dedication event we've had since I became director and have met many of the families and co-workers of those we've lost. But this time was different. I turned around, walked back to the Memorial Wall, and stood there looking at it again. This time, it was as if I were looking at it for the very first time.

Or for the first time with my eyes finally opened to the human beings — the men and women — represented by the hundred-plus stars engraved into that Wall."

Duncan paused for effect and looked around the room. "Many, if not most, of you know someone who is memorialized by a star on that wall. I realized, as I stood there, that I may have only met one or two of them. Many of you in this room may never leave the comfort of your desks or ever find yourself in harm's way, and that's fine. Truly, I hope that's the case, for most of you. Others here may very well find themselves in dire circumstances as soon as next week. Having held the reins of this Agency for several years, now, I thought that I understood the dangers you face better than I actually did. I know that now. This whole experience has opened my eyes to the perils of the work you routinely perform for our nation. Too often, that work and those risks go unacknowledged. That sailor will not receive a star on our Memorial Wall, but she is being recognized by the Navy in their own way for her sacrifice. She was a few years younger than my youngest daughter, and it really hits home to see such a promising life cut short."

The CIA Director ran his hands down the front of his suit, straightening his tie.

"I could continue standing here and talking about my own loss and the death of my wife, but I won't. Today we're here to recognize the successes of the Agency and its exemplary employees. Before I get to that, though, there is one personal thing that I do want to mention, and I very much wish that Heather were here to share this with me."

Duncan cleared his throat and continued. "After the hijacking, my three daughters and their husbands were, quite understandably, placed into full-time protective custody. Our youngest, Julia, having just been married, tells me that there's not a whole heck of a lot else for a newlywed couple to do while under house arrest and kept isolated by teams of CIA SPOs and Deputy US Marshals. So, I'm pleased to announce that I'm going to be a grandfather."

Waves of applause rose from across the auditorium.

After the cacophony died down, Duncan went on. "Today, it is my distinct pleasure to present three awards to Agency officers who played direct and significant roles in making the rescue mission a success. These two gentlemen and one lady exemplified by their actions those qualities that make the Central Intelligence Agency not just the premier intelligence organization in the world, but, in my opinion, the most capable group of professionals that has ever been brought together under a single umbrella. It is *you* — those of you sitting in this room and those watching on closed circuit TV from other facilities across the world — who deserve all the praise, all the applause, and all my appreciation. So, to each and every one of you, I offer my very heartfelt thanks."

Duncan took a step back from the podium and applauded the gathered Agency officers. The audience joined him in polite self-congratulations.

Richard Duncan presented the first award to Evan VanStone of the Directorate of Analysis. For his work leading the task force that identified where the Duncans had been taken, he was presented with the Intelligence Commendation Medal. After shaking hands with the Director and General Folson, VanStone sat in the first of the three chairs on the stage.

Director Duncan presented the second award to Dr. Steven Krauss. Krauss had coordinated both among the Agency's task forces and across the dozen-and-a-half agencies of the US Intelligence Community that were brought together to contribute their most sensitive intelligence and most fragile sources and methods — frequently against their will — to locate and rescue the Duncans.

Krauss was secretly happy that the director did not mention that his work had put him in the hospital. Considering the injuries and deaths of the military personnel that occurred during the rescue, he would have felt publicly humiliated for having been hospitalized for something as trivial as exhaustion. He never would have lived down the embarrassment. For his successes, Director Duncan awarded Steve Krauss the Intelligence Medal of Merit. After accepting his award, Krauss took the middle of the three seats on the stage.

"The third award," Duncan said, turning back to the audience, "is one that is very rarely given and when it is, is usually presented posthumously. I'm very glad that such is not the case today. This award goes to an Agency officer whom I cannot name for performing actions I dare not recount. This officer from the Directorate of Operations was asked to do something that no one should ever have to be asked to do, and she agreed to it willingly. Reluctantly, perhaps, but willingly. It's one thing to ask something risky of an Agency employee. That's not all that unusual, as you know. Many of our officers face danger in the field throughout their careers, especially Non-Official Cover employees like her. Certainly, the SEALs knowingly faced danger on this mission, as well. CIA's paramilitary officers are also routinely sent into dangerous situations around the world, but *this* time things were different. Quite different."

Duncan cleared his throat and continued. "The SEALs, for example, had over sixty operators and sailors participating in this operation, and that doesn't even count the Air Force's bomber crews who crossed into Iran long before the SEALs even landed. Something like ten thousand other sailors on a dozen ships in the Gulf stood by to support them. The military had an effective battle plan—call that Plan A. Not everything went quite according to plan, so the military switched to Plan B along the way. Even then, we had to make up our own Plan C when that became necessary. What this officer was asked to do in Iran, however, went well beyond any of that. General Folson asked her to join the mission in case Plans C, or D, or, God forbid, E became necessary. I can't go into the details, but think for a minute, if you will, about what that means."

Duncan paused before continuing. "This amazing woman was asked to be the last-ditch fail-safe just in case the men and women of the US Air Force and US Navy, with all their resources, could not get the job done. She was the Hail Mary pass, truly the last possible act of the Agency's desperation. She knew right from her initial mission briefing here in the OHB that if the Department of Defense failed in the rescue mission and it turned out that she needed to act, then it was almost certainly a one-way trip."

Duncan looked across the audience. The generalities in which he spoke could not convey the full measure of difficulty of the mission that General Folson sent Eden on. How to make this particular point, which he had to blunt for security reasons, had been challenging him all week as he prepared for this presentation.

"I have never asked that of anyone before and am not sure I could even do so. It's one thing to ask an employee to undertake a mission that involves risks, but asking someone to undertake what has significant potential to be a one-way trip is quite something else. I regret that for reasons of operational security and maintenance of her cover, this officer cannot be here with us today. For her actions, professionalism, and willingness to undertake missions of exceptional difficulty, danger, and importance to the United States of America and the Central Intelligence Agency, it is my pleasure to present our highest honor, the Distinguished Intelligence Cross, to this employee."

Duncan lifted a wooden box from the shelf under the podium. He stepped to the side of the podium, lifted the top of the polished-wood box, and tilted it forward so the audience could see its contents. Inside, a three-inch metal disc gleamed against red velvet padding. The seal of the CIA was embossed into the center of the disc, surrounded by a plus-symbol-shaped cross.

The rarity of the award struck a chord with the audience. Fewer than two dozen Distinguished Intelligence Crosses had ever been awarded, and most of those were given in honor of deceased officers. Most of the employees in attendance had never seen one presented before, and very few of the recipients were still actively employed by the Agency. To have one recipient still walking the halls — even if only a handful of people would ever know her identity — was a special thought for the officers in the auditorium. To be in the presence of greatness was their own vicarious reward.

As if of a single mind, the gathered CIA employees rose as one and broke into ear-piercing applause.

Michelle clapped along with those around her, more to avoid standing out than to pat herself on the back.

Steven Krauss stood on the stage and, clapping enthusiastically, locked eyes with Michelle as she stood against the far wall of the auditorium. Smiling broadly, he beamed with pride at the well-deserved recognition that the love of his life was receiving from the men and women of the Agency they both served with all their hearts.

A tear streamed down Michelle's cheek at the unexpected honor being bestowed upon her. She thought she was attending the ceremony to watch Steve receive his award. No one ever mentioned she would be receiving one herself. *Michael must have known. That must be why he asked if I was going to be here to support Steven. Michael can be so damned sneaky when he wants to be!*

Michelle looked around the audience as the clapping subsided. This was as close to a ticker-tape parade as she would ever get for the work she did for the Agency. No one ever rewarded people like her for doing the work in which she specialized.

If she had actually executed Directive One — executed Director Duncan — there would have been no award ceremony. There would have been no Agency-wide mention of her existence. There would not even have been bodies returned home to bury. Deafening silence interspersed with official denials — the usual language of the intelligence profession — would have been all anyone ever heard.

Tears streamed from Michelle's eyes and fell across her red-flushed cheeks. She smiled across the expanse at Steven and walked out of the Bubble to dry her face in the ladies' room.

Chapter 30

Lynda Moorefield slid her chair closer to her desk on the fifth floor of CIA's New Headquarters Building. She moved her computer mouse and clicked the "X" to close the window in which she had watched the director's award presentation online.

It's cool to see analysts finally getting recognized for the hard work we do. It's not just the Operations employees who do important things.

Moorefield opened another window on her computer to read the latest batch of cables from FINCEN, the Financial Crimes Enforcement Network. The Treasury Department's analysis center traced and analyzed global financial transactions, Suspicious Activity Reports, Cash Transaction Reports, and classified intelligence relating to transnational crime groups and terrorism suspects. To the extent they can, FINCEN also tracks the transfer of gold, silver, and jewelry as they are common proxies for illicit cash transactions.

Moorefield scanned through the list of report titles and clicked on one that got her attention. She read the brief report of counterfeit US currency being processed through yet another Central American bank. One million dollars in fake hundred-dollar bills passed through the Panama City branch of *Banco Internacional de Costa Rica*. She punched a few buttons on her computer and bit her lower lip as she read the results. The US Treasury's database confirmed that the Federal Reserve had destroyed the legitimate currency with those serial numbers over eight years earlier.

Moorfield opened a spreadsheet she created to track similar recent transactions. She scanned down the list and noted that each of the transaction amounts was for the same one-million dollars, except one. That transaction was for ten thousand dollars less. *Hmm, ten grand got lost in the mail. Close enough for government work.*

A million counterfeit dollars here, and a million counterfeit dollars there. Add it all up, and soon you're talking about real money. Lynda clicked the screen to find the name of the bank that had initiated the transaction. She drilled down through the FINCEN report and the answer appeared on her screen: *Banco Nacional de Havana.*

There it is, again. Havana. Ten one-million-dollar transactions in the past ten weeks. One per week. Even one of those Operations employees can see that pattern. Why have so many counterfeit superbills been flowing through Havana recently?

Moorefield clicked the "Query" button on the report and filled out the form that appeared. Only two countries are known to be able to produce such high-quality counterfeit US currency: North Korea and Iran. It was time to pull this thread and find out which nation was behind the latest batch and what they were using the money for. She could think of several possible reasons, including sponsoring terrorism in the western hemisphere or maybe trying to destabilize the US money supply. Either way, as analysts always do, she wanted to know more.

With a press of the "Submit" button at the bottom of the form, she tasked the US Secret Service to analyze the fake bills and determine their country of origin. Even if the bills are visually identical to US currency, slight variations in the inks used to print the bills made it possible — most of the time — to determine which country had manufactured the fakes. *Most* of the time, anyway. The Secret Service had the best lab in the world for doing just that kind of analysis on US currency, real or fake, and Lynda just set them to work.

Chapter 31

Michelle sat on the leather couch in her team lead's office and looked at the wooden box perched on the corner of his desk. She picked the hefty box up and lifted the brown lid gently. She carefully removed the Distinguished Intelligence Cross from the red velvet padding and admired the embossed CIA logo on the front. Holding the disc on its edges to not smudge its face, she turned it over and read the inscription engraved into the reverse side.

"For a voluntary act or acts of extraordinary heroism involving the acceptance of existing dangers with conspicuous fortitude and exemplary courage."

"That's definitely you," Michael said. "Heroism and courage. They got that right."

"Too bad nobody will ever see it, since I can't take it home."

"I'll tell you what. I'll keep it right here on the shelf in my office and you can visit it anytime you want. How's that for a compromise? Oh, and there's this to go with it."

Michael lifted a manila folder from his desk. From it, he withdrew an award certificate preserved inside a page protector. He leaned across his desk and handed the plastic-encased paper to her.

The certificate accompanying the Distinguished Intelligence Cross bore the seal of the Central Intelligence Agency, the signature of Director Richard Duncan, and Michelle's true name. She recoiled involuntarily at the sight of three words she had not seen printed together in one place for several years: Michelle Elizabeth Kopechne.

"It's a beautiful name," Michael commented, his fading West Texas drawl emphasizing the word *beautiful* for a few extra heartbeats. "It's a shame you don't get to use it that often."

"And whose fault is that?" Michelle asked with a laugh. Michael had given her the cover name *Reagan* when she joined his team many years before. "Anyway, *Michelle* was my father's mother's name and *Elizabeth* was my mother's mother."

"It truly is a lovely name, and it's no one's fault. That's just the way it is in this business. I had to sweet talk the director's protocol office into giving me that certificate with the line for the name left blank. They don't just hand those things out to anyone who asks, but I managed to convince them that your cover status required it. I must have gone through fifty sheets of practice paper on my laser printer before I got the size and spacing just right. I spent hours getting it to line up just right."

Michelle told him how much she appreciated his efforts on her behalf as she handed the certificate back to him. Just like the boxed medal, she could not keep anything so incriminating at home. If she were lucky, she might get the award and certificate back at her retirement ceremony. But probably not even then.

"This will go into your True Name file, if I can remember where I put it...." he joked. "I haven't seen it in a few years."

"Forgetting where you put it... maybe that would be a good thing," she said. Part of her thought that her old self was so long gone that losing the paperwork that proved that any part of her pre-CIA existence still remained would be apropos.

A deep voice from the doorway interrupted the conversation. "What would be a good thing?" Alex Ramirez asked as he entered the office.

"You, learning to knock," Michelle quipped. She drew her lips back into an exaggerated sarcastic grin.

"I saw you on TV at the award presentation," Alex said. "You looked good sitting in the chair up there on the stage."

Michelle's head tilted slightly. "What are you talking about? I wasn't on the stage. I was in the back of the room. The cameras were right above me. There's no way I could have been in their field of view."

"You were right up there on stage," Alex continued, stone faced. "I could see it all. You were doing your best Invisible Girl impression. Just like in the field, no one ever sees you coming. But *I* saw you up there. I know what to look for, and you were spec-*tac*-u-lar!"

Michelle smirked, finally getting Alex's joke. "Oh, okay. Thanks, I guess."

"There's one more thing," Michael said to Michelle. "Well, two things, actually. Along with the Distinguished Intelligence Cross, the director is awarding you a cash bonus of twenty-five thousand dollars."

Alex let out a loud *whoop*. "You done good, girl! That's some tall coin!"

"And," Michael continued, "two weeks of paid leave. To take a nice vacation and relax."

"You earned it," Alex said, offering a fist bump to Michelle.

Michelle met Alex's hand half-way and asked Michael to thank Director Duncan for her.

"Where are you going to go?" her boss asked.

"I don't know. Steven wants to go to one of those all-inclusive resorts in Puerto Rico. I guess we can go there. I've never been there before. He keeps wanting to take me to Aruba, but I just can't bring myself to go back there. I just don't think I'd be able to relax at all."

Michael nodded. Michelle's first assignment on his team had been to Aruba where she killed a Peruvian drug trafficker and his girlfriend. He understood her reluctance to return to the location of her first real-world mission — the site of her first kill.

"Well," Alex offered, "going with you to a tropical island paradise and lying under some palm trees on warm, white sand sounds like a real good time, to me. If your boyfriend don't want to go, give me a call, you know?"

Michelle smiled silently. She didn't relish her professional globetrotting with Alex, but did what the job required. A vacation with him was the furthest thing from her mind.

Chapter 32

The stainless-steel elevator doors slid open and the tile-covered hallway of the seventh floor of CIA headquarters materialized in front of Michelle. She walked briskly down the corridor towards Director Duncan's office suite.

Michael's text had said only that Duncan wanted to meet with her alone. She was starting to feel like a regular in Seventh Heaven, as the executive floor was derisively called by lower-ranking employees. Being in the Director and Deputy Director's office suite so often might have been a good sign for an employee looking for a promotion or to rise into the executive ranks of the Senior Intelligence Service, but for Michelle, it began to worry her that her cover could be jeopardized by the visibility of these visits.

She entered the outer office and was greeted by the familiar dark paneling and harried front-office staff. Duncan was shaking hands goodbye with Senator Finn Roberts, the Chairman of the Senate Select Committee on Intelligence. The SSCI — pronounced "sissy," much to the delight of many CIA officers — had been holding seemingly endless hearings since the director's rescue and safe return from Iran. The committee members took turns scoring political points on national television and cherished the many opportunities hearings gave them to publicly bludgeon the current administration.

Michelle waited until Senator Roberts had left the suite before she approached Director Duncan. He stood at his secretary's desk going over his schedule for the remainder of the day as she approached. He smiled broadly as Michelle got closer.

"Shelly," Duncan said to the woman seated at the desk, "I'd like you to meet Eden."

Michelle greeted the director's Executive Assistant warmly.

"If she ever comes up here and asks you for something," Duncan continued, "give it to her. Whatever she needs. Just let me know afterwards."

Clearly impressed with Michelle's cachet, Shelly replied simply, "Yes, sir."

"Let's talk in my office," Duncan said to Michelle, pointing the way.

In his office, Michelle took the seat offered to her by the chief of the world's most powerful intelligence agency. Well, one of the two most powerful, anyway. The Russian intelligence service, the *Federal'naya Sluzhba Bezopasnosti*—the FSB—had been getting quite aggressive and effective over the past few years.

"How have you been?" Duncan asked.

"Doing well, thanks. I took an absolutely wonderful vacation to a tropical island with the money from the bonus. Thank you for that, by the way. It was completely unnecessary."

"On the contrary, you more than earned it."

"And of course, thank you for the award. It's truly special. Naturally, Michael gets to keep it in his office. It looks terrific on his bookshelf. Maybe someday I can file for joint custody."

Duncan laughed. "I guess that's one downside of being undercover."

Michelle nodded. "Oh, and congrats on Julia's becoming pregnant. That's great for your family, but I'm sure that's not why you asked me to come up here."

"Thank you, and no, of course not. Down to business, then. Well... have you been keeping up with the ongoing search for O'Doherty?"

"No. My involvement pretty much ended after Iran. I know that there was a change in the task forces. One or two were ended, and one new one stood up, I think." Michelle knew from Steven Krauss exactly what changes had been made, but she didn't want the director to know that she was the significant other of the man running the task forces and briefing Duncan routinely. She preferred to keep *that* aspect of her personal life private.

"The best lead we have now," Duncan explained, "is that Evelyn O'Doherty is in Cuba. Or, at least, was there for some time after she left Bermuda. There's been a lot of counterfeit US currency working its way through Latin American banks, and it all originates from Havana. The bills themselves are characteristic of those we know are produced by Iran. The Secret Service tells us that detectable properties of the ink used to print bills is unique for every batch made—kind of like a fingerprint or a signature. Fakes can be very good and indistinguishable to the naked eye, but the Secret Service's lab in Maryland can tell them apart, if given enough time for the analysis. Real US currency has one signature, the North Korean fakes have another, and the Iranian fakes have their own. These are Iranian."

"And it's too coincidental," Michelle stated the obvious conclusion, "that Iran was behind the kidnapping performed by someone they had to pay—almost certainly in cash—and now counterfeit bills from Iran are turning up in large quantities. Cuba's not all that far from the site of the hijacking. I get it. Has she been spotted there?"

"No," Duncan said with obvious disappointment, "and, of course, there's no guarantee that she's actually there. That's why I wanted to speak with you. I've ordered a large search effort for her to be conducted out of our Havana Station. I've told the Chief of Station that he can have whatever resources he needs to find her. Naturally, the Cuban government isn't going to help, so we're going about it *sub rosa*."

"I'm not a collector, sir, there are people better trained—much, *much* better, actually—for that kind of work."

"No, Eden, that's not what I need to ask you to do." Duncan paused to collect his thoughts. "I want you there in case they're successful and *find* her. O'Doherty is responsible for the deaths of hundreds of people. Everyone on the airplane, the Navy SEALs, Valerie Shepard—"

"And your wife."

Duncan nodded slowly. "Yes, and Heather, too." The director took a deep breath and grimaced. "I guess this is going to be another conversation that I tell you we never had."

"This is getting to be a regular thing between us, isn't it?" Michelle pointed at the model of a sailboat on the director's credenza. "I was hoping that maybe our thing could just be stealing boats." She smiled. "That worked out rather well in the end, didn't it?"

Duncan didn't take the bait. "If she's there, in Cuba... I want you to get rid of her. Will you do that?"

Michelle sat silently for a moment. "Is that really the most desirable outcome? Shouldn't she be put on trial for all the world to see that no one gets away with what she did? Or just stick her in Gitmo where she can rot for all time. Hell, she's already in Cuba. Well, maybe she is...."

"As you can imagine, I've been speaking with the Attorney General quite a bit about this whole thing. As odd as it sounds to me, I'm told that prosecuting Evelyn O'Doherty would not be all that easy or certain of getting a conviction. Even after all that has happened, there's relatively little physical evidence against her. There are five eyewitnesses: the four women who smuggled the guns and explosives through airport security, and me. That's it. Three of the four women, however, have criminal records of their own. Two have felony convictions for fraud and one has several misdemeanor convictions for drugs."

"Okay, but you'd be a credible witness, I'd think."

"Yes, but it turns out that absolutely nothing I would say can be backed up by any physical evidence. Nothing from the plane is left. The only evidence that she and I were ever together was the video from the runway in Bermuda, and that's too low resolution to make a positive ID of any of us."

"Just the fact that you and she are the only survivors of the flight should be enough to show that she was in on it. Wouldn't it?" Michelle had no basis for judging what would make a good court case or not. She was grasping at straws, and she knew it.

"The US Attorney's Office has been theorizing what kind of defense her lawyers might use. One of the most effective arguments they've thought up would be for O'Doherty to claim that she was actually the victim of an attempted Extraordinary Rendition by us, which went horribly wrong and therefore we're blaming the whole thing on her. The claim is bogus, of course, but would most likely lead either to us having to make too much of the old terrorist rendition program public or dropping the charges against O'Doherty entirely. It's too big a risk."

"*Hmmmm,*" was all that Michelle could think of to say.

With an unexpected outburst, Duncan slapped his hand on the conference table. "That bitch killed my wife, dammit! I want her dead!"

Michelle remained quiet and waited for the director to regain his composure.

Richard Duncan rubbed his eyes and wiped a drop of spittle from his lower lip. He looked up and asked Michelle the question that had been burning in his gut for the better part of a week. "Eden, will you go to Cuba and get Evelyn O'Doherty for me? For my wife?"

Michelle chose her words carefully. Duncan was in an emotional state, and she did not want to be thought of as unsympathetic to his feelings.

"No." Michelle replied simply, and let the word hang in the air for the span of a single heartbeat. "*But...* I will go to Cuba, and if she's there, I *will* kill her."

Duncan ruffled his brow and scrunched up his face. "I don't understand—"

"I can't do it for your wife. I can only imagine how hard this has been for you, and I'm not making light of a tragedy. I've never experienced the kind of loss you have, and I hope I never do. I've lost close friends—co-workers for whom stars have been engraved on the Memorial Wall downstairs—but I've never lost a spouse. I can't imagine what that feels like, and I'm truly sorry for you and your daughters. But O'Doherty didn't kill your wife. Not directly."

"But she—" Duncan protested.

Michelle interrupted him. "Yes, what she did *led* to Heather's death. I know. But she didn't *kill* your wife herself. She did, however, kill the two Security Protective Officers on the AllSouth flight with you. And for them, I will do it. They were CIA officers and deserve justice. I don't want to see O'Doherty get away with this any more than you do. Besides, I've never arrested anyone. I'd probably screw it up if I tried."

Michelle donned a feeble smile but didn't feel the action carried the emotion she was really feeling. She let the grin drop quickly.

Duncan nodded. "Oh. I understand. I know I'm too close to this situation. I've been warned about that by a few people. Some were more polite about it than others, but I get it."

Michelle sat silently.

"Thank you," Duncan said softly.

"Don't thank me, yet. The fat lady hasn't even begun warming up, much less finished her song."

Chapter 33

Eden boarded the Number Five bus at Havana's Plaza de la Revolución and took her seat in the middle of the dilapidated motor coach along with two dozen rush-hour passengers on their way home for the day. She settled into a sideways-facing seat and watched the statue of José Martí disappear in the distance as the bus traveled east along Avenida Paseo.

She opened her large purse — almost a suitcase in its own right — and slid the bag part-way into the aisle, propping it open between her ankles. She adjusted her sunglasses and stared through the window across from her.

Two stops to the pothole. I hope this works. Not having used some of the tradecraft techniques she required for this mission in her usual fieldwork, she thought back to the refresher training she and Alex conducted on Washington, DC, metro busses the previous week. She had the easy role on the bus, although she wondered if she'd even notice when it happened.

At each of the next two stops, men and women boarded the bus while others departed. Most looked entirely disinterested in the others aboard, except for one elderly man with a dark, leathery complexion. He didn't try to hide his ogling of the women near him at the back of the bus.

Eden scanned the length of the bus with her eyes while keeping her head still. She tried to pick out the undercover CIA officer from Havana Station and any officers from the Cuban Directorate General of Intelligence who were certain to be following him. The DGI was exceptionally diligent — perhaps excessively so, from the stories she'd heard in the mission briefings — in following American government personnel anytime they traveled to the Marxist island. The officer assigned to the US Embassy was certain to have a tail on the bus, not to mention another handful or dozen men in vehicles following both behind it and on parallel streets.

Figuring out who was who proved to be a challenge for Eden. Many of the men on the bus wore a combination of casual slacks, colorful shirts, and timeworn dress shoes. The women, as was Eden, were almost uniformly dressed in long skirts and full, loose blouses. Other than a pair of Canadian tourists wearing khaki shorts, there was little to distinguish any of the passengers. Fortunately for her, Eden was not the one under surveillance, and she aimed to keep it that way.

The kidney-jarring thud as the bus's front-left wheel impacted the pothole caught her by surprise. The regulars on the bus lurched and recovered quickly. Eden involuntarily looked at the Canadians who let out a yelp in surprise.

Eden shifted her sunglasses back into place and looked down at the bag between her feet. Lying in the bottom of the bag was a fat manila envelope that had not been there seconds before. *He did it. The pass was successful! It must be that man with the faded blue shirt and tan pants in front of me.*

She squeezed her bag closed with her knees and slid it back under her seat. Its contents were more valuable than gold.

The man in the faded blue shirt departed the bus at the next stop, followed by several other men and one woman. *How many of them are the surveillance team? Probably all of them!*

Eden remained on the bus for another three stops. Just before the doors closed, she rushed off, nearly snagging the hem of her ankle-length skirt on the rusty edge of the bus's bottom stair. Only one other person—a woman in a bright yellow blouse—exited the bus at that stop. Eden kept a close eye on her as the woman rushed off into an apartment building on the opposite corner.

For the next three hours, Eden executed a complex surveillance detection route—a drill in which she excelled. Across dozens of miles of Havana, she switched buses, walked a memorized route, and ducked through alleys, hotels, and a few apartment buildings. On three occasions, she walked in the front door of stores, and out the back, each time, paying close attention to everyone she could see on foot, in vehicles, and on bicycles.

Finally, confident that she was not being followed, she stopped for dinner before stealing a car for the three-hour drive to the coastal rendezvous where Alex would land later that evening.

***

A little after 2 a.m., Eden sat at the designated meeting spot with her back against a large rock and watched one wave after another lap up on the north-facing beach. A half-moon hung low over the horizon behind her, leaving her to *listen* more than *watch* the small waves of the Caribbean Sea break on the marshy shore. Next to her, a small warehouse sat shuttered for the evening and would not open for another four or five hours. The US Navy had chosen the location outside Santa Lucia, three hours west of Havana, as the right spot for their purposes. Earlier in the evening, Eden had found the area enjoyable for a midnight stroll along a deserted beach.

"Boo!"

Eden spun to face the source of the voice only ten feet away. In an instant, her chest tightened and throat went dry. Her heart raced, beating wildly in her chest.

"Son of a *bitch*. Don't do that to me, Alex," Eden hissed at her partner.

"Caught you flat-footed. That's unusual for you. I couldn't pass up the opportunity," he said in a loud whisper. "I might never get another chance."

"When did you get here?" Eden asked, holding her right hand over her racing heart.

"About fifteen minutes ago. We saw you through our night-vision goggles, so I had the SEALs drop me off just up the beach. Couldn't help myself, sorry. The setup was just too perfect."

"Well, don't ever do that again. If I had a gun, I could have shot you."

"Yeah, except you never heard me coming, and I knew you don't have a gun. That's why I had to come in by submarine with a duffel bag full of gifts and goodies." Alex pointed to the large black watertight bag lying on the ground at his side. "Besides, I haven't gotten to practice ingresses and evasions like this since leaving the Navy, so it was fun. Glad to see I've still got it."

Eden tapped her hand on her chest. "I think my heart has finally dropped back down out of my throat. Let's get back to Havana. I got the directions to the safe house from the brush pass on the bus this afternoon. Grab your bag."

"Did you get a car?" Alex asked.

"Yeah, I stole one in the city after dinner tonight. I'll abandon it after dropping you and the gear at the safe house. Have you eaten?"

"Yup. Ate on the sub hours ago. I'm good. Let's head out."

Alex picked up the large gear bag and slung it over his shoulder. On their way to the car, he looked over at the warehouse the Navy's special operations mission planners had selected as one possible safe operating location the CIA or SEALs might use after business hours, if needed. The dilapidated building stood apart from others in the vicinity. With only single lightbulbs for exterior illumination over each of the two entrances, he agreed — now that he could see it in person — that it would do nicely if they had to use it later in the mission.

Eden opened the stolen car's trunk and handed the keys to Alex. "You drive. I'll navigate. If we get stopped by a cop, your accent is more native than mine."

Alex chuckled. "What, just because my parents lived here, you think I sound Cuban? I've never so much as stepped foot on this island before tonight. And coming in on a Navy rigid inflatable boat, I'm not even going to get the tourist stamp in my passport on this trip."

"True, but my Mexican accent would sound a bit more out of place, that's all."

Alex thought for a moment and drew a Beretta 9mm pistol and suppressor from the gear bag and then secured the trunk. He looked at Eden, shrugged, and said, "You know, just in case."

Eden raised her hands palms-up and grinned. "Who am I to judge?"

Ramirez piloted the 1961 Buick Special Deluxe out of the parking lot and followed the signs to the highway — or what passes for highways in Cuba. "Did the brush pass go all right?"

"Uh huh," Eden confirmed. "It was pretty cool. I set up in the middle of the bus just like we practiced in DC. One second, my bag had just my stuff in it. The next, we hit the pothole and, presto, the envelope is right there in my bag. I was thrown about by the bus just enough to never see it happen. No one else did, either, or I wouldn't have made it this far. Pretty cool. We don't get to do real spy stuff like that too often."

"Sounds like fun." Alex slowed down to take a turn on the highway. The old car's shaking as it followed bends in the road bothered him. The antique had probably never had a front-end alignment in its more than a half-century on the roads. "Is that what you were doing in Iran? Real spy stuff?"

"You know I can't go into that."

"Why not? Who am I going to tell? We need to be able to trust each other, right?"

"Then why in the almost two years we've known each other have you never told me why you got kicked out of the SEALs? Can't trust me?"

"I'm not supposed to talk about that, either."

"Guess we're even, then," Eden said.

"Well... you tell me yours, and I'll tell you mine. Will that work?"

Eden thought about it. Secrecy, after all, is relative. "Fine. The Navy did all the real work in Iran. They were the real rescue force in Bandar Abbas. I was there... just in case things didn't go according to plan. If I got to the director but we couldn't get out, I had some forged documents I could use to try to make a land-border crossing. Call that Plan B. But the real reason I was there was...."

Eden thought for a moment about lying to Alex. The real reason was not one that CIA executives would ever want retold over a beer or two in some dusty third-world bar.

"...was that if I could get *to* him but not get us out, then I was to kill him."

"Kill the director! Are you fucking *nuts*?"

"A little louder, if you please. I don't think they heard you in Moscow. Obviously, things went well. Or, well enough, anyway since I didn't have to do that. It was the ultimate fallback option. Not something I wanted to do, but what's the alternative? Let the one man in the world who could do the most damage to us be interrogated by the Iranians? I wasn't happy about it, but, well—"

"And how would *you* have gotten out?"

"Seriously? If I couldn't get *him* out, I wasn't going anywhere, either."

"A suicide mission? I never pegged you for the type."

"I didn't plan it that way, and it worked out just fine, in the end. Besides, I had dozens and dozens of very studly Navy SEALs to rely on. I figured that the deputy director was just covering her bases, and it would never come to that. I'm glad it didn't."

Eden sat in the passenger's seat and stared out the front window. She asked herself if she really would have done it—the same question she had posed herself silently many times since her return. She recalled raising her gun at the Director immediately before the SEALs stormed aboard the *Octopus* and felt like she knew the real answer.

"Okay, your turn, Alex."

"Well, it's because I was bored one day and did something good, but the Navy didn't see it that way. During my last deployment in Iraq, we were always doing patrols in and around this one large village south of Baghdad. We'd already captured or killed most of the high-value targets in that region, so we were training some of the locals, doing the occasional raid, and helping out the grunts. You know, the Army and Marines. Well, there was this one area in the middle of the village. Sort of a public square where there was once a well—you know, from back in the day before running water and indoor plumbing became all the rage. Anyways, around the square were a bunch of small cafes and restaurants, some government offices, a mosque, and the like. Most of the locals would walk there, but some would ride their bicycles into town. So, it turns out that someone was stealing bikes. Not every day, but often enough that it was pissing the locals off."

"You were stealing bikes?" Eden interjected.

"*No*, no. Not me. It wasn't like the military cared about petty theft, but every now and then a couple of us would grab a bite to eat at this one cafe in the square. Some of the guys liked to look at the owner's daughter, you know? Of course, *I'll* never name names. Anyway, the owner's other kid was a twelve-year-old boy who served tea there most days. He and I got to talking over the months I was there on that deployment. The boy'd had his bike stolen twice and was really pissed about it, but there was nothing he could do."

Alex paused and looked at Eden. "Okay, so you know my parents were born in Spain, went to medical school in Cuba, and then emigrated to the US before I was born, right?"

Eden nodded and pointed out the next turn for Alex to take onto the poorly marked highway leading to Havana.

Ramirez turned the large car a bit wider than Eden would have liked. In the absence of stripes on the blacktop, he settled the car down for the long drive on what in the dim headlights looked to him like the right half of the road. "And that's all cool and everything and I don't really talk about this, but it puts what I did later in Iraq in perspective. So, my folks left Cuba with nothing other than their free education and my older brother in tow and emigrated to Florida with *nada*. No money to speak of, no jobs, you know, just the clothes on their backs kind of thing. They worked two jobs each until my dad could get his medical license transferred and blah, blah, blah, raised me to be hard working and blah, blah. Right? So, I get a job in middle-school and save enough to buy myself an old used five-speed bike."

"Oh, I think I see where this is going."

"Yeah. So, one day, my bike gets stolen from outside our apartment building. Sound familiar, yet? Later in Iraq, I'm really feeling for the kid at the cafe, you know? And maybe I went a little too far, but it worked out, in the end."

The words came out of Eden's mouth slowly. *"What* did you *do?"* she asked, almost hating herself for grinning widely and becoming so engrossed in her partner's emotional entanglements.

"So... I bought two bikes. I gave one to the kid because I felt sorry for him."

"That was very generous of you."

"I thought so, too, but it was, you know, kind of the right thing to do."

"Very noble. And the other?"

"So, I had the other bike, right? I took the seat apart and replaced the padding with C-4 explosive and a small remote detonator?"

"No, you did *not!"* Eden exclaimed, amazed at Alex's gumption.

"Yeah, I rode it to the public square one afternoon and sat down at the cafe for tea. I watched for hours until some dude took it and rode off toward the mosque that was way the hell at the other end of this large village square. It was that time of the afternoon when people gathered for afternoon prayers, you know?"

"Go *on....*" Eden said, not entirely sure she wanted to hear the end. In her heart, she already knew what happened next.

"When the guy got to the middle of the square, I triggered the explosive, and it destroyed the bike."

"The *bike?* What about the *guy?"*

"Yeah, well, he came down in three pieces. Two legs and then his torso. It was *so* cool."

"Cool? No, that's disgusting."

"Well, so...."

Eden shook her head at the way Alex seemed to start every sentence with the word "so." *Entirely unnecessary.*

"It wasn't a big explosion, and I made sure the force of the blast just went up — right into him. Lots of locals gathered around this guy and the bike to see what happened and what was left of him. They looked for a bit and then, all of a sudden, they all start backing away and yelling at everyone else to stay away, too. The local police came and found that this guy was wearing a suicide vest."

"Seriously? An S-vest?"

"Yup. The Iraqi Army and local police took it all into evidence, and, a day or so later, US intel traced it all back to the bomb-maker's house. So, of course, they also traced the components from the bike-bomb and found me. I didn't think anyone would ever care, so I hadn't been all that careful." Alex looked at Eden, and said, "Lesson learned."

"Better be more careful next time. And I mean that because it may be *my* ass on the line if they find us."

"Yeah, well, somehow I think the CIA is better at building bombs than I am, but anyway—"

"So, where was he going with the explosive vest on?"

"They think he was going to the mosque. Anyway, DoD publicly took credit for taking out both the bomb-maker and the bomber himself. That meant they couldn't make it public that one of their own—yours truly—had made the bike-seat bomb as a, shall we say, *extracurricular* activity. They wanted to keep it all hush-hush, so they offered me an Article 15 non-judicial punishment. I decided not to take it."

"You can do that? Just say no to a punishment? I didn't know that. I've never been in the military."

"If a sailor declines to accept an Article 15, he's risking a General Court Martial, which can mean a felony conviction on your record and almost certainly jail time. Most sailors will just take the Article 15 because it's not a felony and doesn't completely screw up your future. So, I took the gamble that, this *one* time, the Navy would not want to risk a public trial even though they had me dead to rights. I rolled the dice and won. They transferred me home and told me that the Navy was not going to let me re-enlist the following year. Even though they're hard up for operators, they didn't want me around anymore. So, we came to the mutual agreement that I would muster out of the Navy and we'd just go our separate ways."

"I guess everyone won. You got the bad guy, DoD got credit for two wins, and the kid got a new bike. Not bad." Eden decided to press her luck. "So, how'd you hook up with Michael?"

"I needed a job after leaving the Navy, so I was doing protection work for the Agency as an independent consultant. Lots of former operators do contract work like that. The Special Activities Center pays former Spec Ops folks pretty well. Mike showed up one day out the blue and offered me a job. All he said was that his team kills bad guys. He had me at *kill*."

"I believe you," Eden concluded. She sat quietly as the remaining miles to Havana ticked past them in the darkness. Her partner's easy facility with his chosen line of work left her feeling uneasy.

Chapter 34

On the outskirts of Havana, the early morning eastern sky was easing from black to orange as Eden stepped into the townhouse. Team members in the safehouse were rifling through Alex's gear bag like children clawing at giftwrapped boxes on Christmas morning. A half-dozen CIA officers passed around and inspected the equipment they'd been unable to bring into Cuba on commercial flights. The loot bag included night-vision goggles, lockpicks, encrypted radios, cell phones, two alarm-bypass kits, and four wrapped stacks of Cuban Pesos for bribes.

Maria Ortiz held a small leather case of lockpicks and approached Eden. "I'm glad you're here. It was getting old being the only woman in a house full of Latino men. Most of them are fine, but one or two can be real *pendejos* sometimes. Watch out for Jorge in particular."

Eden nodded. "Thanks for the warning, but I thought there was going to be one other woman here with us."

"Yeah, there was supposed to be," Maria said, "but it turns out she's pregnant and the morning sickness put her in the hospital for a night or two. She couldn't keep anything down."

"That's great for her. I mean being pregnant, not being sick. That part sucks, I'm sure. I wouldn't know."

"Me neither. So, it's just us, sister."

"I'm used to it."

"Yeah, me too, but now I have someone to talk to," Maria said, and bumped shoulders with Eden.

Alex approached the women and handed a blue plastic briefcase to Eden. He held an identically sized black case by its handle. Eden took her locked case and thanked her partner.

"Whatcha got in there?" Maria asked, intrigued by the only two cases in the bag that had combination locks on them.

"More of the same," Eden lied. The fact that the two locked cases contained pistols, suppressors, and other tools of their particular trade was not for public consumption, even among the team of intelligence professionals. The rest were prepared for their roles hunting down Evelyn O'Doherty: conducting surveillances, paying bribes, and breaking into medical clinics to search patient records. Eden and Alex were prepared to go further than just finding her.

A balding man in his late fifties approached the trio. In the rapid dialect of Cuban Spanish famed for its slurring of words together, he greeted Eden. "Hi, I'm Cesar, team lead for Alpha Team. Welcome to Cuba. Do you have the envelope?"

Eden knew that her language skills were being tested and scowled inwardly. She responded in her Mexican-accented Spanish, enunciating each vowel in the way she learned growing up outside Los Angeles. "Yes, here go you. The brush pass went perfectly. There are two copies of the last-minute list of plastic surgery clinics provided by Havana Station. There are also three color photos of O'Doherty, including passport photos and a full-length view from the Miami airport surveillance system."

"*Bueno*," Cesar replied pulling documents out of the envelope. "Looks like they're the same ones we studied in the mission briefings two weeks ago. Why was it you couldn't be at those briefings?"

"We were added to the team at the last minute to handle locks and alarms at the clinics," Eden explained. "Once we got the orders to deploy, we had to scramble. Alex had to get the gear and be helicoptered out to the submarine. I had to practice the brush pass once Havana Station decided how they wanted to get the envelope to me."

"*Bien*, well, Alpha Team has been staking out the *Banco Nacional de Havana*, but haven't seen O'Doherty show up there to move more of the cash. Not yet, anyway."

Maria raised her hand halfway and waved her fingers. "That's what Miguel Beltran and I have been doing since we got here. Real boring, and I think I've gained five pounds in three days just snacking for hours at a time at the various cafes within sight of the bank."

Cesar Romero pointed to a short, dark-haired man sitting at the dining room table. "That's Danny Jimenez over there. He's the lead for Bravo Team. They've been focusing on the two main hospitals in Havana that do plastic surgery work, under the assumption that Evelyn O'Doherty changed her appearance with more than just hair dye. That's the odds-on theory the analysts in the Ivory Tower back home came up with."

"Yeah," Eden replied, "back at Oz I got to speak to the task force focusing on her. It's as good a theory as any, I suppose."

Maria smiled at Eden's referring to the green-glass enclosed Langley headquarters as *Oz* — a common joke-cum-insult levied by Operations Officers on analysts who work in the safe confines of CIA HQ instead of risking life and limb in the field.

Daniel Jimenez joined the group as they settled into to the pair of sofas in the living room. "I'm glad you're here. We lost one of our team a few days ago. Julio couldn't shake the Cuban DGI surveillance team that somehow picked him up. He did what he was supposed to do to keep them off the rest of us — he went to the airport and flew out. You're our lock and alarm specialists, yes?"

"Right," Alex said. "Just so long as you're not expecting us to break into the bank."

"No, no," Jimenez replied, "just the medical clinics on that list. Alpha Team watches the bank in shifts all day, and Bravo has developed several pretty good sources inside the two hospitals to get a look-see at the patient records. Both have turned up *nada* so far. We're going to start working the smaller clinics this evening — a different one each night. We'll break in, rifle through the records of recent patient procedures, and hope they have before-and-after pictures of our subject."

"Roger," Alex said. "No problem."

"I hope you're right. We have a lot of work to do in the next week or two." Jimenez stood up. "Come on, I'll show you to your rooms upstairs. Eden, you'll bunk with Maria. Alex, Bravo Team has one room with bunk beds for the six of us. We sleep all day and work all night."

"I love vampire hours," Alex said, standing. "That's just my speed. Good thing I packed the Ambien."

Chapter 35

A single bare lightbulb in the rusty fixture above the *Clinica Lazaro's* rear entrance illuminated only one side of the dark alley. Eden quickly picked the two locks securing the door and pulled it open. Bravo Team's midnight black-bag job started smoothly.

Alex entered first, followed closely by three members of Bravo Team. The private medical clinic in a western suburb of Havana caters to Europeans and South Americans in search of plastic surgery procedures not as readily available from the nationalized healthcare systems in their home countries. Medical tourism is a multi-hundred-million-dollar source of hard currency for Cuba, and actively supported by the failing Marxist government that perpetually found itself desperate for hard currency.

Alex made quick work unlocking the filing cabinets behind the receptionist's desk while Bravo Team set to work paging through hundreds of patient files.

Jesus Pedrero and Jorge Nunez alternated looking through the medical records and returning the files to their original locations once searched. Nunez looked intently for before-and-after photographs of any female patients who bore even a passing resemblance to O'Doherty's trim figure. Pedrero read through each patient's description and vitals for women who fit the right age, height, or weight range of their subject, in case the photos were falsified or had simply been removed.

Daniel Jimenez gestured for Eden to join him in one of the clinic's offices. "There's a locked safe in the director's office, here. It has one of those circular key locks that I never learned to pick. Think you can get in?"

"Let's take a look," Eden answered. Alex joined the pair and tilted a desk lamp to illuminate the front of the safe.

"That's not a very secure safe," Eden mumbled, mostly to herself. To Daniel, she said, "It's more of a fire-proof filing cabinet, not really designed for protecting valuables." Eden selected a tubular lockpick to fit the keyhole. With a gentle, counter-clockwise motion, she pressed and twisted, applying continuous pressure until the lock sprung open at her fingertips.

"It helps to have the right tools and a steady hand," Daniel said appreciatively.

Eden opened the top drawer of the filing cabinet and stepped back to let Bravo's team lead in.

Jimenez rooted through the filing cabinet's four drawers. The top drawer contained mostly accounting records and administrative logs. The second drawer contained two dozen medical files, which Jimenez handed to Eden to search.

The contents of the third drawer drew a laugh from the intelligence officer. Jimenez held up a clear plastic baggie. He smiled, and said, "It's just for medicinal purposes, I'm sure." The group chuckled as he tossed the bag of marijuana back into the filing cabinet.

The bottom drawer contained more files. Jimenez looked through each carefully. One in particular caught his eye.

"Jorge," Jimenez called into the hallway. "Come take a look at this photo."

Eden looked up from her files to see Jimenez holding up a picture of a middle-aged Hispanic man. She turned her attention back to the files in front of her.

"Is this who I think it is?" Jimenez asked.

"It looks like Oscar Ochoa," Jorge Nunez replied.

Jimenez nodded and placed the file flat on the clinic director's wide oak desk.

"Who's Ochoa?" Alex asked the team lead.

"Foreign Minister of Venezuela," Jimenez replied as he focused his phone's camera on the medical records of Venezuela's chief diplomat.

Nunez sneered. "What was he here for, a testicle transplant? That guy has no balls, I'm telling you. I've done two tours in Caracas and nobody respects him, but he married into the right family."

Eden chuckled as the flash of Jimenez's phone snapped pictures of the politician's medical records. "Nothing here about O'Doherty. Anything in the other files?"

Jimenez closed the Ochoa file and replaced it into the cabinet. "Nope. Alex?"

"*Nada*," he replied, tapping his hand on top of the files he had finished reviewing.

"Okay," Jimenez said, looking at his watch. "Let's close up and head out. We'll hit the next clinic on the list tomorrow night."

The team returned the files to their respective cabinets. Eden used her lockpicks to relock the filing cabinet. Alex made quick work securing the reception area's filing cabinets, and the team quietly made their way out the back door.

Their late-night intrusion would never be noticed by the clinic's employees. Nor would those of the next half-dozen clinics, all of which were dead ends for the search team.

Chapter 36

Alex Ramirez walked briskly into the alley behind Havana's *Clinica de Cirugia Estetica*. Leading his teammate on yet another midnight procession to the rear of a medical facility the team would search that night, Alex hoped that the eighth time would finally be the charm for the CIA's clandestine search team.

Eden followed a few steps behind her partner, thumbs casually tucked under the shoulder straps of her small equipment backpack. Jesus Pedrero and Luis Perazza stood watch at the other end of the alley providing a deterrent to anyone who might want to take a late-night shortcut while Eden bypassed the large clinic's burglar alarm.

The blur bounded from behind a tall, brown trash dumpster half-filled with nose-wrinkling bags of waste and rushed at Alex. The CIA officer side-stepped the short man who dashed past him.

Two paces beyond Eden, the mustachioed Cuban in a tattered black shirt and ripped slacks skidded on his sandals to a halt, spun, and lunged at her backpack.

The impact against Eden's right shoulder drove her forward. "What the—" was all she had time to blurt out in the moment before her head glanced off the clinic's brick wall.

Strong hands yanked at her backpack, lifting her onto her feet. Unable to keep her balance, she stumbled backwards, struggling to regain both stability and composure. She thrust one hand against the wall for reference, looked down, and focused her wavering vision on her boots trying to arrest the spinning.

Two black boots and one brown foot in a sandal. One of these things does not look like the other.

With a swift motion, Eden planted the heel of her right boot onto the top of the sandal. A shrill "*aiiii*" shattered the silence of the alley and was all the proof she needed to know that her attack found its target. Rotating a quarter-turn, Eden drove her right elbow into the source of the scream, silencing it. The crunch of elbow-striking-jawbone changed the tenor of the dark-haired man from vocal pain to muffled anguish.

Eden leaned one hand against the wall's cool bricks and assessed her opponent as he groaned in pain at the edge of the alley. She raised her leg and snapped a kick to her attacker's mid-section. The weak kick to the middle-aged man's rib cage staggered him back two steps but did little in the way of lasting damage. The agony from the shot he took to his jaw masked any pain he might have felt from the kick to his mid-section.

Alex stepped between his partner and her assailant and looked severely at the man he towered over. "¡Vete de aquí!" he said sternly, waving away the man who had picked the worst possible woman in the worst possible alley to try to rob that night.

With one hand on his jaw, the vagrant who thought he might make off easily that evening with a new backpack limped into the night as quickly as his swelling foot and throbbing jaw would allow.

Luis Perazza arrived, huffing from his sprint from the far end of the alley. "Are you all right?"

Eden nodded. "He picked the wrong backpack to try to snatch." She pulled a few errant strands of hair back into her ponytail. "From the stench coming off him, I think he was blitzed. *Borracho*. Drunk as a skunk."

Perazza looked down the street at the receding image of the man disappearing into a park on the next block. "Do you think he's DGI?"

Alex looked around and shook his head. "No, if he were Cuban intelligence or a plain-clothed cop, we would have been swarmed by now for having pummeled one of their own. I think we're still in the clear. No way that guy's going to report to the police that a woman walloped him while he tried to steal her backpack. We're good."

"I agree," Eden said. "No harm done. Let's get into the clinic and out of this alley."

Perazza nodded. "Right. I'll watch this end of the alley. You two do your thing on the alarm."

"On it," she said as she and Alex walked to the rear door of the outpatient surgery clinic. Eden mated a head-mounted flashlight to a Velcro strap from her backpack and flipped the switch to *on*.

At the rear door, Alex cupped his hands and bent down slightly. "Up you go."

Eden took the assist and climbed onto Alex's shoulders so she could reach the alarm's control box mounted above the clinic's rear door.

Picking the lock on the metal box took her only a matter of seconds. Eden looked over the alarm system and recognized it as a knock-off of an old single-zone Honeywell model designed for small businesses. With a screwdriver and three jumper cables, she bypassed the alarm in less than three minutes.

The team of five CIA officers entered the clinic in single file, glad to be out of the alley that had provided them with an unexpectedly warm welcome. Without having to speak the words, each thought the same thing: they would gladly endure a hundred boring nights of records searches to not be surprised by another violent encounter.

Inside the clinic, Daniel Jimenez put his team to work. Alex and Eden easily popped the locks on records storage cabinets. Jimenez, Jesus Pedrero, and Luis Perazza divvied up sets of files to search. Jimenez radioed to Jorge Nunez who watched the clinic's exterior. If the police or employees arrived unexpectedly, he'd alert the team in time for them to make a rapid retreat.

"Eden," Alex said softly. "You might want to find the bathroom." Pointing to her scalp, he said, "You're bleeding a little. Not bad, but it looks like the brick wall got a piece of you."

Eden ran her hand over her scalp at her hairline. Her hand came away with a smear of red across two fingers.

"Ugh," she mumbled, and walked off towards the rear of the clinic.

Alex picked up a stack of files to review and sat down at a desk across from Perazza.

A few minutes later, Eden returned from the washroom and joined the men flipping pages of medical records and scanning though seemingly endless photographs.

Dozens of files and hundreds of before-and-after photos crossed the desks of the CIA search team each hour. One by one, the Clandestine Service case officers looked at the faces and body parts of patients from across the globe who had flocked to Cuba for reconstructive procedures or upgrades to their appearances. Most were cosmetic, but the "before" photos of reconstructive surgery patients garnered the occasional groan from the search team.

"You'd think," Perazza said, "that looking at so many boob-job photos would never get old, you know?"

Pedrero chuckled. "Sucks when you can only look, but not touch, eh, *mano*?"

"Beats the shit out of the tummy-tuck photos, though," Eden offered, generating a knowing laugh from her male colleagues.

The many hours and miles of files passed slowly for the search team.

When the last of the medical records had been returned to its cabinet, Jimenez did one last walk-around the facility.

"I can't find a safe or high-security filing cabinet," he said to Eden. "I don't think they have one here."

"I looked earlier," Eden agreed, "and didn't see one, either. Must not be that kind of clinic."

Pedrero stretched his legs to relieve the stiffness from hours of sitting. "Guess it's just tits and tummies here. And the occasional cleft palate. Even after more than a week of this, those still gross me out."

"All right, guys," Jimenez said to the team. "Let's call it a night."

"Works for me," Perazza said. "Beer for breakfast again, I'm thinking."

Eden rubbed her head gently. The bleeding had stopped, but the throbbing continued. "I'll have mine with a Tylenol chaser."

Chapter 37

Maria Ortiz shifted in the wicker chair on the cafe patio that had become her home away from home. Miguel Beltran, her Alpha Team partner, sat across from her as they kept watch on the marbled entrance to the *Banco Nacional de Havana* next door.

The pair of CIA officers blended into the lunchtime crowd easily. Halfway down the block, team members Ruben Hernandez and Moises Lopez shared a bench near two cars they'd rented and wished for relief from the midday heat. Alpha's team lead, Cesar Romero, sat in the shade offered by the awning of another cafe four doors down the street.

The noon-time crowd of tourists and local shoppers sitting near Ortiz and Beltran enjoyed the cafe's specialties of toasted pressed-ham-and-cheese sandwiches served with the strong coffee for which Cuba is well known. Beltran sipped his coffee sparingly, scanning his eyes in a practiced pattern along Avenida Paseo. The strong drink was loaded with caffeine, and he knew from eighteen years' experience that was the very definition of *frenemy* to a surveillance professional. Too little of nature's miracle pick-me-up and you risked missing your subject as your eyes drooped and concentration succumbed to boredom. Too much of it and Murphy's Law guaranteed that the subject would appear only while you were off on another trip to drain the lizard.

For the thousandth time in the past two weeks, he looked over the statue of a Cuban general who had been a hero of the 1895 War of Independence and subsequently elected as Havana's first mayor. The sculpture of Alejandro Rodriguez y Velasco on horseback occupied a place of honor in the median of the wide avenue and was a favorite with visitors to the island nation. It bored Beltran to tears, but was a large draw for locals and visitors alike, so he dared not ignore its effect on passers-by.

Maria Ortiz adjusted the brim of her hat to block more of the sun that the table's umbrella only partially obscured. She was grateful for the light but steady breeze coming off the Caribbean, five blocks north of the cafe.

The bustling mid-day traffic along the avenue hid the arrival of the yellow-and-black taxi. Its sole passenger was already stepping out of the back seat before Ortiz noticed her. The woman adjusted her sunglasses and hefted an oversized Michael Kors purse onto her shoulder as she closed the taxi's door with a dull *thunk*.

She could be a model, Ortiz thought with a tinge of jealousy. The CIA officer watched the woman's jet-black hair sway in the breeze, flitter over her shoulders, and brush against her white, sleeveless blouse. *Maybe she is. That's a gorgeous skirt, too, and if I had an ass like hers, I could rock it with those heels —*

"I'm going inside," Maria announced to her partner with a quiet urgency.

Beltran looked up at Ortiz and made silent a "Why?" motion with his mouth.

"That woman — the one with the large, expensive purse — is *not* a local. She's too pale to be a Latina, and those shoes cost more than you and I make in a week... combined."

"What shoes?" Beltran countered, not following her train of thought.

"You drive Harley Davidson motorcycles back home, right? Hogs? You know the years and models and options and all that, right?"

"Yeah, so?"

Ortiz leaned in to whisper to her partner. "Well, *I* know shoes. And *hers* are top-shelf. Everyone knows the Jimmy Choo and Manolo Blahnik brands, but those are Christian Louboutins. Some of those go for two grand. *A pair.* That woman did *not* buy them on this bankrupt hell hole of an island. I'll be back soon. I'll give the signal if I think it's really her."

Beltran nodded his ascent. Through the corner of his eye, he watched Maria stride up the marble steps and through the bank's elegant entrance. He raised his hand to catch the waitress's eye and asked for the check.

Inside the bank, Ortiz picked up a small brochure from a narrow literature rack. She leaned gently against a table and pretended to read the description of services offered by the *Banco Nacional de Havana* while keeping a trained eye on her subject. The well-dressed woman sat in an oversized leather visitor's chair against the wall opposite the bank's entrance, keeping her heavy purse in her lap, protectively. A young bank employee stood at a respectful distance, greeting her with a wide smile and over-acting his appreciation for his VIP client.

Maria slowly turned pages in the brochure as if she were bothering to read it. With the woman's sunglasses removed, Maria got a better look at the face she was following. The woman's trim, athletic figure fit the general description of Evelyn O'Doherty, but the face was not quite right, Maria thought, slightly dejectedly. Alternating her gaze between the woman and brochure, Ortiz thought hard about the woman across the room. *With a nose job and some work around her cheekbones, that could be her. Maybe.*

Even if only a "maybe," the CIA case officer knew, it was closer than they had been in the two weeks since arriving in Havana.

Less than a minute later, the door labeled "Offices" opened and an older man approached the seated woman. A brief wave of self-satisfaction and hope lifted Ortiz's spirits. The faces of both the bank manager and the seated woman lit up as the pair greeted each other— obviously not for the first time. The manager led his visitor through the oak door and into the bank's private area. Ortiz knew she could not follow the pair any farther. She took a clipboard from the table and a form from the literature rack, sat in a visitor's chair against the wall to bide her time and, by all appearances, settled in comfortably to complete a loan application form.

Let's see, how about if Rudolf Anderson applies for a car loan today? Would anyone on this shitty little island even know the name of the US Air Force major who was the one and only combat casualty of the Cuban Missile Crisis all those years ago? Probably not.

At the café next door, Miguel Beltran counted out his change and wedged a few Cuban Pesos for a tip under his coffee cup. He pulled a small cellphone from his pocket and speed-dialed the second number in its memory.

"*Sí?*" Cesar Romero asked.

"She's been in there a while. The three of you should get set to follow the brunette if Maria comes out and gives the signal."

"We're on it," Romero responded, ending the call. Cesar headed to his car and motioned for Moises Lopez to join him. Ruben Hernandez took the cue and headed to his own vehicle, parked one block over on a parallel street.

From her seat in the bank, Maria Ortiz watched the large black walnut door for what seemed like an hour but was at most only half of that. Three times she had politely declined employees' offers to help as she appeared to struggle to complete the loan application. *Ugh. There's only so much time someone can sit alone in a bank before becoming suspicious.*

Ortiz let out an audible sigh of relief when the office door finally swung open. Both the bank manager and his now-favorite customer were all white teeth and handshakes, having successfully consummated their illicit transaction. The CIA officer watched as the dark-haired woman shifted her large purse from arm to arm with ease.

Whatever had weighed it down earlier is gone, Maria thought with a great deal of satisfaction at having been correct. *All that cash is now safely in the bank's vault and you feel like a million bucks, don't you, honey? Another million high-quality counterfeit bucks.*

Ortiz flushed with pride knowing that with the rest of the surveillance team here in Cuba all being men, it was she who had identified the woman making a large cash deposit. *Well, maybe it's not the woman, but certainly a woman, anyway,* she corrected herself. *Maybe she's just some Colombian drug lord's girlfriend and not O'Doherty, after all.* The hard part was yet to come, she knew. Ortiz rose and walked out to the street before the subject could exit the bank.

Outside, she stepped to the side of the bank's ornate front door and fiddled with her sunglasses to bide her time. The black-haired woman with the large—and now far lighter—purse exited the bank moments later, walked down the steps, and hailed a cab. The CIA officer reached up and curled both sides of her hat's brim down with her hands.

Ruben Hernandez saw Maria's signal and started his car. He now "had the eye" for the surveillance team. He pulled away from the curb and took up position three cars behind the black-and-yellow taxi as it pulled away from the bank and made a U-turn around the statue of General Velasco. Hernandez keyed the team's encrypted tactical radio and spoke into the clip-on microphone affixed under his shirt.

"We're on. I've got the eye. Subject is the same brunette with the white shirt in a new taxi." He read the license plate number to his teammates.

The team kept its distance, following the taxi in a loose formation as it passed through Plaza de la Revolución in central Havana and turned south. At the botanical gardens, the taxi turned east on Via Blanca, a major thoroughfare in the Cuban capital. The volume of traffic on Havana's central artery made it both easier for the CIA team to avoid detection by their quarry, yet riskier because taxis can so easily blend into the visual noise of a bustling city and be lost by its pursuers.

After three miles, Miguel Beltran and Maria Ortiz took the eye from Ruben Hernandez, who turned off onto a side street and out of sight of the taxi. Beltran coordinated the maneuvers of the team by radio, preparing them to reacquire the cab if it started making sudden counter-surveillance turns. The CIA officers were very well trained to counter such tactics and fully expecting maneuvers like that would be coming at any moment.

While sudden turns intended to lose a tail are a dead giveaway and effectively an admission of guilt, they can still be highly effective if the rabbit's intent is simply to escape *that* particular surveillance on *that* particular day. If it happened to Beltran's team, he'd be unlikely to ever reacquire the woman again—she'd be in the wind for good.

The miles passed quickly as the taxi continued straight on Via Blanca. Ortiz keyed her radio from the passenger seat. "She's continuing straight. No changes." She glanced at Miguel in the driver's seat and finished her thought with a note of frustration edging into her voice. "This woman's the closest we've seen to anyone looking like the subject, yet. I don't know if it's her for sure, but keep going, anyway. Let's see where she goes. Judging by how light her purse was when she came out of the bank, I'm confident she made some kind of large cash deposit. That much I *know* is true. Maybe it really is just some random woman who got lucky at the Roulette table last night. I don't know."

"Not to look a gift horse in the mouth, here, Maria, but if she did have plastic surgery and has been making these cash deposits for two months, you know, maybe she has gotten complacent? We don't know if she started out on her first half-dozen trips running a full surveillance detection route on her way *to* the bank. Maybe she just doesn't do it on her way home? I don't know, either. Let's see where this ends. It's the closest thing to a lead we've had so far." Miguel Beltran frowned. "I would have expected a few rapid—"

Beltran slowed his car as the taxi pulled off the road and into the circular driveway of the Hotel Madrid. Miguel called out the turn over the tactical radio. "*There* we go," he said quietly, his interest in the surveillance growing rapidly. "That a girl. What are you up to, now?"

"Pull up and you follow her on foot," Maria said. "I went into the bank. She might remember me."

"*Bien*," Beltran agreed, and brought the car to a stop. He followed the woman in the white blouse into the hotel lobby.

The lobby of the century-old Hotel Madrid had the elegance of a stately landmark built in the days before air conditioning. Long fans with tan, woven-straw blades hung from the two-story-high ceiling by thin dark-brown poles and rotated slowly. Glass tables and plush leather chairs filled the expanse of the lobby for guests to enjoy in comfort while waiting for friends or the concierge.

Miguel Beltran followed his rabbit as she turned the corner past the reception desk. A sign perched high on the wall advertised that one would find the bathrooms down that hallway. Beltran rounded the corner to find the doors to both the men's and women's rooms closed. He placed his hand on the door to the men's room, preparing to enter. Glancing quickly around the empty dead-end hallway, he quickly backtracked and found a tall-backed wicker chair that offered him an unobstructed view of that part of the lobby. With no service exit in the hallway, the rabbit had to come back out the same way she entered. Beltran picked up a newspaper from a nearby table and settled in to wait for his brunette subject to reappear.

A pair of middle-aged tourists speaking German emerged from the hallway first. It would not have been bad tradecraft at all for O'Doherty, if it were indeed her, to strike up a conversation with another woman in the restroom and depart with her as if they were old friends. A surveillance team looking for a single person might pay less attention to a pair who appeared to be very familiar with each other. Neither of these rotund women bore any resemblance to the far more athletic Evelyn O'Doherty.

Beltran continued his over-watch of the restrooms as a half-dozen men and women came and went.

As a quartet of young tourists entered the ladies' room, the hair on the back of Beltran's neck rose. *What if the bathroom has a rear exit?* He considered taking the calculated risk of checking the layout of the men's room to see if it had more than the one entrance he was watching. *Crap, with such a small surveillance team, we can't cover every possible avenue of escape.*

Beltran decided to remain seated, knowing that if there were a rear exit to the bathroom—a trapdoor, in effect—he would lose the rabbit this time, but the team would be prepared to put on a full-court press the following week. *If she keeps following the same pattern, that is. At some point, she has to run out of money to deposit, doesn't she?*

Five women exited the restroom and walked smartly along the length of the reception desk. None wore a skirt like the rabbit. Two wore long, flowing floral dresses, two sported shorts, and one a pair of light-brown trousers. All had colorful tops, and none wore the white tank-top for which he was watching closely. Three of the women trailed the *slap-slap* sounds of sandals. One of the women in shorts had white sneakers on, that silently glided over the tile lobby floor. The one in brown pants at the back of the group, trailing a step or two behind the others, *click-click*ed as her cream-colored—

Beltran rose quickly and followed the group of women. Or, more specifically, he followed the pair of expensive high-heeled shoes with the bright red soles Maria had made such a fuss over earlier. *The rabbit must have pulled a change of clothes from her bag and put her hair up in a bun, but she wore the same pair of expensive Christian WhoeverTheFuckHeIs shoes. Got you! This shitty mission in the ass-end of the Caribbean is finally turning into something fun.*

Miguel trailed the rabbit back through the hotel entrance and watched her get into a taxi. As he signaled for Ortiz to follow the cab, Beltran called to Ruben Hernandez over his concealed radio to pick him up at the hotel.

"Things just got real, eh, Miguel?" Hernandez asked with a smile as Beltran got in the car. No surveillance team enjoys sitting in their cars on the side of the road all day. Each hopes for enough action during their shift to make the job enjoyable, without it turning into something they'd have to mentally file under the heading of "We fucked up and lost the rabbit."

Maria's announcement over the team's radio brought Beltran's focus back to the job at hand. "The cab doubled back and they're heading west, now. Back to the center of the city along Via Blanca. I have the eye."

"You think this is her?" Ruben asked Miguel, already knowing what his response would be.

"Well, it's either her or another woman who matches the general description, is making large cash deposits in the same bank, and knows at least the basics of how to run a surveillance detection route." Beltran paused to think about the possibilities. "*Sí*, I think it's her."

Ruben nodded. "*Bueno.* It'll be nice to wrap this up soon. I want to get home for my niece's baptism next Sunday."

Beltran chuckled. "While you're in church, say a prayer for my Miami Dolphins. I'll be watching from the couch in my lucky t-shirt and a beer in each hand. This season, the Dolphins need all the divine help they can get."

Maria's voice over the encrypted radio broke through the male bonding. "The cab's turning left," she reported. "They're going to be heading south onto Calzada de Guanabacoa. Can anyone take the eye?"

"Not us," Beltran said. "We're too far behind you."

"I can," Moises Lopez responded. "Maria, take the turn and then burn off. I'll take the eye as soon as I'm on Guanabacoa."

A double-click of the radio was the only response Ortiz needed to send her teammate. Maria slowed and made the turn far enough behind the cab that she was unlikely to be seen but disregarded the request for her to discontinue the pursuit. She followed two-blocks behind the taxi and watched as the cab took a right-hand turn onto a side street.

"They made a right about a half-mile down Guanabacoa and stopped in front of a restaurant. I'm continuing straight. I'm off. Can you pick her up?"

"I'm on it, Maria. I see you. Burn off," Moises affirmed. "Cesar and I have the eye."

On the next block, Ortiz turned right off Calzada de Guanabacoa and parked out of sight of the taxi discharging its passenger in front of the restaurant.

Lopez turned onto the side street and passed the restaurant. Cesar Romero radioed a status update to the rest of the team. "Subject exited the cab and went into a restaurant called Teresa's. We're parked half-way down the block. Moises will stay with the car and I'll follow her inside."

"Shit," Maria said under her breath. To an empty car, she stated the obvious. "That's three of us exposed to her already. We need more people for this."

Miguel Beltran's voice came over the radio, the strain of the afternoon abundantly clear. "Maria, stay frosty. You may have to pick up the eye again quickly. Ruben and I are ninety seconds out. We can *not* lose sight of her!"

Maria clicked her radio twice and adjusted the rearview mirror to give her a better view of the car-lined street behind her.

Cesar Romero hurried down the block and pushed through the restaurant's front door with more force than he intended to use. The lightweight wood door flew open faster than he expected. The few mid-afternoon patrons in the restaurant looked up at the harried CIA officer with clear disapproval at the disruption of their meal. Romero scanned the room quickly. No rabbit.

He made his way towards the bar and studied the half-dozen customers closely—mostly men, two older women, and one ten-year-old girl drawing in a notebook. No rabbit.

Romero looked at the end of bar and the pair of doors leading to the restrooms. He paused to weigh his options. The woman they were following had already gone into the restroom at the hotel earlier to change her appearance. *Maybe she did the same here?*

The Alpha Team leader made a command decision to sacrifice his anonymity and pushed the door to the women's washroom open. If he were right, maybe he could apologize and play drunk. If he were wrong, he figured, he would be leaving the restaurant right away, anyway. Cesar stepped into the bathroom and stopped cold. The small, single-person room was empty. No rabbit. "Fuck me...."

Maria's voice came through the tactical radio clearly. "I've got her, I think. On the next block past the restaurant. She came out. Must be the back door to the restaurant. Be advised, she put her hair into a ponytail. It's no longer in a bun, but she's wearing the same shoes."

"*Gracias a Dios,*" Cesar said under his breath, and headed back out the front door. In the open air, he sprinted down the street to the car.

"Maria," Miguel Beltran commanded over the radio, "do whatever you have to do to stay with her. Just don't lose her!"

"Okay, Miguel, but we need more people."

"I know," Cesar replied to his team. "I'm on that. Just keep her in sight." The Alpha Team lead pulled his cell phone from his shirt pocket. He punched the code to speed-dial the first number stored in the phone's memory and pumped his fist in relief that Daniel Jimenez answered on the second ring.

Chapter 38

The sun hung low over the green tops of the Cuban Royal Palm trees lining the west end of the park Cesar Romero had chosen for the impromptu meeting between Alpha and Bravo Teams. He needed to brief the others about the woman Alpha Team had been following since mid-day before they continued the surveillance.

Alex Ramirez arrived last. He plunked himself down at the opposite end of the picnic table from Eden—the only seat left open by the other five CIA officers. The four other men in the group gravitated immediately to the pretty brunette and sat brushing against her repeatedly in the cramped confines of the picnic bench, much to Maria Ortiz's disgust.

Eden, for her part, ignored the men and looked forward with anticipation to getting her mission completed soon—possibly that evening if she could believe the surveillance team's report.

Alex pulled red cans of Tropic-Cola from the plastic rings one by one and handed a cold, Coca Cola knock-off to Eden, Cesar Romero, and Maria Ortiz. Alex eyed his teammates as Daniel Jimenez and Jesus Pedrero sipped from the bottles of beer they brought with them from the safe house.

Romero filled Bravo Team in on Alpha's busy afternoon in pursuit of their rabbit. He described in detail her changes of vehicles and clothes, techniques well known to surveillance and counter-surveillance professionals worldwide. "Then, once she got into her own car behind the restaurant, she made a couple of routine surveillance detection route maneuvers. With such a small team, it was risky keeping up with her while she ran the SDR, but we did it. I don't think she spotted us."

Maria chimed in with her assessment. "It's as if she read about SDRs on the Internet rather than having had much in the way of training or experience running them in real life. Maybe she has had a little bit of practice, but it's more likely she did some superficial research and has been winging it. She didn't try anything that would lose even a first-year surveillance specialist. It would have helped if we had more follow vehicles, though."

"So," Alex said, "she's definitely up to something shady, then? Likely a strong match for O'Doherty, but not confirmed, is that it?"

"It's her," Ortiz answered confidently.

"No," Cesar Romero countered immediately, "it's *not* confirmed, yet."

Ortiz pursed her lips at Romero's retort. "It's *her*. It *is*. I'll bet you anything."

"Sure sounds to me like you found her," Jesus Pedrero said, and smiled. "Great work. Let's call it a success and go home, then. We're here to find her and report back home, right? You followed her to where she lives, and the rest of Alpha Team is watching her house right now. You know what she looks like with dark hair instead of red and what car she drives. Sounds like a full report to me. *Bueno.*" He lifted his beer in salute to Romero and Ortiz. "*Salud.*"

"Not so fast," Romero said. "It's not confirmed until *I* say it is. I'll admit that it all looks promising, but I'm not certain. Not yet. I'm not burning off this job until we have something more definitive. The cost of staying another day or two is nothing compared to how hard it'd be for the Company to send teams back here if we're wrong. Even if we're ninety percent sure, I want to get to ninety-eight percent. There are no guarantees in life, but we can still do more."

"Like what?" Eden asked.

"We wait until she goes out tonight and then we'll enter her house. While one team is following her, two or three of us enter the house and look for, well, whatever we can find. Certainly, she'll have more cash on hand—probably hidden. She can't have deposited it all, yet. Maybe she'll have something more incriminating like an address book, photographs, a picture of her family, or something. I don't know. We'll photograph whatever we find so we'll have something tangible to point to."

Eden shrugged. "Sounds good to me." Looking at Alex, she directed the conversation in the way she wanted Cesar Romero's plan to evolve. "You and I can break into a house with our eyes closed, right?"

Alex followed Eden's lead. "*Pffff*, yeah. Child's play."

"Good, that's perfect," Romero responded as if Eden had written the script for him. "Bravo Team should go get dinner now and be ready to relieve Alpha Team at 6 p.m. Alpha will then go grab a quick bite to eat and be ready to pick up the rabbit if she leaves the house."

"What do you want to do if she doesn't go out tonight?" Daniel Jimenez asked.

"Then, we'll burn off around midnight," Romero answered. "If she doesn't go out tonight, we'll set up on the house again at 6 a.m. tomorrow. If we have to, we'll make a daylight entry after she goes out tomorrow or the next day. She has to go out eventually." He looked at Eden and asked, "Is a daylight entry a problem for you?"

"Nighttime is preferable, of course," she answered, "but daytime's fine. I have a pick gun and can get in within ten seconds. It's noisier than manual lock picks, but nothing the neighbors would hear. No problem."

"Good," Romero concluded. He looked over at Daniel Jimenez, and said to the Bravo Team lead, "Go get something to eat and be back at six." Slapping his hand on the wooden table, Cesar smiled, his eyes bright. "This is going to work!"

***

Alex looked at the luminous dial on his watch. The hours of sitting idly in a car had taken its toll on his patience. "Eleven forty-five. Ugh. I hope Cesar calls it a night soon."

"Not too much longer," Eden answered hopefully. "We'll be done with this tonight and, with any luck, sailing home tomorrow. Won't that be nice," she said stretching her arms behind her head.

The team's radio chirped as Jesus Pedrero's voice came across in digital clarity. "What do you think, *jefe*? Can we call it a night now, or is she likely to finally go out for a late night of dancing and drinking on the town? The lights went off an hour ago. What do you say, Cesar?"

The Alpha Team leader's voice sounded annoyed. "A few more minutes. We'll stick to the plan."

Eden grunted. "What do you think, Alex? Is Cesar trying to be the Alpha Team *lead* or the alpha *male*?"

"You've got him pegged," Ramirez said and smiled. "But, hey, it hasn't been a bad couple of weeks. Other than the knock on the head you took in the alley, it's actually been pretty boring here."

Eden rubbed her scalp, running her fingertips over the scab that had formed along her hairline. "Thanks for reminding me," she said sarcastically.

"I *will* miss the food, though," Alex added.

"Oh *yeah*, I'll give you that, but I'm looking forward to going home. As soon as the surveillance teams burn off, we do what we have to do and meet everyone back at the safe house for a beer or three."

"You know it, sister."

Cesar Romero's voice came through the radio clearly. "Listen up, folks. Let's all go get some sleep, and we'll start again in the morning. I'll establish the schedule when we all rendezvous back at the town house. See you there."

One by one, members of the surveillance team radioed their acknowledgements. Alex called his in.

Eden nodded. "Good. Give 'em a few minutes for Jesus to get out of the bushes across the street and everyone will be very happily driving back to Havana. Anything you need from the trunk?"

Alex shook his head. "Nope, got it all right here."

"Me too." Eden hung her elbow out the car's front-passenger window and peered up at the half-moon. There was more moonlight than she would have preferred for what she planned that night. She would just have to make do.

Alex lifted his night-vision goggles—NVGs—to his eyes and looked at the rear door of the target's house. Satisfied that the electronics worked properly, he put the light-intensifying lenses down and inserted a paddle holster into his pants on his right hip.

Eden opened her blue case and checked over her own equipment. With practiced motions, she distributed her equipment into pockets, belt pouches, and her elastic shoulder holster.

"Porcupines—" Alex said, and extended his gloved fist toward Eden.

"—and ponytails," Eden replied with a grin. She smacked her fist on top of her partner's and held her arm in the air as he returned the motion.

The pair crossed the unlit street quickly. The single lens of Eden's small NVGs made looking at what was in front of her a claustrophobic affair—like viewing the world through a soda straw. She greatly preferred the two- or four-lens goggles her team routinely used on other missions, but space had been at a premium when packing Alex's duffel bag for this mission.

Eden rotated her head from side to side—keeping her head on a swivel, as her tactics instructors always said—as she approached the house. At the rear door, she knelt and picked the lock in eight seconds flat.

Alex drew his silenced .45-caliber Glock 36 semi-automatic pistol and led the way into the house. Eden drew her own sidearm—her preferred Sig Sauer—and followed her partner inside.

The sparse array of furnishings looked bland in the green glow of night-vision goggles. Sofas and end tables in the living room contrasted with the empty spot in the center of the dining room. Bare walls spoke to the recency of the new owner's occupation of the house.

The duo of CIA operators cleared the first floor of the house silently. Having found nothing of interest, Alex pointed toward the stairs. Eden nodded her agreement and led the way. As she ascended the wooden staircase, the bottom two boards creaked more than she would have liked. Eden slowed her pace to maintain the conservative sound discipline she had perfected through more than a decade of training and practice.

Alex left enough distance between himself and his partner that he could take the stairs a few at a time—skipping over the noisy ones—and not bump into Eden from behind.

At the top of the stairs, Eden peered down the straight hallway in front of her. Open doors to bedrooms and a bathroom lined the hallway. A single closed door sat the far end of the hallway. Alex and Eden quickly and quietly cleared the other rooms on the second level and found each unoccupied and largely unfurnished.

At the end of the hall, Eden stopped and listened intently for any sign of life beyond the sole closed door. She wished they'd had enough space in Alex's gear bag to bring a thermal scope to see any heat sources through the walls of the house. That would have shown them exactly where their target was.

Through the wall to her left, Eden heard the muffled sound of rushing water as a toilet flushed. Eden took a deep breath and allowed herself a small grin. Now she knew where her target was. With her pistol in her right hand, she twisted the doorknob with her left and slowly pushed it open part-way. The door opened smoothly and quietly.

Bathed in the green glow of her NVGs, the bedroom furniture in the part of the room she could see through the half-open doorway sat arrayed against the wall to her left. A dresser and tall chest lined one wall. A door to her left—the bathroom, she judged from the hissing sound of the toilet tank filling—sat closed. Light streamed from underneath. She focused intently on the bathroom door, entered the bedroom, and angled to her left.

The quick movement from her right was only a blur. Sharp pain seared across the back of Eden's right hand. She yelped as the metal rod impacted her a second time, this time across her forearm. Eden's pistol dropped from her gloved hand and clattered on the hardwood floor.

She spun to her right, took a half-step back for distance, and faced her attacker. The woman's long hair—tinted green in the NVGs—flew about her head as she swung the metal bar down at the CIA officer's head. More out of instinct drilled into her in training than from conscious thought, Eden raised both arms, crossed at the wrists, and blocked the bar above her head with the back of her hands. The metal bar clanged loudly as it struck Eden's wristwatch.

Eden twisted her wrists and grabbed the bar—*probably the towel rod from the bathroom*, she thought as she rapidly assessed the situation—and twisted. Eden pulled the bar towards her and planted a kick in the woman's mid-section. The pajama-clad woman let out a grunt but held tightly to the metal bar, unwilling to yield her improvised weapon.

A bare foot kicked at Eden's head. The CIA officer shifted, and the blow struck her shoulder. The attacker lifted her leg again and aimed a round-house kick at Eden's ribs.

Eden counter-attacked into the kick, striking the woman's thigh a few inches above her knee, rendering the attack ineffective.

Seeing that she was up against a skilled adversary, the attacker changed tactics. She pulled the bar for leverage and spun like a dancer twirling into her partner's arms. She tucked the metal bar under her right shoulder and struck Eden in the chest with a well-executed blow from the bony tip of her left elbow.

Eden held her quarry tightly as she staggered backwards two steps from the assault.

The woman landed two elbow strikes to Eden's mid-section and cocked her arm for another strike.

Unable to wrest the metal club from the woman, Eden pulled herself against her attacker to minimize the effectiveness of another blow. With a circular wave of her hand, Eden grabbed a fistful of the woman's loose hair and yanked it back sharply, causing her to yelp in pain.

Eden spun to face the woman towards Alex. "Shoot her!" Eden commanded.

Alex lifted his pistol towards the pair of writhing women. Three arms in front of his target struggled for ownership of the metal bar.

The pajama-clad woman twisted, trying to reverse position with Eden, but Eden held her attacker fast.

Alex aimed his Glock at the middle button of the thrashing woman's pajama top, but hesitated, not convinced he could get a clean shot. A chill ran down his spine as the former SEAL pictured the devastating effect a .45 caliber hollow-point bullet would have if it passed through his target and into his partner.

With a smooth motion, he holstered his weapon and stepped forward. The woman he approached kicked out at him weakly, but from an unbalanced stance since Eden was bending her backwards. Alex easily blocked the kick with his left hand and drove the top two knuckles of his right fist into his adversary's gut. His punch landed three inches below her sternum. The air in her lungs rushed out, escaping with a gravelly *whoosh*.

The woman crumpled to the wooden floor in an ungainly cascade of flailing limbs and whirling hair. Her raspy, wheezing attempts to inhale pierced the quiet of the Cuban night. The metal bar clattered to the floor and skid to a stop under the bed.

Eden drew a square, silver packet from her back pocket and sat down roughly on the woman's back. The CIA officer opened the zip-locked packet labelled "Product Strength 4" and pulled a moist towelette from the resealable pouch.

Alex looked at his partner, his head tilting slightly. "Aren't we going to shoot her?"

"Not yet," Eden said haltingly, still catching her breath. "Change of plans."

Eden held the moist towelette over the woman's mouth. Even with her uneven breathing, the vapors from the CIA's version of a chloroform-coated handkerchief made their way into the woman's lungs. Her muscles relaxed slowly, and her breathing became more regular as she lost consciousness.

Eden stood, stretched, and rubbed several body parts she knew were going to be black and blue the next morning. Eden retrieved and holstered her weapon while Alex looked on.

"What gives?" he asked.

"Did you see how she fought?"

"Yeah, she was pretty good, but you're better."

"That's not the point. The fact that she was any good at all means that she's been trained. That's not something like the half-assed SDR she ran earlier or something she picked up from watching old Bruce Lee movies. Someone trained her, and she was good. Think about it. First, she heard us coming up the stairs. Then, she used the toilet to get us — to get *me* — looking to the left while she attacked from the right. Her hand-to-hand techniques were practiced. She fought from close-in and didn't try to disengage for distance like an amateur would. She knew *exactly* what she was doing. When someone comes at you with a knife, you backpedal for distance. But when someone in the same room comes at you with a gun, what do you do? You rush in so they can't get a clean shot at you and maybe you'll have a chance to tear the weapon away."

"Sure, everyone knows that—"

"No, everyone does *not* know that. You and I know that because we've been trained by the best in the world. Someone trained *us*, and someone trained *her*. I want to know who it was."

"That's not the plan."

A man's voice from the hallway startled both operators. "What *is* the plan, then?"

As if choreographed, Eden and Alex drew their weapons and spun towards the doorway.

Cesar Romero raise his hands and stopped in his tracks. "*Whoa*! Hold on. Good guy here, folks. Good guy alert! I'm on *your* side, remember?"

"What are you doing here?" Eden asked.

"Me? What the hell are *you* two doing in here? The plan was for us to wait until the rabbit went out again and *then* search the place, not to risk getting caught in the act like you just did. And can you please put those guns down? You're making me nervous."

Alex and Eden lowered their pistols.

Alex holstered his Glock, and asked Eden, "What now?"

"Now," she replied calmly, "since he's here, he can help you load her into the trunk of our car."

"Are you *nuts*?" Romero asked. "What the hell are you going to do?" The CIA officer looked down at the woman sleeping on the floor, and then back up at the members of Bravo Team. The realization came to him with a twist in his gut. "You're not here to just *find* her, are you? You're here to—"

"Cesar," Eden said interrupting the career case officer, "your job here in Cuba was to find her. You've done that and done it very well. You and Alpha Team were brilliant, actually." Eden hoped that pumping up the man's ego would make the next part more palatable. "Now you're done. Congratulations, Cesar. You get to go home tomorrow and do what the Company tasked you to do: report that you successfully found Evelyn O'Doherty. Tell the task force back home how you found her at the bank, followed her home, and give them her address. Give them a description of her car and its license plate number. Give it all to them. But you're going to leave this part out of your report."

Cesar stood silently in the bedroom doorway and stared at the woman on the floor. "Did you find anything that ties her to the hijacking? Anything that shows who she really is? Maybe it's not her."

"No, we haven't looked around, yet," Eden answered, "but since you're here, you can help us search."

Romero didn't take his eyes off the unconscious woman. "What did you hit her with?"

Eden showed him the silvery packet. "It's one of DS&T's knock-out formulas. It's like chloroform, but they make it effective for a predictable amount of time. This is Product Strength 4. She'll be out for about four hours."

"And then?"

"And then," Eden responded, "you'll be fast asleep back at the safe house looking forward to a flight home through Panama City or Lima or wherever."

"How are you getting home?" Romero asked.

"There's nothing about our exfiltration that you need to know. Now, help us look around for anything you can use as proof that it's her."

The trio of CIA officers spread out and searched through closets, dressers, and under the bed. As he searched through the dresser, Romero looked over at Alex. "What did that whole porcupines and ponytails thing mean?"

Alex chuckled. "It's like a pre-game good-luck tradition. It's just something that some soldier at Fort Bragg said to us in training last year. That day, Eden was wearing a ponytail, but he said that my short hair stuck up and looked more like a porcupine. It became our pre-mission ritual. Kinda like saying 'good luck' or 'break a leg' or something."

"You heard that?" Eden asked Cesar. "Where were you?"

"I was rounding the corner of the house you were sitting in front of, down the street. I heard Alex's reply on the radio to burn off, but not yours. I came to make sure you were all right."

Eden paused her search through the night table. "Well, I guess that was chivalrous of you. Didn't find what you were expecting, did you?"

"No, definitely not."

Alex pulled a large suitcase from the corner of the bedroom closet. "This thing weighs like a hundred pounds," he said, his voice strained. He lugged the valise into the center of the room and pushed it over with a hard shove. The bag landed on the wooden floor with a reverberating thud. Alex pulled back the zipper and opened the top of the case revealing bundles of hundred-dollar bills.

Cesar's eyes blinked rapidly. "*Wow.*"

"Guess she wasn't done with her trips to the bank, after all," Eden concluded, admiring the millions of dollars of US currency at her feet.

Romero picked several bundles of cash out of the suitcase. "That's a lot of money," he said softly.

Eden corrected him. "Actually, that's a lot of *counterfeit* money."

Romero turned his head towards Eden slowly and nodded.

Eden anticipated what Cesar Romero was thinking. "Cesar, do you really think you could get even the few stacks you're holding through Cuban customs on the way out?"

Romero thought intensely for a moment. "No, I suppose not." He hefted the bundles of cash in his hand as if weighing them and dropped the funny money back into the suitcase. He withdrew his cell phone from his pocket and took a photo of the open suitcase. "Guess a photo will have to suffice as my souvenir."

Eden pulled a dozen bundles of cash from the suitcase and put them into a thin nylon backpack she found in the closet. "I'm sure the Secret Service will be able to analyze these and determine whether or not they're the same as the Iranian superbills that led us to the *Banco Nacional de Havana* in the first place. That'll be pretty good confirmation."

"But how are *you* going to get them through customs?" Romero asked.

"I'm not. Alex and I have another way to get home. Sorry, Cesar, I can't give you the details. Need to know, and all that."

Romero nodded. "But still, maybe she *is* just some drug dealer's girlfriend. How can you be sure she's the Irish woman?"

Eden looked at the slender female form lying quietly on the wooden slats of the bedroom floor. "Well, there's one way to find out for sure, isn't there?" She knelt next to the prostrate woman, pulled the pajama pants down to the rabbit's knees, and rolled her face up.

Chapter 39

A warm, moist breeze wafted through the drafty coastal warehouse as Eden watched Evelyn O'Doherty slowly regain consciousness. O'Doherty's head bobbed a few times as she fought off the residual effects of the chloroform.

O'Doherty tugged against her restraints, still only half-awake. A violent shudder made its way down the length of her body as she instinctively pulled against the duct tape securing her arms and legs to the metal chair. Her struggle against the improvised restraints proved futile, but she continued to pull, anyway. Overlapping lengths of reinforced strapping tape kept her firmly anchored to the chair.

Eden greeted O'Doherty in English. "Welcome back, Evelyn. My name is Michelle."

Evelyn silently looked around the dimly lit warehouse in which the two women sat facing each other; the same warehouse Eden and Alex had spotted on the beach two weeks earlier.

O'Doherty replied in lightly accented Spanish. "I am not whoever this *Evelyn* woman is. Let me go. You have me confused with someone else."

Michelle responded gracefully in Spanish. "Yes, you *are* Evelyn O'Doherty. We followed you from the bank where you were depositing the cash the Iranians paid you. We knew that you'd change your appearance, so we also spent quite some time looking for your plastic surgery records in any number of clinics. We never found them. I must say, though, personally, I think you were prettier as a redhead."

"This is my natural hair color," Evelyn insisted, maintaining the façade.

"No, it's not. I checked while you were unconscious," Michelle responded in English, pointing to O'Doherty's lap.

O'Doherty glanced reactively towards her groin and grimaced in disgust. Venomously, she spat out in Irish-accented English, "*Ohhhh*, seriously? Have you no common decency, woman?"

Michelle shrugged and reached a gloved hand into the black backpack laying on the table next to her. She withdrew two plastic-encased cotton swabs, which she held up for O'Doherty to see.

"My partner, Alex, behind you, and I also took two swabs from your mouth for DNA analysis."

"Gee, thanks," O'Doherty said sarcastically, craning her neck to get a glimpse of Alex as he stood sentry duty twenty feet behind the prisoner. "What happens now? You read me my rights and take me back to America?"

"No," Michelle said with a straight face. "You won't be going back to America. In fact, you're not going to leave Cuba. Right now, it's just after 4 a.m. At 5 a.m., a small boat with two US Navy SEALs will arrive. They'll take Alex and me to a submarine sitting off the Cuban coast, and we'll sail home. Before he and I leave here, though," she said with no inflection or emotion in her voice, "I'm going to kill you."

Michelle looked at Evelyn and paused to let her last statement sink in. The CIA officer knew O'Doherty would not believe her immediately. It would take some time for the magnitude of the situation to feel real to the restrained woman.

"Is that some kind of bad interrogation technique?" O'Doherty asked. "You threaten to kill me, and I'm supposed to just crack wide open and tell you all my secrets? You play bad cop and Alex comes around later playing good cop?"

"No, it's not an interrogation technique," Michelle said calmly, "and I'm not interrogating you. We're just two women talking. I'm not going to yell at you. I'm not going to hit you. I'm not going to insult you. In fact, I'm not even going to lie to you. If you want to talk for the next hour, then we can talk. If not, that's your choice. Either way, in—" Michelle looked at the watch on her left wrist and continued in an even tempo, "—forty minutes, I am going to kill you."

"Do you even know what it means to kill someone?" O'Doherty sneered. "Do you have it in you to pull the trigger of that gun in your shoulder holster? Have you ever even fired that weapon anywhere other than a training range?"

"Yes, Evelyn," Michelle replied stoically, looking O'Doherty directly in the eyes. "I've killed more people than you have, although fewer than your father did when he crashed that airliner into the Atlantic Ocean."

"Who are you?"

"My name is Michelle Reagan. I'm a CIA officer assigned to the Special Activities Center. Most recently, I went into Iran with our military forces to rescue Richard Duncan and his wife. We were only partially successful, as I'm sure you've seen on the news. My mission here in Cuba is to locate and then kill you. We brought a dozen of our best officers here to hunt you down. It took a lot of hard work, but we did it. Nobody gets away with kidnapping a CIA Director, much less killing two of his bodyguards. Did you really think that *you* were going to get away with it?"

Evelyn pondered the question for a moment. She glanced again at her surroundings, looking for any avenue of possible escape. "Yes, actually, or I wouldn't have done it. It was a very good plan. And why are you telling me all of this, anyway?"

"We're just two women talking, that's all. In a half hour, it won't matter what I may have told you. What else would you like to know?"

"So, how are you going to do it?"

"I don't know, yet. I haven't decided," Michelle answered with a calmness in her voice that sent a shiver down Evelyn's spine. "I could shoot you in the heart, but it would no doubt be quite painful. I could shoot you in the head, which would be quick, but very messy, and then you wouldn't get an open-casket funeral. I have a plastic bag and more duct tape, so suffocation is an option. But I'm afraid that'd be slow and, even if not exactly painful, still agonizing in its own way. And believe it or not, I don't actually want you to suffer. Or there's one other way, but I'm not sure about that."

"Well, thank you so kindly for your concern for my feelings," Evelyn said with a snip in her voice.

"I could try to snap your neck, but I've only done that once before, and I can't guarantee I'd do it quite right from that angle—with you sitting in a chair."

"Aren't you just an encyclopedia of death. A real *femme fatale*?"

"Unfortunately for you, yes. Is that also how you would describe yourself?"

"I thought you said you weren't going to insult me?"

"I didn't intend it to be an insult. How do you view yourself, then? What's your own self-image?"

"What are you, my psychiatrist? Are you going to shrink my head or blow it off?"

"No, I'm not here to psychoanalyze you," Michelle said with a chuckle. "Just making conversation. I appreciated the sophistication of your plan to kidnap Director Duncan and get away. The way you used four obese women to smuggle firearms and explosives through airport security was extremely creative. How did you know which flight the director would be on?"

Evelyn looked at Michelle sternly. "So, now you get to the questions that you really want to ask, is that it?"

"Yes," Michelle said, and then sat silently.

Evelyn considered the question and lost herself in thought for a few seconds as she decided whether or not to answer it. "I guess it doesn't matter, anymore. You've already bombed Iran once. The videos on the tele were quite spectacular, I must say. I doubt you'll do it again anytime soon. It was them. The Quds force has computer hackers that have gotten into all the major travel reservation systems worldwide. Or at least that's what my contact told me. He may have been bragging a bit, but I think it's most likely true."

"Iran's planning must have started long before the Duncans' plane tickets were booked, though."

O'Doherty nodded. "They got back in touch with me about a year ago—about eight months before the wedding. The Iranians must have been planning it since the Duncans' daughter announced her engagement on Facebook the year before. What parent is going to skip their own daughter's wedding, right? So, they knew the Duncans would be there. Once the Iranians knew it was going to happen, they put their plans in motion. I found the four women early on. That part was surprisingly easy. Thirty grand apiece and they were bought and paid for. The Iranians eventually found the right flight number and told me which one to be on."

"You said the Iranians 'got back in touch' with you. What did you mean by that?"

Straining against the tape holding her arms to the chair, O'Doherty said, "This is getting rather uncomfortable. Can you at least loosen it a bit?"

"No," Michelle said flatly.

"Then why should I tell you anything else?"

"You don't have to. Like I said, we're just talking and in twenty minutes, it will all be over."

"You're *serious*?" O'Doherty asked in disbelief. "You're going to *kill* me? You're just going to kill me and sail off into the sunset?"

"Well, sunrise might be more accurate. And yes, I told you the truth. That's exactly what's going to happen."

"That's not the way America does it, though, is it?" O'Doherty asked with concern growing in her voice. "Aren't you supposed to arrest me and make a spectacle of the trial to show that the good guys always win?"

"I'm glad you realize that we're the good guys," Michelle said appreciatively, knowing full-well O'Doherty didn't mean it that way. "But no. Not this time. It wasn't my decision."

"Is that how you justify it to yourself?" Evelyn said accusingly. "Since 'it wasn't your decision,' it's not your responsibility?"

"Sometimes. But in this case, you killed two CIA officers in cold blood and were directly responsible for the death of Heather Duncan. That's enough reason for me not to mind killing you," Michelle said.

"So, you strap me to a chair and put a gun to my head?"

"Yes."

"Not very sporting."

"No."

The two women sat in silence for a few minutes to let the tense atmosphere dissipate.

"What's the other way?" Evelyn asked. "You said there was some other way, but you weren't sure about that."

"Oh, that." Michelle pointed to the watch on her left wrist. "Concealed inside the stem of my watch is a poisoned needle. This is what the CIA sometimes provides to our officers in the field to use on ourselves if the situation gets bad enough. I've never seen it used, though, so I hesitate to even consider it."

"Feel free to test it on yourself, first," Evelyn said with a grin.

Michelle smiled in return.

"What is it supposed to do?"

"It's made from the same chemicals as military nerve gas. I'm told that it stops all electrical communications between nerve cells. Death is supposed to occur in three seconds. The nerve cells stop talking to each other, so there's no pain. The brain simply shuts down. It's supposed to be peaceful."

Evelyn turned away and stared off into the wall of the warehouse, alone with her thoughts.

Michelle moved to get conversation back on track. She pulled a piece of white paper from her backpack and unfolded it. "We have fifteen minutes left. I wanted to show you this. I wrote a note to leave with you."

She faced the paper towards O'Doherty who read aloud the block letters written in black ink. "Please return my remains to Ireland. — — Evelyn Meara O'Doherty"

Tears welled up in Evelyn's eyes and coursed down her face. Flowing over her surgically enhanced cheek bones, the river of silent pain flowed along the curve of her chin and rained wet sorrow upon her pajama top.

As the tears silently descended, Michelle saw upon Evelyn's face the reaction she'd been hoping for. Evelyn had crossed the mental threshold needed to break loose her willingness to talk more openly. She had clearly accepted that her demise was imminent.

"What was the previous time you were in touch with the Iranians?" Michelle asked, finally willing to press the questioning more firmly.

"Please," Evelyn implored. "You don't have to do this, Michelle. I can give you millions of dollars. *Ten* million, even. You can just walk away—"

Michelle shook her head slowly—as much in disgust as in rejection of the offer—and pulled four bundles of cash she and Alex had retrieved from Evelyn's house from her backpack. She dropped them one at a time, so each landed with a *thud* on the table. "Oh, you mean this money?"

Evelyn looked at the currency wordlessly.

"We left the rest back at your house. I don't need the money. That's not why I'm here. It's all counterfeit, anyway."

"*Mmm.* I suspected as much," Evelyn said softly with resignation. "The Iranians are rather infamous for their so-called superbills. I watched a documentary about it on Netflix before all of this. But I figured that in Cuba it'd be too hard to tell the difference and the banks here wouldn't notice."

"You were right. They didn't. But that much US currency suddenly appearing at Cuban banks caught the attention of our analysts. At first, of course, everyone thought that it was drug money. The local banks never figured out it's counterfeit, but our Treasury Department got samples and the Secret Service has ways of telling. Later, the possibility that *that* many high-quality counterfeit bills—the kind Iran is known to make—were suddenly flowing through Cuba made the Iranian connection too hard to ignore. You crafted a good plan, overall, though, I do have to admit."

Letting her praise for Evelyn's strategy sink in, Michelle continued to press for answers to the questions she most wanted to know. "You couldn't have known in advance that the Iranians would torpedo your yacht, the *Blue Ayes*. But you had your getaway planned, just in case."

Evelyn nodded. "I didn't trust them. I convinced myself that they would not want to leave behind any witnesses to something as big as this, and it turned out I was right. I figured that even if I were wrong, the extra expense of the second yacht as insurance was well worth the cost."

"You were right not to trust them. You must have had good training. Where did you get your training?" Michelle asked. "From the IRA and your mother's family?"

"You don't know?"

Michelle shook her head.

O'Doherty debated taking that secret to her grave. As she contemplated her few remaining options — silence or conversation — Evelyn quickly realized that she now believed that this CIA officer meant everything she said. Michelle Reagan was indeed going to kill her in just a few minutes' time. Evelyn pushed from her mind the thought of spending the last few minutes of her life in silent protest. With the end upon her, Evelyn knew in her heart that what she wanted at this moment was companionship — human-to-human contact and someone to connect with before her time was up. If this polite and pretty woman from the CIA was the only choice she had, there wasn't anything left to lose by sharing the time she had left with her to-be angel of death.

"It was the Iranians. Who trained us, I mean."

"'Us'?"

"I was seventeen when I was selected by my mother's cousin to go. It was all the Iranian intelligence officer's idea. Five pairs of men and women traveled to Tehran where we spent almost a year training in firearms, hand-to-hand combat, insurgency tactics, urban agitation, counter-surveillance, clandestine communications, explosives, and the like. We learned to make homemade bombs, build detonators, and craft various triggering mechanisms from everyday electronics. You know, things you can buy from grocery and hardware stores without raising suspicion. Skills needed by the soldiers of the cause back home. When I returned, I joined the Active Service Unit of the brigade my mum's cousin commanded."

"How did you connect with the Iranians in the first place?"

"They approached the Provisional IRA. The Iranians wanted to support various groups around Europe and the Middle East that oppose the nations Iran dislikes. Five pairs of men and women went. One pair each from Ireland, England, France, Saudi Arabia, and Palestine. After the year of training, we were all supposed to go home and train our own people. There was a little bit of political rhetoric every now and then, but really they just kept saying we were to 'continue the Revolution'. That was their refrain, although fortunately they were not overly obnoxious about it. We Irish have our own reasons for resisting England. I didn't really care why the Iranians didn't like them. I suppose we used each other for our own purposes. In Iran, the intelligence and military trainers treated us extremely well. Including all five women, which rather surprised us all. But they did."

"So, the Iranians trained you as both soldiers and instructors, then sent you home to pass on their knowledge. In the end, your groups would all be that more sophisticated at harassing Iran's enemies. I get it. It's creative. But you were so young. Why not send older, already experienced soldiers from each country?"

"Two reasons, at least that's what they told us. First, the more experienced people were already known by too many law enforcement agencies. Even if they had never been arrested, they were more likely to be watched closely because they associated with people who had. Teenagers had not made it onto anyone's radar, yet, so we could travel freely, and no one ever noticed. Second, the price for agreeing to the training was that we would agree to do the occasional job for Iran. We were told up front that we would never have to kill anyone for them, but we would have to agree to do anything else they asked. I guess we're all more gullible when we're younger."

"What did they have you do?"

"My only one was a seduction job in Lucerne. Some Swiss banker on vacation that Iranian intelligence wanted to make into a spy for them. I'm pretty sure it worked."

Michelle nodded.

"And Iran got back in touch with you when they'd cooked up this plot against Director Duncan?"

This time, it was Evelyn's turn to nod.

Michelle said, "This was quite a bit bigger than the other job, and they paid you a lot for it, even if it did turn out to be funny money."

"Yeah, this was outside of that previous arrangement. But since they already knew me, they were comfortable enough that I could carry it out. And being Irish, I could travel freely throughout America without bringing any extra attention to myself. After the Troubles ended back home, only a few of the others in the brigade shared my passion for continuing the fight against our English oppressors. Even then, their hearts were just not into it anymore, and I got fed up with the lot of them. Like the saying goes, they became all talk and no action, so I wanted to get away from there. The Iranian money was supposed to be my retirement fund. I couldn't very well work again after this job, now could I? Of course, the Iranians had other ideas, and I was suspicious of them from the start. Who wouldn't be?"

"True. How did you get your father to go along? He wasn't in the IRA."

"No, but he was a believer at heart. That's why my mother married him. It was his head that was too weak to do anything but talk after some drink, though. That's why my mum took me to live with her cousin. When my father was diagnosed with cancer, well, he got very depressed. He was already in stage four. There was no treatment for him, then. It was too late. I gave him a way to give his life meaning. It took some convincing, but, in the end, he went along. He didn't want to crash an airplane—he loved flying. He'd been doing it his whole life. I told him that all he had to do was one landing and one take off. Then, just set the autopilot for home and take his pain pills. He was probably unconscious when the plane ran out of fuel above the Atlantic. The rest was physics."

"And how did you get the weapons and explosives into the US?"

"Me? I didn't. They gave all of it to me. Even the special underpowered bullets that are made for shooting on airplanes. I met up with the Iranian courier in Orlando, Florida. He said they brought it all in through Diplomatic pouches via their United Nations mission in New York City. I didn't really care, but he bragged more than he probably should have. I preferred that they provided what I needed. That way, I wasn't taking any risk of exposure in trying to buy the kit in America, so that was all *foine* by me."

Beeping from Michelle's watch interrupted the conversation. All eyes in the room focused intently on the timepiece as Michelle depressed the crown to silence the timer.

"It's time," Michelle said matter-of-factly.

"Please, Michelle, I can tell you more."

Michelle shook her head briefly and stood up. "Do you have a preference?"

"That's not a fair ques-*tion*," Evelyn replied, her voice cracking on the final word.

"You're probably right."

Without giving it any more thought, O'Doherty said softly, "The needle."

Michelle stepped behind O'Doherty's chair and stood behind her seated and bound prey. With a twist of the false crown of her watch, Michelle carefully extracted the inch-long needle from its concealment. Holding the poisoned pin between the thumb and index finger of her right hand, Michelle looked closely at the instrument of death that she had carried in her watch for years and never in the past so much as removed from its concealment outside of the DS&T lab in which it had been issued to her. The thought that the CIA intended the needle to be used on one of its own officers sent a chill down Michelle's neck.

"Do you have any last words?" Michelle asked.

O'Doherty simply shook her head.

"Lift your chin up," Michelle instructed O'Doherty.

Looking at the needle held between her fingers, the image of some trapped and helpless CIA officer having to use the last-resort option to avoid capture and a brutal interrogation flittered through Michelle's mind. The thought of killing O'Doherty with a poison created by CIA officers for use on a CIA officer — even as a last resort and an act of mercy — did not sit well with her. Some things, Michelle reasoned, should be reserved for those who deserve an honorable exit.

Gingerly, Michelle reinserted the needle into the case of her watch. Slowly, she screwed the crown back in and ensured it sealed tightly.

Michelle bent down behind the chair and wrapped her right arm around Evelyn O'Doherty's neck. O'Doherty flailed, bucking her head at the betrayal. "What are you —"

Evelyn's fingers scraped at the metal arms of the chair. Veins on her neck protruded prominently in her struggle against Michelle's arm as it slid under the Irishwoman's chin.

Michelle held tightly against O'Doherty's squirming. The duct tape kept the prisoner's arms and legs secured, but her head and hair thrashed wildly. Michelle held tightly, pressing her body against the back of O'Doherty's head to stabilize it for the few seconds she needed.

With her arm encircling Evelyn O'Doherty's neck, Michelle positioned her elbow directly in front of the captive woman's trachea leaving her windpipe surrounded, but not squeezed. O'Doherty's heavy breathing as she lashed out violently was all the proof Michelle needed that the woman secured to the chair could still breathe.

With her right arm around her target's neck, Michelle wrapped her left arm behind the seated woman's head. She locked her right hand onto her left bicep and with her left hand, grabbed her right shoulder and squeezed.

Michelle pulled firmly with her right arm and pressed with her left. Her forearm compressed the left side of O'Doherty's neck pinching off the flow of blood through the carotid artery but leaving her airway open so O'Doherty wouldn't suffocate.

"Breathe, Evelyn. Just breathe," Michelle said as calmly as she could, but not as calmly as she would have liked. "This won't hurt."

O'Doherty's head bobbed forcefully forward and back, glancing off Michelle's jaw.

"*Mmmph*," was the only indication Michelle gave that the blow had connected.

Evelyn's vision narrowed as the diminished level of oxygen reaching her brain began to take its toll. The walls of the warehouse faded into the distance. O'Doherty struggled to focus her eyes on the chair Michelle so recently occupied. The Irish hijacker's head bobbed gently. Her raven-dyed hair fell over her right eye, further obscuring her view. Out of reach and out of time, she looked longingly at the bundles of cash sitting on the table next to the tent of paper Michelle had propped up. Her eyes blurred as they scanned over the words "Evelyn Meara O'Doherty," and then closed as she lost consciousness.

Michelle maintained the pressure on O'Doherty's neck for three minutes. After releasing her grip, she shook out her arms. O'Doherty's head drooped and tilted to the right.

Alex checked for a pulse along the left side of Evelyn's neck. He looked up at Michelle and shook his head. Evelyn O'Doherty was dead.

"Okay, Alex," Michelle said, "that's that." She walked to the table and packed the cash and hand-written name sign back into the nylon backpack.

Alex looked at Michelle, puzzled. "You're not going to leave the name tent, like you said?"

"Nope. She'll end up as nothing more than an anonymous and unclaimed corpse in some Cuban morgue. She doesn't deserve any recognition for what she did. I just used that sign to pry her open again when she wanted to stop talking."

Michelle looked at O'Doherty's lifeless remains securely taped to the chair. The dead woman's chin rested limply against her chest and her mouth drooped open.

Michelle lifted the backpack over her shoulder and looked at her partner. "Let's go home."

Chapter 40

Michelle sat alone in the darkened office on the fourth floor of CIA headquarters and focused on her breathing. She missed the peaceful state she achieved during yoga classes. The month of mission prep and travel to and from Cuba put a big dent in her workout routine.

The familiar voices of two men approaching brought her focus back to the present.

"I'm telling you, Steve, the Washington Nationals need the pair of relievers they got from the Phillies more than the one rookie and two prospects they traded away."

"I think Thompson is going to become the kind of slugger they'll need next season," Dr. Steven Krauss replied. "He has the swing. He just needs more consistency. That'll come with experience. Getting rid of him was a mistake."

The motion-activated lights turned on as the men entered Krauss's office.

Michelle's voice startled both men when she said, "You can't have enough extra-base hitters, but the Nats still lack depth in the bullpen."

Startled, Krauss backed into the handle of his office door. Jon Brady laughed as his best friend yelped in pain.

"*Owww*," Krauss said reflexively. His eyes flew open fully when he saw Michelle. He put one hand over his palpitating heart and rubbed the sore spot in his back with the other. "Were you sitting here alone in the dark? Sneaking up on people is not a nice thing to do." Steve moved forward quickly and embraced his girlfriend once she'd gotten to her feet.

Returning his hug, Michelle whispered in his ear, "Sneaking up on people is kind of what I do." She kissed him and stepped back, holding his hand in hers.

"What about me?" Jon asked from the doorway, smiling. "Do I get a kiss, too?"

Michelle put her hand to her lips and blew a kiss to the CIA division chief. "That'll have to do, Jon. Good to see you, too. How's Linda?"

"She's fine. I'll let her know you said 'hi.' See you later, Michelle. Good luck at the debrief, Steve."

"Thanks."

"Well, kids, I'll leave you two to get reacquainted. Don't do anything I wouldn't do." Jon Brady grinned wickedly as he pulled the office door closed behind him.

"Word's getting out," Steve said to Michelle while he maintained his grip on her hips, "that the team must have been successful in Havana. No one has any details, yet, but the rumor is that both surveillance team leads came back all smiles. I've been dying to hear the debrief. We've had to delay it twice so far. Was that to wait until you got back?"

Michelle shrugged. "I don't know. Alex and I took the slow way home, so maybe that's why. We flew into the Naval Air Station at Oceana late yesterday, stayed there overnight, and drove up very early this morning. When I got here, I figured you'd be at lunch, so I waited in here to surprise you before the debrief. I should have known you'd be hanging out with Jon."

"You should have called yesterday. You know I worry about you when you travel. And what in the world happened to your head?" Steve ran his fingers across the scab on Michelle's forehead.

"Oh, that's just a scrape. It's nothing. I got pretty banged up after that, though, but it's nothing I can't handle. I've had worse. You'll see all of my bruises at home."

"I'll kiss each and every one of them better."

Michelle smiled. "*Oooh*, I'm looking forward to that."

"Are you going to the debrief?" Krauss asked. "The director himself is going to be there. He never does that, but nothing about the last few months has been business as usual."

"No. I'm scheduled to meet with him afterwards."

"Once you found O'Doherty, did you—"

"Steven... let's not. It was a successful mission, and I'm home safe. Let's just leave it at that, okay?"

Krauss bit his lip and nodded.

"I don't think my meeting with the boss will go very long," Michelle said. "I'll meet you at home tonight. I have a feeling there's a refrigerator full of half-eaten take-out from Hunan Garden for us to dine on. Am I close?"

"*Zing*. You know me too well. Now that you're back, I won't stay late tonight."

"Love you."

"You too," Krauss said, and squeezed his girlfriend hard enough to elicit a grunt. It was going to take a few more weeks for the results of Evelyn O'Doherty's elbow strikes to heal completely.

***

Michelle browsed through the stacks of used books arrayed on tables set up along the hallway outside the secure conference room on the fourth floor of the New Headquarters Building. The odor of fresh paint wrinkled her nose as she waited for the primary debriefing session to end. To pass the time, Michelle rummaged through the assorted titles for sale as part of the Combined Federal Campaign's annual charity fundraiser. Old books about Cold War political jousting sat next to worn children's books covered with unicorns and talking cats, each selling for just a buck.

The door to the conference room opened and voices filtered into the hallway. Congratulations were exchanged loudly, and the departing crowd beamed their smiles up and down the corridor. Cesar Romero exited the conference room amidst handshaking and backslapping. Michelle grinned at the sight of the Alpha Team leader reveling in his success.

Daniel Jimenez stepped out of the conference room and locked eyes with Michelle. She grinned and gave a slight nod to the Bravo Team lead. As the crowd dispersed, Jimenez took Romero by the elbow and led him in Michelle's direction.

"Anything good for sale?" Danny asked as the men approached the table.

Michelle picked up a book with a black-and-white cover. "I like this one. It's a ghost story my dad used to read to me as a kid."

"You must have learned a lot from that book. You disappeared like a ghost in Havana," the Bravo Team leader said. "Where did you go?"

"Alex and I had to dispose of the equipment he'd brought in," Michelle offered, not really caring if he believed her story.

"We could have used your help the next day," Jimenez said, his eyes narrowing. "We lost the rabbit and never reacquired her again. We made entry into the house the day after and found a suitcase full of cash, but no woman in expensive shoes. Cesar took a photo of the cash and declared the mission a success. Personally, I would have liked to have a little more to use to make the confirmation."

Jimenez looked at Romero and then back at Michelle. "Why do I get the feeling, now, that there was more to it than that, Eden? Why are you here?"

"To congratulate you both on a terrific mission." Michelle patted Jimenez on the shoulder and started to walk towards the conference room. "You did great. I look forward to working with both of you again someday."

The men watched from behind as she walked away.

She cleans up well, Jimenez thought as Michelle's high heels clicked on the tile floor. *Damned well.*

Dozens of mementos of past CIA successes hung from the walls of the conference room. Engraved plaques with demilitarized rifles, photos of paramilitary teams behind enemy lines, and duplicates of medals awarded to CIA officers adorned the walls. Director Richard Duncan sat at the head of the wooden conference table and waved at Michelle as she entered the room.

"Thank you, Steve," Duncan said, dismissing Dr. Krauss. "I look forward to reading the task force's final report. Wonderful work on this. I owe you a personal debt of gratitude for everything you've done on my behalf over the past few months."

"My pleasure, sir. I'm glad the surveillance team was successful in Havana. I'll have the report on your desk by the middle of next week. I'll make sure it has all the distribution restrictions you asked for on it. Few people outside your office will be able to access it."

"That's how I want it, Steve," Duncan asked.

"Yes, sir."

Krauss turned towards Michelle Reagan and greeted her.

"Eden, is it?" he asked.

"Yes, Dr. Krauss," Michelle said, maintaining a poker face. To make the mention of her name not seem unusual to the director, she added, "I sat in on a few of the task force briefings over the summer representing the Special Activities Center. Dagmar Bhoti introduced us. Good to see you again. Congratulations on finding O'Doherty."

"Thank you," Krauss said, giving her a wink. "I'll leave you two to talk." He closed the door behind him, leaving his girlfriend alone with the CIA Director.

Michelle took a seat at the corner of the conference table and faced Richard Duncan.

"Everything went well, I heard," he said.

"Yes. Cesar's team found Evelyn O'Doherty at the bank when she arrived to deposit more counterfeit currency. Then they followed her home. She did what she could to lose the surveillance team along the way, but they're real pros and she was not. I'm sure you got the play-by-play from Romero and Jimenez. They did good work."

"Mm hmm. I heard all about it from them. I'd like to hear *your* version, too." Duncan pointed to Michelle's scalp. "What happened here?"

Michelle ran her fingertips lightly over the healing head wound. "Oh, that's what happens when a skull meets a brick wall."

"Brick *wall?*" Duncan asked excitedly.

"It's nothing. I'm fine." She filled the director in on the surveillance and the conversation she had with O'Doherty in the warehouse. She left out any description of O'Doherty's death.

"So, Tehran trained western subversive groups, huh?" Duncan asked. "We watch them run large-scale military training throughout the Middle East for terrorist groups all the time, but I've never heard of anything like what you described. They haven't trained any foreigners on Iranian soil — that we know of. Probably to maintain plausible deniability. That's an interesting development."

"The way she described it, it sounded to me like an experiment being run by the intelligence service, not the military," Michelle said. "O'Doherty didn't know if there had been groups before hers or afterwards. Either her cohort was the only class ever run, or the Iranians used good compartmentation within their program. None of what she told me is going to be in the task force's report, though. I'd hate for it to go to waste."

"No, we don't want it to be for naught, do we? I'll call my counterparts in Britain, France, and Israel and let them know about this *rumor* we picked up, so they can run with it. It affects them more than us, anyway. If they end up finding something, they can take all the credit. It's small potatoes to us. What did you do with the counterfeit cash and DNA samples?"

"This morning, I turned them over to the DS&T point of contact Michael gave me. I used the new case number he created for those items. It's a different number than one used for the rest of the Cuban surveillance mission. Michael said that the report will be sent directly to your office and classified for the Director's Eyes Only."

"Thank you. I'll let you and Mike know what the results are."

"No need. I know it was her."

"Did she... apologize? Did she really think she could get away with it?"

Michelle shook her head. "No, she never expressed any remorse. She stated flat out she thought we'd never catch her. After the surgery, she looked different enough that it might very well have worked. She didn't count on the fact that we have the world's best bloodhounds. It took the FBI a decade-and-a-half to find the Unabomber, but they never gave up. It took us longer than that to find Osama bin Laden, but we did. She was naïve to think we wouldn't be able to find her, even in Cuba."

Duncan nodded. "In the end, how did you... I mean...."

For all the years that Michelle had known Richard Duncan, she was still surprised that he found it impossible to utter the word *kill*. Since he first sent her to shoot a Canadian traitor in South Africa, and now to this mission in Cuba, he could readily ask her to commit the act, but he could not bring himself to utter that singular, irrevocable word. Michelle recognized the schism that existed inside the man who found the gritty reality of his position as Director of the Central Intelligence Agency to be in conflict with his sense of self and need to be thought of by others as a gentleman.

Michelle saved him the trouble. "Perhaps it's best if you don't know all the details."

"I want to know —"

To be merciful, Michelle cut him off. "Since the September 11th attacks, CIA Directors have given orders like these more and more frequently. In large measure, the agency has been turned into a hunting machine to find and eliminate High-Value Targets around the globe. You've signed off on I don't know how many orders to kill HVTs before, and I don't want to know. But this is different. It's not like watching a flash on a video monitor or reading about an explosion in a task force report. Anytime it's up close and personal, it's *personal*. It doesn't look like a video game. You can't hit the reset button and you don't get do-overs. You can't turn away or shut the screen off. You're forced to stand there and look at your own hands as you do things with them that you'd rather not talk about. Messy things. I've learned the hard way that when you have to look your target in the face, you never get that vision out of your head. I think it would be best for *you* if I didn't put that image in your head in the first place. That may disappoint part of you today, but someday, the rest of you will thank me."

Duncan sat quietly and contemplated Michelle's attempt at comfort. Most of the time, agency employees simply did as he ordered. He was not used to hearing words of wisdom from employees half his age.

Duncan leaned back in his padded leather chair. "This whole thing has just been so... intimate. With Heather and me locked in our cell in the submarine for so long, we got very close again. Not having anyone else to talk to for two months, except when the captain came in to practice his English, Heather and I reconnected like we were young again. Then, not being able to say goodbye before she died... the insanity of that battle and our escape... it's just all so...." The director's voice trailed off. He looked at his hands as he wrung them together. "It was all so sudden and... jarring. I've had a lot of time alone at home since we got back to think. The hunt for O'Doherty and gnawing feelings of uncertainty have been eating away at me the entire time. More than anything, Eden, I just want to know for sure that it's all over."

"I understand. Trust me. It's over. Instead of thinking about the woman I left behind in Cuba, think instead about the wonder of the grandchild you have coming early next year. Focus on the positive."

Duncan leaned back in his plush leather chair and looked at the ceiling. He closed his eyes and sat silently in thought. A tear formed in the corner of his left eye. He let out a slow, deep breath. "If it's a girl, Julia wants to name her Heather. If it's a boy, they're talking about the name Heath."

"I think that's beautiful," Michelle said with a lilt to her voice.

Duncan looked around the room at the wall-mounted trophies and hero-pose photos. "There won't be any plaques made for this mission," he said softly.

"No, there won't. No one will know."

Richard Duncan scanned the trophies and mementos on the walls around the room and let his gaze come to rest on Michelle. "The official story is going to be that Evelyn O'Doherty died in the yacht explosion when the Iranians torpedoed it. We'll let Tehran think that they were successful in silencing her. The FBI has the bloodstained blouse she wore that day, and when you see it on the TSA videos from the Miami airport, it's obviously the same one. Only the surveillance team, a few senior members of the task force, and, of course, you will know the rest of the story. As far as the world is concerned, she was killed by Iran."

"I'm sure you made that clear at the end of the debrief just now."

Duncan nodded.

"What about O'Doherty's helicopter pilot?"

"Well," Duncan said, "he was just the hired help, really — a pawn in her game. I'm sure he'll spend the rest of his days looking over his shoulder and afraid of his own shadow. We've let the Irish Garda Síochána know to look out for that specific type of counterfeit US currency, just in case he went back to Ireland. If he shows up passing funny money and they catch him, maybe he'll be prosecuted for the counterfeits. I doubt he'll want to admit where he got those bills from, since that'd tie him to a capital murder charge here in the US. I imagine he'll prefer to do his time quietly in Ireland."

"I'm sure you're right." Michelle stood up and flattened the front of her skirt. "Since it doesn't sound like you'll be sending me after him, I think this is where I say my goodbyes." Michelle took a step toward the conference room door.

"One last thing, Eden." Duncan paused, hesitant to ask his next question. "I know I asked you this when we got to the aircraft carrier, but... would you really have carried out Directive One?"

Michelle turned to face Duncan directly. "Think about it this way... if the Iranians had captured us after your escape, what would they have done? A public trial in which they admit to the world that they kidnapped the Director of the Central Intelligence Agency? No, I don't think so. It would have been a very secure pair of cells for us deep inside a mountain, or maybe inside one of their own black interrogation sites, if they have such things. If not, I'm certain they would have created one just for us. Then the torture would start, and, I'm sure you've heard from our own officers on the matter, everyone cracks eventually."

Duncan sat stone-faced, listening to Michelle's description of an alternative future he might have had to endure.

"After your years as Director of the CIA, how much critical information do you have locked up in your head? How valuable would that be to the Iranians? The Russians? The Chinese? How many ongoing intelligence collection and covert action operations would be compromised once they tortured the information out of you? Dozens, if not hundreds, I'm guessing. How many lives would have been lost if agents-in-place were compromised? More than few of our Crown Jewels, I'm sure."

Duncan pursed his lips and nodded his head, agreeing with Michelle's summary of the situation.

"After the interrogations," she continued, "what would they have done with you? With *us*? A first-class ticket home, saying 'thanks for sharing all of those stories, we'll take it from here'? No, of course not. If we were lucky, it would have been a quick death. If not, I'm sure there would have been a lot of suffering involved for both of us."

Duncan's face paled at the thought.

"The sad truth is that once they took you and your wife aboard the submarine, there was no other way it could possibly have ended for you. No matter what, they *had* to kill you both to cover their tracks. Just like they planned from the start to kill O'Doherty aboard the yacht. They were not going leave any witnesses behind, you and me included."

Michelle stood still and looked on as the CIA Director slowly rose.

"I suppose I owe you my thanks," Duncan said.

"For the rescue? That was the Navy's doing."

"No, for the sacrifice you were willing to make by accepting the assignment and going into Iran in the first place. No one would have blamed you if you had said 'no.' After all, if carrying out that directive had been necessary, I think I know where your next bullet would have gone."

Michelle nodded. "I like to think I would have gone down fighting. But when it's my time," Michelle said, tapping her wristwatch, "I have a trick or two up my sleeve for how to take the off-ramp from Planet Earth if it ever becomes necessary. I hope with all my heart that it never does."

Duncan smiled at her thought. "I hope so, too, Eden."

"And I hope you get to spend many years enjoying time with your grandchildren."

"Well, then, thank you for that, at least," Duncan said.

"You're most welcome."

Michelle turned on her heel and walked towards the door.

"Eden," Director Duncan called after her. "The least I can do for you is to give you some time off. Take a couple of weeks. Or, hell, take a month. You've earned it. You'll probably enjoy that more than another medal."

Michelle turned her head and smiled at him. "And for that, Mr. Director, I thank *you*."

Chapter 41

Michelle and Steven ate their dinner of reheated Chinese take-out while catching up on the news of family and friends that she missed during her Cuban excursion. She had decorated the dining room table of their Arlington condominium while the microwave oven did the hard work of preparing their evening repast.

"The candles are a nice touch," Steve said as he finished his General Tso's Chicken. "I wouldn't have thought of that."

"You probably didn't know we even had candles in the bottom drawer over there," Michelle shot back with a teasing smile.

"Yeah, well, I'm pretty sure they're a fire hazard, anyway," he said with a smirk, not willing to concede that his girlfriend was correct. Krauss changed the subject. "So, the official story is going to be that Evelyn O'Doherty died in the yacht explosion off Bermuda. Do you think the surveillance team will keep the rest of the story under their hats?"

Michelle nodded. "They're professionals." She didn't tell her boyfriend that Cesar Romero knew at least the basics of how O'Doherty really died. Even if the Alpha Team leader hadn't seen it happen, he knew in his heart that either Michelle or Alex killed Evelyn before leaving Cuba. "Besides, other than one photo of some cash in a suitcase, there isn't really any evidence of another outcome, is there? And that money could have belonged to any drug dealer in the Caribbean, right? There's nothing to say it was even hers."

"I suppose so. That's what the financial analyst suspected it was in the first place—drug money—before they were determined to be Iranian counterfeits. I guess it doesn't matter. Once the FBI makes the yacht story public, the whole matter will be put to rest. Only half of the bodies of the crew were ever found, so there's no need to produce hers."

Michelle drained the remaining red wine from her glass.

"Did she put up a fight?" Steve asked.

Michelle looked across the dining room table at her love and contemplated her response. Returning the wine glass to the table, she paused as if examining the few red drops of Merlot that remained in the vessel. It was not her habit to go into the details of her kill-missions with Steve. She found mixing that part of her job with her personal life to be distasteful conversation and distracting to their relationship. Steve didn't have a stomach for too much operational detail—especially the gore—and she didn't want him to worry excessively every time she deployed. She pressed her fingers down on the base of the glass and slid the stemware in small circles as she decided what to say.

Without a word, she slowly stood up and unbuttoned the cuffs of her white blouse. She undid each button down the center and let the garment drop to the floor behind her.

Krauss gasped. Standing in front of him, wearing only a blue skirt and white bra, the half-naked form of the love of his life sported a dozen large, deep-purple bruises up and down her torso.

Steve Krauss rose and approached Michelle. Tenderly, he ran two fingers across the bruises Evelyn O'Doherty's elbow caused to Michelle's side and upper chest. "Do they hurt?"

"Uhhh, *yeah!*" Michelle answered snidely.

"I'm so sorry. Can I get you anything?"

"No, they'll heal. I suppose I won't be going to yoga class for a few more weeks. I wouldn't know how to explain these."

With a light touch, Steve wrapped Michelle in his arms. His gentle squeeze was loose enough to not draw a complaint, yet firm enough to let her know how much he loved her. "You're home safe, now. That's all that matters."

"I'm always safe when I'm in your arms," Michelle said softly, hugging Steve and nestling her head underneath his chin.

Climbing into bed later, Michelle pulled back their old blue bedspread and got under the covers. She laid her hand on Steven's chest, settled her head onto her favorite spot on his shoulder, closed her eyes feeling peaceful and safe, and just smiled.

ABOUT THE AUTHOR

Scott Shinberg has served in leadership positions across the US Government and industry for over twenty-five years. He has worked in and with the US Air Force, the Department of Homeland Security, the Federal Bureau of Investigation, and most "Three-Letter Agencies." While in government service, he served as an Air Force Intelligence Operations Officer and a Special Agent with the FBI. He lives in Virginia with his wife and sons.

Website: www.ScottShinberg.com
Facebook: @ScottShinbergAuthor
Twitter: @Author_Scott

WHAT'S NEXT?

Don't miss the next thrilling installment of this series, which is perfect for fans of Tom Clancy, Robert Ludlum, Dean Koontz, Brad Meltzer, and Len Deighton.

FLY BY NIGHT
Michelle Reagan – Book 3
(Releases in 2020)

To remain up to date for plans and schedules related to this book, and to all works by Scott Shinberg, please subscribe to his newsletter at:
www.ScottShinberg.com

MORE FROM SCOTT SHINBERG

Is *Confessions of Eden* drawn from today's headlines, or are the headlines drawn from what little is visible of Eden's footprints?

CONFESSIONS OF EDEN
Michelle Reagan – Book 1

Michelle Reagan—code name Eden—is the CIA Special Activities Division's newest covert action operator, an assassin, who struggles between wanting to succeed in her new profession for herself and her charismatic boss, and the moral quandaries of what she must do to innocent people who are simply in the wrong place at the wrong time. Although she faces seemingly intractable decisions as she executes her missions across the globe, the adversary most difficult to overcome may very well be her own conscience.

Through it all, only one man has ever called her an 'assassin' to her face. Someday, if she has her way, she'll marry him—if she lives that long.

WINNER: Pinnacle Book Achievement Award - Best Spy Thriller
WINNER: Literary Titan Book Awards - Gold Medal

"This novel is purpose-driven; it is written for those who enjoy action, but the strength of the characters is one of the irresistible elements of this well-crafted thriller. ... Fast-paced and filled with action, it is one of those books you feel compelled to read nonstop."
~ Christian Sia, Readers' Favorite Book Reviews (5 STARS)

"For fans of crime and espionage, *Confessions of Eden* comes across as a tour de force in entertainment."
~ Romuald Dzemo, Readers' Favorite Book Reviews (5 STARS)

MORE FROM EVOLVED PUBLISHING

We offer great books across multiple genres, featuring high-quality editing (which we believe is second-to-none) and fantastic covers.

As a hybrid small press, your support as loyal readers is so important to us, and we have strived, with tireless dedication and sheer determination, to deliver on the promise of our motto:
QUALITY IS PRIORITY #1!

Please check out all of our great books,
which you can find at this link:
www.EvolvedPub.com/Catalog/

Thank you!

CPSIA information can be obtained
at www.ICGtesting.com
Printed in the USA
BVHW030450051219
565722BV00010B/35/P